CW01391115

Secrets in St Ives

By Deborah Flower

A St Ives Christmas Mystery

Secrets in St Ives

Secrets in St Ives

DEBORAH FOWLER

Best wishes

Allison & Busby Limited
11 Wardour Mews
London W1F 8AN
allisonandbusby.com

First published in Great Britain by Allison & Busby in 2025.

Copyright © 2025 by DEBORAH FOWLER

The moral right of the author is hereby asserted in accordance with
the Copyright, Designs and Patents Act 1988.

All characters and events in this publication,
other than those clearly in the public domain,
are fictitious and any resemblance to actual persons,
living or dead, is purely coincidental.

All rights reserved. No part of this publication may be reproduced,
stored in a retrieval system, or transmitted, in any form or by
any means without the prior written permission of the publisher,
nor be otherwise circulated in any form of binding or cover
other than that in which it is published and without a similar
condition being imposed on the subsequent buyer.

A CIP catalogue record for this book is available from
the British Library.

First Edition

ISBN 978-0-7490-3109-1

Typeset in 11/16 pt Sabon LT Pro by
Allison & Busby Ltd.

By choosing this product, you help take care of the world's forests.
Learn more: www.fsc.org.

FSC
www.fsc.org
MIX
Paper | Supporting
responsible forestry
FSC® C013604

Printed and bound in the UK using 100% Renewable Electricity at
CPI Group (UK) Ltd, Croydon, CR0 4YY

EU GPSR Authorised Representative
LOGOS EUROPE, 9 rue Nicolas Poussin, 17000,
LA ROCHELLE, France
E-mail: Contact@logoseurope.eu

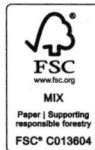

To Bonce – thank you for your wonderful friendship and support over so many years.

PROLOGUE

Trehearne Farm, St Ives, West Cornwall,
July 1992

'Is that you, Philip?' Sarah called out.

'No, it's that Mel Gibson, come to pay you a visit, lovely lady,' was the reply.

Sarah smiled. It was an old joke. 'Supper's on the table, love.'

'I'll just clean up a bit,' said Philip. 'It was a difficult calving but we've a fine heifer at the end of it.' A cheerful, red face appeared round the kitchen door. 'Where are the kids?' he asked.

'They've gone into town with Annie and Dan from down the road. Geoff has passed his driving test now so he's going to drop them all home later.'

'I hope that Geoff is a careful driver, particularly now the visitors are about – most of them drive like maniacs – they just don't understand narrow lanes. What are the kids doing in St Ives anyway?'

'They're just seeing a film, Philip. Stop fussing.'

'At fifteen, I think Gemma is still too young to be gallivanting about in town at night.'

'I seem to remember that you did quite a bit of gallivanting at her age,' said Sarah, with a smile.

'My point exactly!' said Philip, laughing as he disappeared off to the bathroom.

Sarah opened a bottle of beer and, on his return, she placed a hearty plate of stew and mashed potatoes in front of him. 'As I recall,' she said, 'rather than watching a film and behaving yourself, you spent most of your free time cuddling your girl on the beach.' She smiled. 'And look how that worked out – we got ourselves a life sentence!'

Philip stopped eating, his fork in the air. 'Best thing I ever did, marrying you. We're happy, aren't we? No regrets?'

'We are, my love, both us and our wonderful children. Alright, money's sometimes tight and we work too hard, but no one goes into farming just to get rich and sit on their bums all day. I wouldn't change a thing.'

They ate their meal in contented silence for a few minutes and then began a spirited discussion as to whether they could turn one of their large barns into bedrooms to provide bed-and-breakfast accommodation. It was a pipe dream, they couldn't afford it, but they always enjoyed a little gentle bantering around the subject.

'Would you mind if I dropped in at Halsetown Inn for a quick one?' Philip asked as he helped clear the table. 'Jim Ferrell reckons he's sourced some winter feed at a really good price.'

Sarah laughed. 'You know, that almost sounds like a

genuine reason for going to the pub – hardly an excuse at all.'

'You cheeky mare.' Philip grinned. 'Particularly since it's God's own truth.'

Sarah came to the back door with him. Unexpectedly, he swept her into an embrace and kissed her soundly. 'I love you, my darling,' he said, still holding her close.

'I love you too, Philip,' she replied.

In the gathering dusk, as Philip trudged down the lane, Sarah watched him fondly, leaning against the door frame and straining her eyes against the gloom until he was completely out of sight.

She would always be grateful she did that – for she never saw him again.

CHAPTER ONE

Present Day

Merrin McKenzie walked briskly along Porthkidney Beach, deep in thought. It was fifteen months since her policeman husband, Adam, had been fatally stabbed 'in the line of duty'. It was a term she loathed – it wasn't his duty to die at the age of only fifty-four.

As a direct result of Adam's death, in an uncharacteristic knee-jerk reaction, she had sold the Bristol house they had lived in all their married life and returned to her childhood home of St Ives in Cornwall. After initial resistance from her daughter, Isla, they both agreed the move was a good idea – but what now? Having specialised as a solicitor in family law all her working life, she needed a change. There was no way she could retire in her mid-fifties; she had to work at something – in fact, she couldn't imagine ever retiring, she craved the discipline and structure of a working day. But working at what? The problem was on her mind, night and day with no obvious resolution.

Turning to discuss the problem yet again with her childhood friend, Clara, she found her walking companion was no longer with her. Shading her eyes, Merrin saw that Clara was some distance behind her, busy collecting shells, which she liked to use as decoration in her restaurant.

'Come on, Clara,' Merrin shouted above the sound of the breaking waves. Clara waved an arm in acknowledgement but continued picking up shells.

'What's she like?' Merrin addressed the dog at her feet. William, a dog of indeterminate breed, wagged his tail in agreement. 'Still,' she continued, 'there could be worse places to wait.'

It was a sunny day in early July, that sweet spot where the summer had begun but the schools had not as yet broken up, so the beaches were still quiet. The sea was deep blue, turning to fluorescent green in the shallows, the surf, by contrast, a crisp white. It was fabulous, with just a light breeze to make walking comfortable. William cautiously ventured into the sea, but he was no swimmer – 'never above the knees' was William's rule and his knees were very close to the ground. Inspired to follow, Merrin whipped off her flip-flops and paddled in to join him. The tide was coming in so the water was warm as it swirled over the hot sand. Merrin gazed out to sea. It was moments like this, when she was close to nature, that she felt as near to being happy as was possible since Adam's death.

'Here I am, darling Pearl,' said Clara, interrupting Merrin's reverie. 'Pearl' was the exclusive nickname Clara used when addressing her friend, for 'Merrin' in Cornish means 'sea pearl'. 'Look,' said Clara, waving her carrier bag. 'I've got quite a haul today. Come on, we'd better hurry or otherwise . . . oh God.' She pointed ahead of her to where waves were curling round the rocks, known as Hawkes Point, which separated Porthkidney Beach from the beach at Carbis Bay. Already a deep pool was forming.

'I thought you said we had plenty of time to get back to Carbis Bay before the tide cut us off?' Merrin challenged.

They had begun their walk a couple of hours earlier, driving out of St Ives, parking at Carbis Bay and then walking through to Porthkidney and across the beach to the Hayle Estuary.

'Don't fuss, Pearl. There's still a good half hour before we'd have to swim for it,' said Clara. 'At the moment, the state of the tide won't involve anything more than a shallow paddle.'

Clara sounded full of confidence but Merrin was not reassured. 'Why don't we go back on the cliff path?' she suggested.

'Because I haven't got time. I need to get changed and be in the restaurant in half an hour. Stop whinging, Pearl darling, it'll be fine.'

Of course, it wasn't fine. As they waded through the pool, Clara holding her carrier bag of shells above her head, Merrin with a deeply disapproving William firmly tucked under her arm, the sea was up their waists. 'Oh for heaven's sake, Clara!' Merrin began.

Clara turned and their eyes met. Suddenly, like the children they had once been, they were convulsed with laughter, struggling out on to Carbis Bay Beach, doubled up with mirth. Only William did not find it funny. He stood watching them with ill-disguised disdain.

CHAPTER TWO

Chief Inspector Louis Peppiatt had been running late all day. A briefing with his team, concerning an armed robbery at a Newquay sub-post office, had badly overrun. He had then made a mad dash to Falmouth to witness his son's sports day. Edward, aged nine, was not a sportsman and was quite happy for his father not to attend, on the grounds that sports day was boring. Louis, however, felt he should be demonstrating support, whatever his son's views. Meanwhile, his ex-wife, Stephanie, and her new husband, Andrew, were attending the sports day of his daughter, Daisy, who was at secondary school. Sports day mercifully over, he was back in the car heading for Camborne, having been summoned by his boss, Chief Superintendent John Dent.

The summons, according to John Dent's wonderful secretary, Sally, was an urgent one, though Louis could not imagine why. The armed robbery was nasty and had put the postmaster in hospital, though not critically so. An armed robbery was something that very rarely happened in Cornwall and, working with the Met, Louis was now confident that the perpetrators were a gang from London. The investigation was going well and Louis was pretty sure of an arrest within the next few days. There was nothing else major on the horizon, which left Louis a little nervous – he didn't relish an urgent summons from the chief super without knowing the cause.

He took the stairs two at a time and reached Sally's office seriously out of breath. He looked at her clock on the wall, he was ten minutes late and John Dent had strong views on punctuality.

'I'm so sorry, Sally,' he managed between gasps, 'only it was Edward's sports day this morning and, of course, he was in the last race so I had to stay until the bitter end.'

'Of course you did, Louis dear,' said Sally, 'now calm down. I've just taken sir a lovely coffee and a piece of toasted saffron cake with plenty of butter. He perked up no end. How did Edward get on?'

'Not well,' said Louis, 'but he didn't seem to care; sport is not his thing, unlike Daisy.'

'He's still a lovely lad, just like his father. Now what can I get you?'

'You old charmer. Just a glass of water would be great before I face the music. What's up anyway?' Louis asked.

'He'd better tell you himself but don't worry – for once you're not in any trouble.' Sally smiled fondly. 'You know, now you're a chief inspector, you really ought to slow down a bit, let others take the strain for once.'

'That's rich coming from you, Sal dear. How many years are you past the official retirement age?'

'It's extremely rude to refer to a lady's age, particularly if she is a little on the mature side. Get in there, Louis. I hope he gives you hell!'

'I'm so sorry I'm late, sir,' Louis began.

'No problem,' said John. The two men shook hands and the normally rather dour John Dent appeared to be smiling. Clearly, the coffee and saffron cake had worked their magic.

'Come and sit down,' John said, indicating the two armchairs at the end of his office, which suggested the subject matter was not too serious. Louis relaxed a little.

'I want you to take on a cold case, Louis. I want it investigated as a matter of urgency and I want you to re-assign all your other cases and concentrate entirely on this one.'

'I thought cold cases normally went to retired officers?' Louis said. 'You're not suggesting I retire, are you, sir?'

'Of course not,' said John irritably, his substantial eyebrows starting to bristle, which was never a good sign.

'It's just that I'm very much involved with the Newquay armed robbery at the moment,' said Louis. 'I only need a few more days. I'm working with the Met and an arrest is imminent.'

'This can't wait, I'm afraid, you'll have to offload Newquay and everything else you're working on. The case in question is close to St Ives so you can have Jack Eddy to assist. Otherwise you're on your own.'

'Great,' said Louis, with a barely disguised sigh.

'Just listen, Louis, and let me explain. Back in the summer of 1992, a farmer named Philip Trehearne disappeared on his way to the Halsetown Inn from his home, just outside St Ives – a journey by foot of about twelve minutes. He never reached the pub and no trace of him, dead or alive, has ever been found. He was very happily married, the farm was doing well, he was a cheerful chap, very well liked, a positive pillar of the establishment and a true Cornishman.'

'So why are we opening the case after all this time? In any event, I was still in Newton Abbot when this chap disappeared so I can't see I'll be much use, particularly as no one could find him at the time.'

'I'm coming to that,' said John impatiently. 'Ten days ago, Philip's widow, Sarah, killed herself with an overdose of sleeping pills. She left a very brief note for her children, saying how sorry she was to leave them but she just couldn't bear living any longer with the uncertainty surrounding Philip's disappearance. She was seventy-three.

'Their son, Tom, who has run the farm for many years, blames the police for his parents' deaths. He's very angry and bitter, not an easy man at the best of times, so I understand. However, he is getting a huge amount of media coverage, nationally as well as in Cornwall and on the socials. The whole story is really going viral and the "powers that be" want someone senior to clear up the mess as quickly as possible, aiming to vindicate the police at the time from having made a balls-up, whether they did or not. So, naturally, we thought of you.'

'I'm flattered,' said Louis, sounding anything but.

'Look, Peppiatt, I know you are an officer of very high

moral standards, and I admire you for that. However, it is extremely important that we shut down the vitriol that has developed in respect of this missing man, who obviously must have been dead for years. I'm not looking for a solution, it would be nigh impossible after all this time. I just want you to satisfy the Trehearnes that the police did everything they could.'

'Sir, I'll take on the case, but only if you agree that my aim will be to find out what really happened to Philip Trehearne. I'm not prepared to simply patch over the cracks in a thirty-year-old investigation to make the force come out smelling of roses. But assuming that you accept my approach, then I'll do my best. When do I have to start?'

'Right now,' said John. 'There's a fat file for you to take home and read. Whatever you say, I can only repeat that I am not looking for answers as to what happened to the missing man – just a calming-down of what threatens to be a media frenzy.' He buzzed through to Sally. 'Could you bring me the Trehearne file please, Sally?'

Sally appeared in the doorway and gave Louis a brief wink. 'Here's your light reading, Chief Inspector. Could you just sign here to say you're taking the file out of the office?' She turned to her boss. 'Oh, one thing, sir. I've just heard that the Trehearne sister is flying back from Australia to be with her brother and presumably attend their mother's funeral. Her husband's coming too, they're a Mr and Mrs Tripconey. Presumably they'll be joining in the campaign to help discredit the police who originally handled of the case, God help us all.'

'Tripconey!' said Louis, suddenly showing real interest

for the first time. 'They must be related to Merrin McKenzie. She was a Tripconey before her marriage to Adam and now I come to think of it, I believe she said she had a brother in Australia.' He hesitated, frowning in thought. 'Jago, I think she said his name was.'

'Bullseye,' said Sally, 'that's the one.'

'You remember Mrs McKenzie, sir, from the Steve Matthews case?' said Louis. 'I'll start by talking to her to get some background.'

'Of course, I remember Mrs McKenzie, she was a great help with that poor man. However, your starting point should be to try and convince Tom Trehearne to stop stirring up trouble. That's your brief, Peppiatt. I don't care how you do it, but your job is to bring to an end this adverse publicity, and bloody quickly.'

'Nonetheless, I think I'll talk to Mrs McKenzie first, she's a clever woman and very perceptive. She's bound to have a helpful overview.'

'And she's unattached now, Louis, as are you,' said Sally wickedly.

'Don't be ridiculous,' said Louis, picking up the file and heading for the door. 'She's a grieving widow.'

As the office door closed behind him, John smiled at Sally. 'I can't quite understand why, but he does seem to have an awful lot of faith in that woman.'

'The gentleman doth protest too much, methinks,' said Sally and they both laughed.

CHAPTER THREE

Merrin had been both surprised and intrigued by the phone call from Louis Peppiatt. He'd asked if he could come over to St Ives to see her but had refused to be drawn on the reason for the visit, other than to say he wanted to pick her brains.

'I wonder what he wants?' Merrin asked her African Grey parrot, Horatio, who cocked his head on one side as if giving the question serious consideration. This was something that, over their years together, Merrin had come to believe was highly possible. Horatio, without question, was very smart but he was also given to dramatic mood swings. At the moment, he was decidedly disgruntled, having been left alone all morning while Merrin, Clara and William had attempted to drown themselves on the beach. If that wasn't enough, because a visitor was expected, Horatio was not allowed out of his cage. He liked to fly around Merrin's cottage in the afternoon and then, bizarrely, settle down with William in the dog bed.

Reading his mind, which was not difficult, given the black looks she was receiving, Merrin said, 'I'm very sorry, Horatio, but you know it's for your own safety. I don't want you flying out of the front door or being frightened by a visitor. And there will be biscuits for tea.' The look she received suggested that Horatio thought bribery by biscuit was a low blow – deeply insulting and inappropriate.

On cue, there was a knock on the door and Merrin opened it to find Louis Peppiatt on the threshold. 'Come in, Inspector. Horatio and I were just talking about you.'

They had not met for nearly six months and, for a moment, they stood awkwardly staring at one another. Finally, Louis held out his hand and they formally shook hands. 'Thank you very much for seeing me at such short notice, Mrs McKenzie,' he said.

'No problem,' said Merrin. 'Tea and biscuits?'

'Yes, please, to tea, but I should be avoiding biscuits.'

'You can't say no to biscuits, I'm afraid. I've promised Horatio we'd have them.' Horatio gave his bell a mighty bash, as if to make the point.

'So I see,' said Louis dryly. Bending down, he gave William a scratch behind the ears. 'Alright, William?' he asked. William thumped his tail – he was rather picky about the people he liked but Louis was definitely one of them.

They sat down at the kitchen table and while Merrin fed Horatio and William a piece of biscuit each, Louis took out his notebook. 'Heavens, Inspector, I don't like the look of your notebook. Are you about to interrogate me? What have I done?'

'Absolutely nothing to worry about; it's advice I'm after,' Louis replied. 'I should have Jack here really, taking notes, but you know what an old gossip he is and it's a slightly tricky subject.'

'You intrigue me, Inspector,' said Merrin.

'Actually,' said Louis, 'it's "Chief Inspector" now.'

'And I suppose that's a reward for nearly getting yourself killed?' said Merrin, clearly not very impressed.

'Or you could say, it was a reward for catching a major villain,' said Louis, a little tersely. 'Either way, as "Chief Inspector" is something of a mouthful, should we agree on Merrin and Louis going forward?'

'Alright then, Louis.' Merrin relented and offered a small smile.

'I want to talk to you about Sarah Trehearne. I presume you've heard about her death?'

'Yes, of course I have,' said Merrin. 'Sarah's family and ours are related by marriage but then, you must know that or you wouldn't be here. When you say "Sarah's death", you're not suggesting foul play, are you? There is no question that she killed herself, she left a note and, poor woman, it's not surprising really that she'd had enough.'

'Absolutely,' said Louis hurriedly. 'You're right and, sadly, there is no doubt that she killed herself. However, as a result, I've been asked to re-investigate the disappearance of her husband, Philip Trehearne.'

'I see, so you're involved in a police cover-up? You surprise me, Louis, I didn't think you were that sort of policeman, not when you profess to have had such high regard for my husband. Adam would never have allowed himself to be a party to a cover-up.'

'It's not like that,' Louis protested.

'Oh, I think it is,' said Merrin. 'Tom Trehearne is kicking up an enormous fuss in the media generally because he holds the police responsible for his mother's death, since they couldn't find his father. Tom has been a troubled man ever since his father's disappearance but you can't blame him for being so angry. When I lost Adam it was terrible, but at least I knew what had happened to him. I can't begin to imagine how I would have felt if he had walked out of the door one day and simply disappeared without trace. I do know, though, I would never again have found a moment's true peace.'

'Merrin, could you at least listen to me before making such a sweeping judgement,' said Louis angrily. 'I can explain my involvement, if you give me half a chance to actually speak.'

'I'll listen,' said Merrin, 'but you'll have trouble convincing me that you haven't taken on a very shabby job. No one these days seems to be able to accept that sometimes they get things wrong. Why can't the police just admit they failed to find Philip, apologise to the family and admit that their failure may well have contributed to Sarah making the decision to take her own life? That would earn the force far more respect than you attempting to prove that the police aren't responsible in any way.'

'Have you finished now?' Louis said. Merrin nodded. 'Right, then at least listen to what I have to say and then, by all means, you can pass judgement.'

CHAPTER FOUR

Clearly agitated, Louis stood up and walked over to the window. The view looked down onto Fore Street, St Ives's main shopping street. It was late afternoon and a sea mist was rolling in and funnelling up the street, which was now almost empty. He turned round to face Merrin. William, clearly upset by the anger in the room, began to whimper. 'It's alright, William, don't worry,' said Louis, reaching down to pat the dog. He didn't realise it, of course, but his words of comfort for Merrin's dog immediately drained away at least some of her anger.

'My boss, Chief Superintendent John Dent, called me into the office at lunchtime today. I was still based in Newton Abbot when Philip went missing so I knew nothing of the story. The boss filled me in and, like you, I immediately saw it as a cover-up, which I'm sure is what it is intended to be, the prime objective being to get the press off our backs. I was going to turn it down, refuse to take the case, and then the super described Tom as being "very angry and bitter, not an easy man at the best of times". Quite clearly he and his superiors are seeing Tom as the enemy, not as a victim, and it was then that I knew I had to take the case.'

Louis returned to the table and sat down, facing Merrin. 'You confirmed just now that Tom has been troubled ever since his father's death. What sort of man would Tom have been if his father had not disappeared? What sort of man will he become if we simply brush the cause of his mother's death under the carpet? We owe it to him to at least have another serious go at finding out what really happened to his father.' Louis hesitated. 'And that, Merrin, is where my interests lie. No way will this be a police cover-up – not on my watch.'

'I understand and I'm sorry,' said Merrin, 'truly, I'm very sorry to have sounded off at you like that. It's just that I've seen this sort of thing happen before, in fact many times, and it stinks. Also, the fact is that if Tom hadn't kicked up a media storm, the police wouldn't even have considered opening Philip's file when Sarah died. I'm right about that, aren't I?'

'Of course you are. Look, I'm going to say this just once, and then never raise the subject again. We ended up working quite closely on the John Lumley case. I would have liked to believe you could not have thought me capable of hushing up what has happened to the poor Trehearne family. If I'd refused to take this case, in my view, no one else was going to do more than just go through the file and say the police did everything possible at the time. I may be very wrong but I'd like to think I can do better than that – for Tom's sake and the rest of his family. Of course I'm not the sort of policeman to become involved in a cover-up to protect the force's reputation. Of course I'm not.'

'I can only say again that I'm terribly sorry for misjudging you and you're right, I should have known better. I will do anything, everything I can to help you,' said Merrin. She hesitated. 'So where do we start?'

It took Louis a moment to compose himself. When he spoke, he was once more calm and professional. 'I was given the original file on Philip's disappearance and, before coming here, I had a speedy read of it. From what I can see, while the police, coastguards and a huge number of the general public did some impressive searching of the area, there were no apparent background checks on Philip to see if he had any enemies or skeletons in his cupboard.'

'I think that very unlikely,' said Merrin. 'I don't know the family terribly well and I was at university when Philip went missing. However, I am absolutely sure that they were a very loving family – everyone locally was very fond of them. I know my parents were absolutely delighted when Jago married Gemma, Tom's sister, and certainly Dad and Philip got on like a house on fire. Growing up, though, Jago and I had very little to do with Tom and Gemma so most of what I can tell you about them is hearsay. Jago and Gemma are on their way back to St Ives from Australia, incidentally.'

'Yes, they told me at the station. So, why didn't you spend any time with Tom and Gemma during childhood, given your parents were friends?' Louis asked.

'A difference in age – Jago and I are older than the Trehearnes. In fact, Jago is nine years older than his wife.' She smiled. 'A cradle-snatcher, my brother! Tom and Gemma are still only in their mid-forties now whereas Jago and I are old codgers of fifty-six and fifty-four.'

'They must have been very young when Philip disappeared?' said Louis.

'Yes, poor loves,' Merrin agreed. 'They were teenagers. I think Gemma was only about fifteen and Tom two years older. Tom never went to college. He left school immediately after his dad disappeared and began working on the farm to help his mum, and Gemma followed as soon as she was old enough to leave school.'

'So, how come Jago and Gemma ended up in Australia? Presumably, Gemma was badly missed on the farm?'

'Jago, naughty boy, went on a gap year to Australia. He's naturally very clever at IT and he was supposed to be coming back to the UK in order to go to university, where he had a place to study computer science. Instead he stayed on in Australia and founded a business with an Australian boy of about the same age. They were both surfing mad. Firstly, they gave surfing lessons, then they opened a shop selling surfing gear and now they have five shops and, of course, sell on line. Jago came back to St Ives after a few years to tell Mum and Dad he was going to make his home in Oz and go for Australian citizenship. While he was home, he and Gemma got together and she went back with him. In order to cope, soon after Philip vanished, the Trehearnes took on a young farm manager and he still works for them, I believe. There's no way they could ever give up on the farm – it's been in the family for generations – and also they felt they had to keep it going for Philip.'

'In case he ever comes home, you mean?'

'Yes, I imagine so. Certainly if you or I were in the same position, I'm sure we would cling on to hope, even when it became increasingly unrealistic. Maybe the children gradually began to accept that their dad was not coming back but I very much doubt that Sarah ever gave up on Philip – she loved him so much. Actually, Louis, thinking about it, perhaps that's why Sarah took her own life – she had finally given up hope.'

'It's a tragic story,' said Louis. 'Look, I need to really study the file and to think about what you have told me. Then, I'm afraid, I will probably have a lot more questions, if that's OK. When are Jago and Gemma arriving?'

'Tomorrow. What would be really helpful is if you could talk to Jago on his own initially – without Gemma, I mean. Understandably, he knows a lot more about the family than I do. Also, he tells me that Gemma is equally as angry as Tom about what happened to Sarah. She was very close to her mum and, of course, is blaming herself for not being here for her – for going to Australia and leaving Sarah to cope. Shall I suggest to Jago that the three of us meet up?'

'Yes, please do. I want to understand as much as possible about the background to all this before talking to Tom and Gemma. If I go in without a thorough knowledge of the whole situation, it might well appear disrespectful, like I'm not taking their concerns seriously. That mustn't happen.'

'You're not such a bad chap, Louis, and William likes you, which is a major plus point,' Merrin said magnanimously.

'We've had quite a number of battles and misunderstandings one way and another, since we first met, haven't we?' said Louis. 'Are we alright now?'

'We're alright now,' said Merrin, smiling, 'and I'm sorry again for misjudging you. You're right, I should have known better. About the Trehearnes – try not to let what has happened define them in your mind. They were just a very ordinary family, to whom a very extraordinary thing happened.'

CHAPTER FIVE

Sergeant Jack Eddy ended the call with the chief superintendent's secretary, Sally. He rose from his desk and walked over to the very small window in his very small office. He had never received any direct communication from the chief super before, and so surprised was he that the instructions given to him were not entirely clear in his mind. He gazed over the rooftops, trying to work out what could possibly be expected of him. He would be working with Inspector, no, now Chief Inspector Louis Peppiatt, something that pleased him very much. He had always been completely in awe of Louis Peppiatt and now it appeared that the two of them would be working alone together on a cold case – he had been especially chosen, Sally said. Jack was not as intimidated as he once would have been because, just before Christmas last year, he had saved the chief inspector's life and several times the boss had expressed his gratitude. Perhaps this was the boss's way of saying thank you again.

Jack counted himself as having been very lucky over the last few months. He had been much praised by his colleagues for his action in saving the boss's life and Mrs Eddy had even declared herself to be proud of him – something that had never happened before. Secondly, and amazingly, he had passed his latest medical. This time last year, he had quite expected to be pensioned off by now. Instead, although he was overweight and not very fast on his feet, his blood pressure and cholesterol readings were excellent, due, it was decided, to him being not much of a drinker. So, he had scraped through, and now Sally had said he had been specially chosen to help the boss with a tricky case. He felt quite pleased with himself and also hugely grateful. He loved his wife, of course, but the thought of being at home with Mrs Eddy every day of the week was not something Jack relished – in fact, it didn't bear thinking about.

Jack's reverie was interrupted by the arrival of the man himself. 'Ah, Eddy, I'm glad you're here. We have an important and very urgent job to do.' Louis burst into the office, his energy appearing to make the already small space seem suddenly very overcrowded indeed.

'The chief super's office has just rung me. What's it all about, boss?' Jack asked.

Louis explained the details of the Trehearne case and noticed that Jack was starting to look increasingly appalled by what he had to say.

'Bugger, we're not going to have to start tramping all over the moors again, are we, boss?' Jack said when Louis had finished.

'Eddy, this is a case that is over thirty years old. Of course we're not going to be searching the moors for a body. We have to look at it in an entirely different way. I take it, from your unhappy expression, that you were involved in the original search for Philip Trehearne?'

'I was, boss,' said Jack, 'and I can promise you that we left no stone unturned in our search of the moor. We went backwards and forwards along the path Philip would have taken and then we spread the search outwards – widely in all directions. As well as us, the coastguards became involved and the public – Philip was very well liked. It was July but the weather was awful – quite chilly, as well as very wet and windy. I'd just got engaged to Mrs Eddy and I turned up night after night covered in mud. I thought she'd call off the engagement – in fact she threatened to, as I remember. I tried to explain not all police work was the same but she was very displeased at the time, very displeased indeed.'

'Well, you can tell Mrs Eddy that mud is unlikely to be involved on this occasion,' said Louis, failing to suppress a smile. 'What do you know about the Trehearne family?'

'Not much when they were kiddies. Tom and Gemma are quite a bit younger than me so we didn't really play together at that stage.'

'I've just been to see Mrs McKenzie,' said Louis, 'and she said exactly the same thing. Still, as her brother is married to Gemma, she may know the family rather better than you, I imagine.'

'Maybe, maybe not,' said Jack mysteriously.

'What on earth do you mean by that, Eddy?' asked Louis.

'Well,' said Jack, looking pleased with himself. 'Three years before Philip disappeared, I went to work on their farm for the summer. I'm quite a lot older than Tom, but although he was still a boy and I was grown up, we got along very well. I was about to start my police training in the autumn. I lived with the family as it was easier than going home at night – we worked all hours. There was a good harvest that year and they were in the process of increasing their livestock so they were busy times. The children worked hard as well, though Gemma can't have been more than twelve. I shared a room with Tom and I'm ashamed to say I taught him to smoke.'

'This is very helpful, so, in fact, you must know a lot about the family.'

'Yes, I suppose so. There was no time for chit-chat, we all worked from dawn until dusk, including Mrs Trehearne. She was lovely, by the way, so sad she died. Also, a few times Philip took me to the pub for a pint. Spooky really, taking the same path as he did that fateful night.'

'I am aware that your knowledge of the people in this area is encyclopaedic, but I wasn't expecting anything as useful as this. Tomorrow, I want you to think long and hard about your time at the farm and write down any memories you have, good or bad, however trivial, in as much detail as you can. Will you do that, please?'

'Of course, boss. I'll start dreckly.'

'Do you still see much of Tom? It sounds as if you were quite close as boys.'

'I haven't seen him for years,' said Jack. 'When Philip first disappeared, I offered to help out on the farm during the times I was off duty and I did work when I could for a few weeks but, obviously, I didn't have much spare time. After a while, they took on a full-time farm manager and after that I've hardly seen any of them. I was invited to Gemma's wedding to Jago Tripconey but I couldn't go as I was on duty.'

'OK. Just one last question – with your knowledge of the family, did you have a theory, at the time of his disappearance, as to what had happened to Philip?'

Jack was silent for some time. 'Not really,' he said at last. 'I was only a young man and I was courting so I had other things on my mind. During the search, I just did as I was told. The sergeant in charge of the search was ex-army and a very hard man. There wasn't much time for thinking.' There was another silence while Louis waited patiently. 'All I would say, boss, is that no one could believe, not for one single moment, that Philip would have left his missus and the kiddies. It would be hard to find a happier family than those Trehearnes. He either had an accident or foul play was involved and if it had been an accident, then we'd have found him.'

'My thoughts exactly,' said Louis.

CHAPTER SIX

Merrin sped down the A30 as fast as she dared. She had just picked up Jago and Gemma from Newquay Airport. After a loving and joyful reunion with her brother and a big conciliatory hug with Gemma, things had very rapidly deteriorated. They were hardly in the car when Gemma started cross-examining Merrin.

'Do you realise, Merrin, that the police haven't even been in contact with Tom since Mum died?'

'They must have been,' said Merrin gently. 'You must have had the results of the post-mortem and presumably poor Tom had to cope with the formal identification.'

'Yes,' said Gemma, 'they've done all that but they also promised a rapid internal inquiry as to why Dad has never been found. So far, we've heard nothing and Mum died more than four weeks ago. You'd think someone would have had the courtesy to at least call us and tell us what's happening. Surely you must know something?'

'Why me?' Merrin asked. Gemma was sitting in the front passenger seat of the car and Merrin found herself wishing that instead Jago was beside her to give moral support. She felt desperately sorry for Gemma and she was acutely aware that both she and Jago must be exhausted and jet-lagged. She just hadn't expected to be the immediate butt of Gemma's anger.

'Because,' said Gemma, her voice rising a pitch, 'because you were very involved with that cocaine-smuggling case and you must know a lot of local policemen as a result, surely?'

'I do,' Merrin admitted, 'and I know two of them are working full time on your dad's disappearance.'

'Two of them!' Gemma shrieked. 'A woman has died because of their failure and they've put just two policemen on the case! And if you know all this, Merrin, why haven't you told Tom?'

Anxious not to mention Louis by name, Merrin said, 'I believe they're going to make contact with you and Tom within the next few days but, presumably, they first need to familiarise themselves with the details surrounding the search for your father. It was over thirty years ago, Gemma, and I expect they want to study the file and talk to anyone who has any memories of what happened on that awful day.'

'In order to engineer a cover-up, I bet,' said Gemma bitterly.

Merrin had to remind herself that initially this had been her exact reaction. She tried to imagine how she would feel if it had been her and Jago's parents in a similar situation – tried, and failed. It was just too awful.

'In any case, I suppose it doesn't really matter,' Gemma continued, her voice flat with despair. 'My mother's dead and I wasn't there to support her. The fact is, I should never have married your brother and agreed to move to Australia.'

There was a deathly silence. Merrin heard Jago move uneasily in the back of the car, but he said nothing.

Eventually, Merrin spoke. 'Gemma, none of this is your fault. You know Sarah was completely supportive of you and Jago marrying and settling in Australia. Bless her, she loved your dad so much. I don't believe anyone could have stopped her doing what she did – she'd just had enough.'

'You don't know what you're talking about, you hardly knew her. She was my mum and I knew her very well – so just shut up, Merrin, would you, please?'

So, Merrin shut up and the journey continued in a highly charged silence.

As they bumped up the lane to Trehearne Farm, Merrin wondered how on earth she was going to manage a few minutes on her own with Jago. Seeing the level of Gemma's anger, added to Tom's, and she could well imagine them cooking up a raging storm between them. Louis would need as much information as possible, before confronting them, in order to stand a chance of gaining their co-operation and, above all, their help.

As it turned out, the fates were on Merrin's side. As they drew up outside the front door of the farmhouse, Gemma flung open the car door and said, 'I want to see my brother alone for a few minutes. Would you two stay here, please.' She slammed the car door and ran into the farmhouse.

'No problem,' Jago called after her. 'We'll start unloading the luggage.'

'Before we do that, Jago,' Merrin said quietly, leaning over the car seat to face her brother, 'I need to ask you something. Would you come with me tomorrow morning to meet Chief Inspector Louis Peppiatt, who is in charge of re-opening Philip's case? And I mean on your own, without Gemma.'

'Why without Gemma? Surely this is all about Gemma – and Tom, of course?'

'Because Louis wants to gather as much information as possible about what happened, before approaching Gemma and Tom. He doesn't want it to look as if he's just glanced at the file and then pushed the matter under the carpet, which is clearly what they're expecting. He's serious about this case, Jago. He really wants to find out what happened to Philip.'

'Louis, you called him, so he's obviously a friend of yours. Can we trust him? Are you sure he's not just going through the motions – a cover-up as Gemma suggested?'

'Yes, you can trust him, Jago. I absolutely promise you,' Merrin said, placing a hand on his arm.

'Well, that's good enough for me, sis, but what am I going to say to Gemma? As you know, I'm a lousy liar at the best of times, and lying to my wife really isn't an option.'

'There's no need to. Just tell her that you and I are going into St Ives early tomorrow morning to winkle out who's in charge and ask some searching questions – all of which is true. Say you need to make your own judgement about Louis Peppiatt and not just rely on my view. I'll pick you up at nine tomorrow morning and it will also give Tom and Gemma a bit of time on their own.'

'Okey-dokey, I can do that,' said Jago. 'I just feel so sorry for Gemma. She's absolutely riddled with guilt and I don't seem to be able to reassure her in any way. She is blaming herself entirely for her mother's death, without a doubt.'

'But if we can find out what really happened to Philip, then maybe that will help Gemma come to terms with the decision her mother made. Yes?'

'Yes,' said Jago firmly. 'God bless you, sis.'

CHAPTER SEVEN

As soon as Merrin was back in her cottage, she phoned Louis Peppiatt. 'Things are a bit tense in the Trehearne camp at the moment, as you can imagine,' she said. 'So, I had to make a snap decision. I'm picking up Jago at nine tomorrow morning and I'm hoping it will be possible to meet you in town at nine-fifteen? I'm sorry it's so early and on a Saturday, too.'

'That's no problem. I'll be at your cottage sharp at nine-fifteen and thank you for arranging the meeting so quickly,' said Louis.

'Actually, could we meet at Clara's restaurant instead?' Merrin said.

'I would prefer we met at your cottage, or the police station. I don't want to conduct the interview with other people about.'

'Clara and Tristan don't open their restaurant until eleven, which is why I have suggested we meet early. I'll talk to them and make sure they stay in the kitchen for the duration,' said Merrin firmly.

'OK,' said Louis, 'if that suits you best – it just seems rather an odd place to meet when the subject matter is so delicate.'

'I should have explained at the beginning, Louis – apologies. My brother, Jago, uses a wheelchair and the steps leading up to my cottage could prove to be rather a challenge. He is fiercely independent and he can wheel himself straight into the restaurant.'

'Of course, I understand now. Tristan's Fish Plaice at nine-fifteen it'll be.'

Merrin then phoned Clara and made arrangements for the meeting. Clara was immediately very excited. 'Two of my favourite men here at the same time, hurrah!'

'I knew, of course, that Jago was a favourite of yours but I had no idea that Louis Peppiatt had made it into Clara's Hall of Fame.'

'Of course he has, Pearl darling. You've spent far more time with him than I have so you must have noticed that he is seriously fanciable. I know you're not on the lookout for a chap at the moment, but there is no harm in window shopping!'

'For heaven's sake, Clara. You know perfectly well that there can never be another man in my life after Adam. I can't bear the idea; it's absolutely out of the question.'

'And I know your inspector can be a bit grumpy and sharp at times, but he can also be very funny. I think he's lovely.'

'Clara, are you listening to me?'

'No, not really, darling Pearl, actually not at all.'

* * *

41

Louis had planned to take his children out for the day on Saturday but if the meeting went well with Jago, he knew it was important that he collated all the information he had gained so far. Then, it was a question of setting up a meeting with the Trehearnes as quickly as possible, before they became too impatient. He also suspected that, by Monday, he would be under pressure to report back to the chief super on his progress. He called his ex-wife, Stephanie, and as he did so, he felt the all-too-familiar gnawing sense of guilt – how many times had he made this very same phone call?

Stephanie supplied the answer. 'Hello, Louis, I assume you're calling to cancel tomorrow?'

'Yes,' said Louis. 'I'm so sorry, but I've got this rather urgent case about a missing man . . .'

'Save it. We've heard it all before, so many times, it's quite impossible to count. Is there any chance you can take them out on Sunday instead?'

Louis hesitated. 'I think I'd better say no as I'm hoping to see the family concerned on Saturday, but if it's not convenient for them, then it will be Sunday. I could pop over now, if you're free, and maybe take you all out for supper as it's Friday. Does that have any appeal?'

'I'm afraid that won't work. We have Andrew's brother and his son coming for supper and staying the night. I think it might be a little awkward if you turned up – awkward and maybe difficult for Andrew. His brother is not the easiest, I believe.'

'I totally understand, Steph. Give my love to the children. I'll try and do better next time.'

'Don't say that, Louis – I know work always comes first,

the children know work always comes first, so don't try and kid me that things will ever change. And most important of all, don't kid yourself.' Stephanie ended the call.

As he drove to St Ives the following morning, Louis's thoughts were clouded with remorse. He firmly believed himself to be a failure as a father but could see no way to redress the balance. After the separation from his wife, Louis had made his home in Truro, in a small Victorian terraced house, close to the city centre. It suited him very well, and, thanks to his job, he was at home so little, it was difficult for him to judge if he was lonely. What he did know, though, was how much he missed his children, and how difficult it was to work out the logistics for seeing them as much as he would like. Daisy, aged thirteen, and Edward, aged nine, lived in Falmouth with their mother and stepfather, Andrew, and fitting trips to Falmouth around the demands of his job was not easy – particularly in the summer months with so many visitors around.

The traffic was light and so he arrived a little early at Tristan's Fish Plaice. Louis knocked on the door and within seconds, it was flung open. 'Inspector, come in, it's lovely to see you,' said Clara. 'I know I'm not supposed to talk to you today and I promise I will play a very low profile, but you are the first to arrive, so can I say hello and fetch you a coffee?'

'Yes please to both,' said Louis, 'black, no—'

'Black, no sugar, I remember. Look, I've put the three of you on that table in the corner, as far away as possible from the kitchen. No one will disturb you, I promise.'

'I feel slightly awkward,' admitted Louis. 'I made a fuss

about coming here, instead of going to Merrin's cottage because I didn't realise Jago was in a wheelchair.'

'How could you possibly have known if no one had told you? He's wonderful about it, makes no fuss – he's a very special person – well, you'll see.'

Louis sat down at the table and leafed through his notes. Really, there was very little to ask Jago that had not already been covered by a combination of Merrin and Jack Eddy. Still, another perspective, and one closest to the family, had to be useful.

The restaurant door opened and Jago entered, followed by Merrin. He propelled his wheelchair across the restaurant at impressive speed, coming to a grinding halt in front of Louis.

'Chief Inspector, very good meet you. I'm Jago Tripconey.' And with a big grin, he held out his hand.

'I'm very pleased to meet you, Mr Tripconey.' The two men shook hands. 'And good morning, Merrin,' Louis added.

At that moment, Clara and Tristan erupted out of the kitchen, Tristan carrying a tray of coffee and biscuits. Clara ran up to Jago and flung her arms round him and there followed much hugging and kissing between the four of them. Louis looked on with amusement. It was not difficult to imagine them all as children, playing on the beach and yelling and shrieking much as they were doing now.

Finally, calm was restored. Clara, still holding Jago's hand, said, 'He was my first love, you see, Inspector. When he threw me over, I ended up with this dolt.' She left Jago and put her arms round Tristan.

'So, I'm second best,' said Tristan, addressing Louis.

'You don't look too distressed about it,' Louis suggested.

'You're right, Inspector, I'm very lucky – Jago's loss!' Tristan confirmed.

'You two are seriously out of order,' said Jago. 'It's "Chief Inspector" now – so disrespectful.'

'Sorry,' said Tristan and Clara in unison.

'As we only have until eleven, we do need to get on with the interview now,' said the newly titled Chief Inspector.

'So masterful!' said Clara.

'Go!' demanded Louis, smiling.

While everyone said their farewells, Louis studied Jago. He was a very good-looking man, and appeared years younger than fifty-six, which Louis knew him to be. Possibly because of his years in Australia, he had a mop of fair hair, so unlike his sister, whose hair was dark. However, like Merrin's, his eyes were a startling blue, which very easily crinkled with pleasure. *This is a good man*, Louis thought and, despite his injury, he seemed full of enthusiasm and zest for life. He was also, Louis felt immediately, a man he could trust.

Silence reigned at last as Clara and Tristan retreated to their kitchen. 'Before we begin, Mr Tripconey,' said Louis, 'can I first offer my condolences for the loss of your mother-in-law, in such very sad circumstances. I imagine it must be particularly hard on your wife, being so far away when her mother died.'

This is a decent bloke, perceptive and kind, Jago thought, *and Merrin is right to trust him*. 'Thank you,' he said.

* * *

'I'm just going to ask you questions at random, Mr Tripconey. I suppose the first one is where were you when Philip disappeared?'

'I was in Australia. I knew Gemma, of course, St Ives is a small town, but we were not involved in any way at that time. I heard the news from my parents, and I was particularly upset for Dad, as Philip was a great pal of his. Before we go on, could you possibly call me Jago?'

'Thank you, I will,' said Louis. 'In a way, this is not a very promising start to an investigation. You were in Australia, Merrin was in Bristol and I was in Newton Abbot when Philip vanished. However, we are saved by Jack Eddy, who was in St Ives at the time and was also involved in the search.'

'Dear old Jack, how is he?' Jago asked.

Louis and Merrin looked at one another and smiled. 'I think we can say he's just the same,' said Merrin.

'Very diplomatic and absolutely accurate,' said Louis, laughing. 'So, apart from the family and Jack, is there anyone else you think I should talk to, just really for background?'

'I've been thinking about that,' said Jago. 'I believe it might be worth talking to Jim Ferrell. He was the farmer Philip was going to meet at Halsetown Inn that fateful evening. Philip, of course, never turned up, but the two men were contemporaries, friends and both farmed nearby. Jim's wife died about ten years ago. He struggled to keep going on his own but his heart wasn't in it. He sold the farm but kept one of the cottages for himself. He's out Ludgvan way, not far. You won't find him easy, he's pretty much a recluse, so no great conversationalist, but he's straight as a die.'

'I'll give you the details as to how to find him,' Merrin offered.

'Thank you,' said Louis. 'Is there anyone else I should talk to? What about the farm manager who works for the Trehearnes?'

'David, not much point, really. He came to work on the farm after Philip had disappeared. Sarah and Tom just weren't coping and so advertised for help. Also, he's not even local, he comes from somewhere in Devon – up Dartmoor way, I think.'

'Jago, do the family have a theory as to what happened to Philip? I'm including Sarah in this as well as their children,' Louis asked.

Jago was silent for a while. 'The trouble is,' he said, 'the family's view was very much coloured by Sarah. You see, she never gave up hope that one day Philip would walk back through the kitchen door. I think it was the only way she could cope – over thirty years on her own, battling to keep the farm going, raising the kids as a single parent – she managed it by believing that Philip would return one day. It's my belief, for what it's worth, that the reason she killed herself was because she was so worn out, she could no longer keep hope alive.'

Louis looked at Merrin. 'You said something very similar, didn't you?' She nodded. 'That's very sad,' Louis continued, 'but also interesting. Do you think her hope died purely because she just gave up, or do you think it could be because something happened, a trigger that made her give way to despair?'

'I honestly don't know,' said Jago, 'but it's a question you need to ask Tom. I'm not sure what Tom and Gemma really believe happened to their father, but Gemma held the party line – even to me. Because their mother kept hope alive, for Sarah's sake they went along with it – apparently also believing he would turn up one day. There was no body, you see, so there was no closure.'

'This is a question I've already asked your sister – is there anything you know of in Philip's past that could have rebounded on him in some way?' Louis asked.

'Absolutely not, so far as I know,' said Jago. 'It's a pity our dad's not alive; he would be able to answer that question better than me and Merrin. They were lads together but I never heard anything about them getting up to no good. Did you, sis?'

Merrin shook her head.

'Jack Eddy is working with me on this case. While I've been gathering background information, I've not involved him. However, when I meet your wife and Tom, I will need to bring him along.'

'That's fine,' said Jago. 'He's a local man, which helps. Also, it might reassure Tom to see you have someone else working on the case. I know Gemma was not overly impressed when Merrin told her that there were only two policemen involved in the new investigation, but two is definitely better than one!'

'Could I come out to the farm this afternoon?' Louis asked. 'If I arrive at about four, by then, hopefully, I will have had a chance to see Jim Ferrell.'

'I know that'll be fine. They are very anxious to see you,' said Jago.

'Finally, Jago,' said Louis, 'please be assured that I'm not trying to wind up the case in a hurry because it's an embarrassment to the police – which, of course, it's certainly proving to be. I promise you, I'm going to do my utmost to try and find out what really happened to Philip Trehearne. I may not succeed but it won't be for the want of trying.'

'Thank you for telling me,' said Jago, 'but, of course, I already knew that.'

There was a sudden banging on the window of the restaurant, a face peering through the glass and waving madly. 'It's Max!' said Merrin. 'Can I let him in, Louis? We're finished here, aren't we?'

Max Richards had been in the same year group at school as Clara and Merrin. He was a serial lothario, with an unbelicvable number of past loves. Now, at fifty-four, he still behaved like a teenager, so far as women were concerned, but he found time to run a very successful independent estate agency. Clara had managed to escape Max's advances but when they were very young teenagers, Merrin had enjoyed a brief and innocent period as his girlfriend. Her heart had been broken when he dumped her, of course, but swiftly mended, since when they had become very good friends.

Max let out a whoop as he ran into the restaurant, made a beeline for Jago and swept him into a huge bear hug. 'Welcome home, boyo, I've missed you.' He stepped back and studied Jago, grinning widely. 'You look great, boy, apart from the obvious – being stupid enough to end up on wheels. Plonker!'

'I love you too, Max,' said Jago, laughing.

'What are you all doing here?' Max turned round and spotted Louis. 'Oh, Lord, I'm sorry. You must be Inspector

Peppiatt and you're all here to talk about poor darling Sarah? Then I come barging in – humble apologies, I'll leave immediately.'

'No need, our meeting's over,' said Louis. 'I'll leave you all to have a catch-up.'

'I need to go, too,' said Merrin. 'I have to drop Jago back and I've promised Isla a FaceTime at midday, which is the time she can get a signal in some bar, they've discovered. She's on Corfu at the moment.'

'I'll drop Jago back to the Trehearnes' to save you a trip,' said Max. 'We might manage a sneaky pint on the way, what do you say, Jago.'

'A bit early for me, Max, but no doubt you'll talk me into it.'

'Come on then, race you to The Sloop!'

Having said their goodbyes to Clara and Tristan, Louis and Merrin walked out onto the Wharf. 'I'll walk you home,' said Louis. 'My car's in the Sloop car park. That Max is a live wire but he certainly knows just how to handle Jago.'

'Totally,' said Merrin. 'Jago wants absolutely no concessions made for his disability and yet you would be surprised at the number of people who grab his wheelchair and start pushing him around, without even asking.'

'The "does he take sugar" brigade – well-meaning, of course, but I imagine very humiliating for someone trying to regain his independence,' suggested Louis.

'Exactly.'

'How and when was he injured, if you don't mind me asking?' said Louis.

'It was a surfing accident. He and Gemma live and work

close by the Northern Beaches, near Sydney. He went up to Bondi because some good surf was forecast. In fact, the waves were massive. He got into trouble and his spine was seriously damaged. To be honest, he was much too old to be surfing such big waves. It all happened just over three years ago. He's worked so hard to get himself fit – you must have noticed how strong his arms are and he has a great barrel of a chest now.'

'It must have been hard for Gemma,' Louis said.

'Yes, of course, although once Jago came out of hospital, he was pretty independent. They have two children, both in their early twenties. Their son, Remy, still lives at home and works in the family business. He's been a great help, I believe.'

'We part here, I think,' said Louis, as they reached the slipway. 'You and your extended family have had a lot to cope with over the last few years. Let's hope we can resolve what happened to Philip. It would be something.'

'It would be a lot,' said Merrin.

CHAPTER EIGHT

Andrew Stevens still couldn't believe his luck. After so many struggles and difficulties, set against his spectacular lack of confidence, everything had changed and he was now truly happy for the first time in his life. After kissing his lovely wife goodbye, exchanging high-fives with his stepson, Edward, and giving his stepdaughter, Daisy, a hug, he climbed into his car and headed for work, even though it was a Saturday. His wife, Stephanie, didn't mind him working at the weekend because he had promised to be home by 11 a.m. sharp, and so he would be. Stephanie was almost paranoid about punctuality and Andrew understood why. Having been married to a very conscientious policeman, who rarely returned home when he said he would, Andrew made sure he was always reliable where time was concerned.

There was also another reason why he was anxious to

get home. His elder brother, Peter, and Peter's son, Henry, had stayed overnight and Peter, in particular, was driving them all mad. Andrew needed to get them out of the house as quickly as possible. An hour's paperwork should see him back home.

From a very early age, Andrew had been aware that he was something of a disappointment to his parents and that Peter was the star of the Stevens family show. Peter was exceptionally good at everything, while Andrew was not particularly good at anything – a fact that was cruelly pointed out from time to time. Peter's A-level results were outstanding and obtained him a place at Cambridge to read pure maths. No one from the Stevens family had ever been to university before and the boys' parents were beside themselves with joy.

At the same time as Peter headed for Cambridge, Andrew left school at sixteen and joined a building firm in Bodmin, the family's home town. He began at the bottom – in those days carrying hods of bricks up rickety ladders – but he immediately loved the work and, much to his own astonishment, his boss told him he was very good at it.

Fast forward six years and Peter was in Futures in the City of London, earning a fortune. Andrew, meanwhile, had bought his first house, renovated it and sold it on at a substantial profit, which enabled him to buy two more houses. After a solitary holiday in West Cornwall, Andrew fell in love with Falmouth and saw the potential for building decent homes in the area. So, he sold his two houses, moved to Falmouth and started his own building firm. He now employed a full-time workforce of six men and had a highly successful business. Peter, now approaching sixty, was immensely rich, pompous, entitled and extremely unpleasant. His son, Henry, was not much better.

Andrew had never married – that is until four months ago, at the age of fifty-seven. There had been girls, of course, but his lack of confidence often got in the way of him progressing a relationship. His upbringing had left him with the feeling that no one could possibly rate him much and, of course, he had worked so hard in the early days of establishing his business, there had been little time for a social life. And then he met Stephanie Peppiatt, newly divorced and looking primarily for security and comfort in any new relationship. Andrew found he could provide both. Having never had children of his own, he was already immensely proud of his stepchildren and found them very easy to love. He could hardly believe it, but he and Stephanie appeared to have created a happy family. He utterly adored her, of course, and he was even starting to believe that maybe she loved him, too.

Peter had been married and divorced three times. Henry, aged thirteen, was his only child, the product of his second marriage. Henry lived with his mother but, reluctantly, had come on holiday to Cornwall with his father. Mercifully, as Peter favoured upmarket hotels, they had only stayed one night with Andrew and Stephanie and that was more than enough. At dinner the previous evening, they had been forced to sit through Peter showing off about his success, and contrasting it with his brother's. It was excruciating but when, once or twice, Stephanie, outraged, had tried to intervene, Peter simply talked over her.

'The trouble is with Peter,' said Stephanie, when, exhausted, she and Andrew finally climbed into bed, 'he is so up himself, there is absolutely no point in trying to argue with him. He doesn't think he's marvellous, he knows he's marvellous. Sorry, darling, but he really is ghastly.'

'I know,' said Andrew, 'I am very, very sorry for inflicting him on you all. It won't happen again, I promise. There's no point, anyway – Peter and I don't like it each and, sadly, never will.'

So, it had been arranged that the two brothers and the boys, Henry and Edward, would go over to St Ives for lunch as Peter and Henry were staying at the Carbis Bay Hotel that night. They therefore travelled in two cars, Andrew hoping that he and Edward could make a hasty exit as soon as lunch was over. Stephanie and Daisy were staying in Falmouth – mother and daughter had decided they needed a little retail therapy to get over the whole Peter experience. Andrew completely understood.

Lunch had been booked at Tristan's Fish Plaice. Peter was predictably awful, being rude to the staff and criticising the wine list. Eventually, they ordered and when the main course arrived, Peter asked for a second bottle of Chablis.

'I'm not going to drink any more, Peter,' said Andrew, 'so do you really want another bottle?'

'Turned into a bit of a lightweight, have you, old boy?'

'No,' said Andrew, 'but I'm driving with a very precious cargo on board.' He winked at Edward, who grinned back.

'Well, if you won't join me, I'll just have to drink alone.' Peter was already slightly slurring his words.

Predictably, as the meal continued, Peter became louder and more embarrassing to the point where Andrew could see that even the boys were starting to feel uneasy.

'After all these chips,' Peter announced, 'what we should do now is walk to Zennor on the cliff path and grab ourselves a cream tea.'

'Not a good idea,' said Andrew firmly. 'It's a good three hours' walk, particularly for the boys.' As he spoke he tried hard not to consider the merits of Peter almost certainly falling over the cliff, in his current state of inebriation.

'Henry and I have done the walk before. It's nothing like three hours,' said Peter, who, one had to remember, knew everything and was always right.

'Actually, Dad, we went the field way, which is quicker,' Henry piped up.

There was a pause, while clearly Peter was considering what *he* actually wanted to do. 'I suppose you're right, Andrew,' he conceded magnanimously. 'The walk is too far for Edward. He's rather young and not very sporty, I understand. It's a shame for the rest of us, but it can't be helped. We'll drive over there instead.'

'Edward and I need to get back to Falmouth, so we'll give Zennor a miss,' said Andrew, just managing to contain his anger. 'And I'm sure you can have a cream tea at your hotel, without having to go to Zennor.'

'Why don't you two boys get yourselves an ice cream and do a bit of shopping,' Peter suggested. He drew out his wallet and peeled off two twenty-pound notes for each of them.

'I don't need all this,' Edward began.

'Don't be churlish, boy, off you go.'

'Hang on a moment, let's fix a time when you'll be back here. Let's say fifteen minutes at the most.' Andrew looked at his watch. 'By two-thirty.' Both boys nodded and scampered off.

'I just want to make the point, Andrew,' said Peter, 'that I don't like being told how I should spend the afternoon with my son. As soon as the boys are back, Henry and I will drive over to Zennor. You're obviously under instruction from Stephanie to go back home. I have never allowed myself to be bossed around by any wife of mine, like that.'

Andrew let it go. Peter had already ordered coffee and brandies for them both. Andrew would not be drinking his brandy, so clearly Peter would drink the two of them. Not wanting to cause a scene, Andrew decided he would leave the drink-driving issue until they were out of the restaurant. So instead, he then had to endure a lecture on how to run his business, how to run his finances and even more advice on how to have a successful marriage, which was particularly rich considering Peter had three failed marriages behind him.

At last, Andrew could stand it no more and, looking at his watch, saw that the boys had been away for over forty minutes and it was now three o'clock. 'Peter, has Henry got a mobile?' he asked.

'Yes, of course,' said Peter.

'Could you call it, please?'

Peter fumbled in his pocket and after a few false starts, the number rang out from the pocket of Henry's jacket, which was still hanging on the back of his chair.

'Damn the boy,' said Peter. 'You'd better call Edward.'

'Edward doesn't have a mobile yet,' said Andrew.

'Extraordinary! Well, I suppose one of us had better go and look for them.'

CHAPTER NINE

It took Andrew nearly half an hour to establish where the boys were likely to have gone. With information obtained from two very helpful shopkeepers, a kindly man selling ice cream from a van and, finally, a member of the St Ives Bowls Club, he established that the boys had apparently decided to walk to Zennor.

He could hardly believe it but the information he received was compelling. The shopkeepers and ice-cream seller had heard snippets of conversation between the boys that suggested that was what they were planning to do, and the member of the bowls club was able to describe the boys in detail, as they walked alongside the bowling green and headed up towards the cliff path – now about an hour previously.

'I nearly shouted after them,' the elderly man said, his face creased with concern. 'The little one can't be very old.

I just assumed they were meeting their parents up there. I'm so sorry.'

'It's not your fault; you've been very helpful. Thank you but I must dash now.'

Andrew started running back towards the restaurant. On arrival, he saw that Peter was still slumped at the table. He went straight to the till. 'I'm sorry about him,' he said to the waitress, nodding in Peter's direction. 'I'll pay the bill and then move him.'

'It's a monstrous bill, I'm afraid,' she said, smiling, 'and mostly down to him.'

'I don't doubt it,' said Andrew. 'Also could you tell me where to find the nearest police station?'

'Yes, of course. What's wrong, can I help?'

'Our two boys, who were eating here earlier, have started walking on their own along the coastal path to Zennor. They've been gone over an hour and I think I need some help to find them. The sun's disappeared and it's getting very misty.'

'You certainly need help. Look, here's your receipt. I'll call the police right away.' She picked up her mobile and seconds later she was through. 'Jack, it's Clara. There are two young boys who are attempting to walk the coastal path to Zennor, all on their own. They've been gone over an hour.' There was a pause, as she listened. 'Our local constable is going to alert the coastguards,' she said. 'Jack says when this happens they usually have two teams searching, one starting from Zennor and one from St Ives, so don't worry, they'll find them.' Another pause. 'Jack says can he have the names and ages of the boys, and your name too, please?'

'Yes, of course. My name is Andrew Stevens; the boys are Henry Stevens, aged thirteen, and Edward Peppiatt, aged nine.'

'Peppiatt!' said Clara. 'Any relation to Chief Inspector Louis Peppiatt?'

'Yes,' said Andrew, 'Edward is his son.'

'Goodness,' said Clara, 'that's not good, poor Louis. Actually, I think he still might be in the area today. I'll get Jack to track him down. I hope the boys are alright.' Clara suddenly had images of the cliff edge and the mine shafts. 'What are you going to do with your friend there?'

'It's my brother, I'm afraid. I'm going to dump him in my car, which is just up the road at the Sloop. Then, I'm going to join the footpath and hope I catch up with the boys. It's a nightmare, someone else's child. You know Louis Peppiatt, then?'

'Yes, I do, in fact he was in the restaurant earlier this morning,' said Clara. 'Look, let's exchange numbers and I promised I would pass yours on to the police. If the boys come back here, I'll obviously let you know and please tell me when you find them. My name's Clara Tregonning.'

'Thank you so much for your help, Clara.' Andrew went over to the table, picked up the boys' jackets, none-too-gently dragged Peter to his feet and left the restaurant as quickly as escorting a drunk would allow.

Louis's meeting with Jim Ferrell had not been very productive, in fact not really productive at all, except to confirm what instinctively he believed he already knew. Louis was not allowed inside Jim's cottage so the two men sat outside on a bench. It was very pleasant, the sun was shining and the view spectacular – looking towards the moorland one way and Mount's Bay the other, St Michael's Mount, back-lit by the sun and looking like something out of a fairy tale. However, Jim was both grumpy and monosyllabic.

Louis tried to engage the old man in topics unrelated to Philip Trehearne – modern farming, retirement, the old collie dog who sat by his side – all a waste of time. Finally, Louis asked him the question he had asked everyone else. 'So, Jim, what do you think happened to Philip?'

'Well,' Jim said, without hesitation, 'Philip would never have left Sarah of his own free will, nor the children, nor the farm, come to that. So, either he had an accident or he was took.'

'What do you mean by "took"?' Louis asked.

'How should I know? That's your job. But we searched every square inch of land around the path to the pub. No sign of him and no body, so he must have been took – stands to reason, don't it, copper?'

'Put like that, it does sound about right, Jim,' said Louis.

'I'd have thought you'd have been able to work that out for yourself.'

Suitably chastened, Louis returned to his car. He still had an hour before he was due to see Tom and Gemma Trehearne, so he decided to call in on Jack Eddy and use the office for a final look through his notes before they both headed to the Trehearnes.

Louis was still driving down the lane leading from Jim's cottage, when his phone rang. It was Jack Eddy. 'Hello, Eddy,' he said, 'I'm just on my way over to see you.'

'Where are you, boss?' Jack asked

'I've just left Jim Ferrell's, I shouldn't be more than ten minutes. Why do you ask?'

There was a moment's hesitation, which Louis immediately picked up on. 'What's going on, Eddy?' he asked.

'There's a bit of a flap on, boss. Two young boys are on the coastal path, apparently trying to walk to Zennor on their own. The thing is, boss' – he hesitated again – 'one of them is your son, Edward.'

Louis jammed the brakes on, stalling his car. 'How long have they been on the coastal path?' he asked.

'About an hour and a half, no, maybe two hours by now. Boss, the coastguards are on the job – one team have just left St Ives, the other is going to Zennor and will start walking from that end.'

Louis felt his sense of unease bolting towards panic. 'What's my son even doing in St Ives? Does his mother know he's missing? Who is the other boy and why is no one with them?'

'I don't know all the answers, boss, I'm sorry. He was with his stepfather, Andrew Stevens. The other boy is a nephew of Andrew's, I think. His name is Henry Stevens and he's thirteen. I don't know why they're in town, boss and I don't know if Mrs Peppiatt has been informed.'

'Mrs Stevens, not Mrs Peppiatt,' Louis replied savagely. Some part of his brain registered that it was completely out of order to be angry with Jack Eddy but somehow he was unable to control himself. He took a deep breath. 'Do you have Andrew Stevens's phone number, and where is he at the moment?'

'I have his number, boss, and he is on the coastal path

himself but he is a long way behind the boys.'

'Right, Eddy. Call Andrew and find out if he has rung his wife. If not, tell him to do so immediately. Also, ask him if the other boy, Henry, I think you said, has ever been on that section of the coastal path. I'm fairly sure Edward has not been there before.' He stared through his car windscreen. 'It looks like there's a sea mist coming in. How's it down with you?'

'Very thick, boss, and it's starting to rain – a right old Cornish mizzle.'

'I'm heading your way right now – you'd better call the Trehearnes and explain what's happened. We'll have to postpone the meeting.' Louis was about to start the engine again and then paused for a moment, trying to calm the wave of panic sweeping through him. Edward was a sensible boy, but what about this Henry, that much older – was he a good influence or a bad one? *Pull yourself together*, he thought, *Ed will be alright, of course he will.*

As he drove off, his thoughts turned to Stephanie. Why did he suggest Andrew should call her? Because he was Stephanie's husband, he supposed. Now he wished, with all his heart, that he had been the one to break the news to her. Together they had produced this beautiful boy. Stephanie was the only person he wanted to speak to right now – she was the only person who would understand. And he knew, without a shadow of doubt, that she would feel the same.

CHAPTER TEN

Tom Trehearne strode into the kitchen, waving his mobile in the air, his face like thunder. His sister, Gemma, and Jago Tripconey were sitting at the kitchen table. David, who worked on the farm, was washing his hands in the sink.

'Jack Eddy has just rung to say the police can't come this afternoon. Apparently, they have a more important case on their hands. They are going to try – "try", mind you, no promises – to be with us tomorrow morning.' Tom collapsed in a chair and struck the table with his fist. 'It's just not good enough. Bastards!'

'Did they give a reason for cancelling this afternoon's meeting?' Jago asked, surprised at this development.

'Yes,' said Tom. 'Apparently, two young boys have got themselves lost on the coastal path to Zennor and one of the boys is the son of Peppiatt, the man allegedly heading up the inquiry into Dad's death. Typical, isn't it? They always look after their own.'

'Come on, Tom, be reasonable,' said Jago. 'I don't know exactly how old Peppiatt's boy is but I think he's quite young. Of course he needs to give priority to finding his son. We've waited over thirty years to find out what happened to Philip, another day will make no difference.'

'That's not the point,' said Tom morosely.

'Who's for tea?' David asked, picking up the kettle. 'Tom, did Jack give you any details about the boys, as to where they might be?'

'Of course he did, you know how Jack witters on. I stopped listening properly after a while, I was just so angry. Let me think for a moment.' Tom put his head in his hands and rubbed his eyes. 'They've been missing for over two hours and they started from St Ives. The coastguards are on it. They have split into two groups – one on the coastal path from St Ives, and one on the field path from Zennor, so the little buggers are bound to be found soon.'

'Why the field path?' Gemma asked.

'Apparently, the older boy, not Peppiatt's son, the other one, has walked to Zennor before but on that occasion, he was taken on the field path. Bloody fuss about nothing, if you ask me.'

'Two hours is a long time to be missing on that stretch. I bet I know what they've done. They've left the coastal path to find their way across to the fields, and got lost,' said David. 'Gemma, would you mind making the tea? I'm going to try and find them.'

'How, where and, for God's sake, why?' Tom demanded.

'I'll drive to Wicca Farm; I bet they're somewhere near there,' said David.

'But why should you even bother?' Tom repeated.

David picked up his coat. 'Look out of the window – there's a thick sea mist coming in fast and it's started to rain. The sooner they're found, the better. It wouldn't be too difficult for the boys to go over the cliff edge in this.'

'You're such a good Samaritan,' said Tom, and, somehow, it didn't sound like much of a compliment.

David jumped into the Land Rover and hurtled down the drive. He had walked the coastal paths of West Cornwall many times in the years since he began working for the Trehearnes. As a boy of about seven, he had once got lost on Dartmoor, wandering off on his own during a school outing. He had never forgotten his mother's face when he was found. How her expression had turned from terror, to relief, to absolutely unconditional love. When she died, it wasn't the cuddles, kisses, bedtime stories, nor, as he grew, her encouragement and pride in him that lingered in his mind. It was the look on her face the day he'd been lost that he treasured most. He might never have had children of his own, but instinctively, David knew exactly how these boys' parents would be feeling. His mother had taught him that.

And, David mused, if he could find the boys, it should make Peppiatt work a little harder to finally close Philip's case, which in turn might help Tom to calm down. While Sarah had always held on to the belief that her husband would one day come home, her children had been more circumspect. As the years went by, David's view was they had come to accept that they would never see their dad again. However, since his mother's death, Tom seemed to have picked up her cudgel of hope, which was making him both very angry and very unhappy. It was distressing to watch but, in David's view, it was time Tom realised that his father was now never going to come back home. Maybe Peppiatt could help him see that.

David turned into the car park at Wicca Farm. He was about to get out of the car when he realised he did not know the boys' names. He found the number for the police station and Jack Eddy answered. 'Jack, it's David from the Trehearnes'. I'm at Wicca Farm and I'm going to have a look for the boys – I assume they're still missing?'

'Yes, they're still out there somewhere,' said Jack, 'and it's a worry – the mist is awful thick, there's no wind and the tide's dead low – a very bad combo.'

'I don't quite follow,' said David.

'Can tell you're no Cornishman. If the tide's low, if there's no wind and with this mist and rain, the boys won't be able to hear or see the edge of the cliff. Easy to go over the top in those conditions and there'll be no one else walking on the cliff path to help them when the weather's like this.'

'I hope the boys' parents aren't with you, Jack. They certainly don't need to hear that.'

'No, only the boss is here and he's taken his phone outside. What can I do for you, David?'

'I just need the names of the boys. Obviously, if I find them, I'll let you know immediately, and could you do the same for me if the coastguards track them down?'

'Right-oh,' said Jack. 'The boys' names are Henry and

Edward. Edward is the boss's son. Give me your number and I'll keep you in the loop.'

David headed down the path between Wicca Farm and the cottage opposite, but instead of turning left onto the field path, he began picking his way down towards the sea. The way was tortuous. He seemed to have completely missed the path, the ground was littered with large boulders, which were difficult to navigate, and the mist was so thick, he could barely see where he was going. Stopping to catch his breath, he realised Jack had been right. There was an eerie silence, no wind, no sound of the waves and the mist was acting like a blanket, covering all sight and sound. To add to the general discomfort, the rain was now pelting down. It would be very easy to become disorientated up here, he realised – even for someone like him, who knew the area so well. But for two young boys . . .

He began shouting their names – 'Henry, Edward, can you hear me? I've come to rescue you. Shout if you can hear me?' Silence. He stumbled on.

After about ten minutes, he reached the coastal path. He was right on the cliff edge now but could still only just hear the sea as it broke over the rocks below. *Now what?* he thought. Instinct told him to head back towards St Ives. Despite the length of time the boys had been missing, he doubted in this weather that they would have made a great deal of progress. He decided to walk a short way along the coastal path and then head back up again towards the fields. And where were the coastguards? He began shouting again, his voice hoarse now. The search was beginning to feel a great deal more difficult than he had first thought.

* * *

Louis was striding up and down Jack's tiny office, beside himself with frustration and rage.

'What's up, boss?' Jack asked.

'The coastguards don't want me to help in the search for the boys. In fact, they pretty much forbade it. They say the conditions are too dangerous and they don't want anyone else up on the cliff path. I reminded them it was my son they were looking for, but they seemed to think I would be a hindrance rather than a help. I can't just stay here and wait, I just can't.'

'You'll have to wait for your wife, boss. You can't leave her here, worrying herself sick. She won't be long now. She called me from Camborne and that was at least a quarter of an hour ago.'

'My ex-wife, Eddy. Did she say what she was doing about Daisy?'

'Don't think so, boss. Is Daisy your dog?'

'For God's sake, Eddy. Daisy's my daughter!'

Mercifully for Sergeant Eddy, at that moment Stephanie burst through the office door. 'Any news?' For a moment her expression was full of hope.

'Not yet,' said Louis, his anger completely vanishing as he watched his words replace hope with anguish. 'It's alright, Steph, they'll find him. Two teams of coastguards are out there, aren't they, Eddy?'

'Yes, boss, and David from the Trehearnes' is up on the cliff too, and Mr Stevens, of course.'

'Mr Stevens – you mean my husband, Andrew?' said Stephanie.

'That's right,' said Jack.

'Why's he still up there and yet the coastguards won't

let me join in the search?' Louis raged. 'And what the hell is this David doing? Why's he even involved?'

'Mr Stevens has been up there a while, of course, way ahead of the coastguards. As soon as he'd raised the alarm, Clara said, he was going to try and catch up with the boys. He rang Mrs Stevens, I understand, and then went straight on up. As for David, he knows the cliffs well and has an idea where the boys might be.'

'I'm going up to join them,' said Louis, reaching for his coat.

'No,' said Stephanie and Jack in one voice.

'He's my son, I can't leave him up there in the hopes that someone will find him. I have to go.' He looked at them both, appealing for understanding.

'You can't, Louis,' said Stephanie. 'When it comes to crime, you're the expert. You know exactly what you're doing. When it comes to rescue, the coastguards are the experts, you have to respect that. Anyway, look at you, you need walking boots for clambering over rocks, which will be very slippery in this weather. You're just not dressed for the cliff path.'

'Neither is Ed, I imagine,' said Louis.

Louis and Stephanie stared at one another for a moment. Then Stephanie burst into tears and ran into Louis's arms.

'I'd best get a brew on,' said Jack.

CHAPTER ELEVEN

Of course, it had been Henry's idea and, like his father, he was used to getting his own way. 'Let's walk the coastal path to Zennor without waiting for my dad and Uncle Andrew.'

'Why?' asked Edward.

'To show them that you can do it, of course. Dad said it was too far for you to walk, which was spoiling things for the rest of us. Don't you want to prove him wrong?'

'Not really,' said Edward. 'I'm sorry, but I don't like your dad very much. He's too shouty and he's nasty to Andrew.'

'Oh, don't be such a wimp, Ed, you're almost as pathetic as Uncle Andrew,' said Henry. 'I know the way to Zennor. Honestly, it doesn't take long over the fields. They'll still be having drinks at the restaurant by the time we get there.'

'Andrew wants us to go back to Falmouth,' said Edward. 'I think Mum is expecting us home.'

And then Henry played his trump card. 'Your real dad, he's the policeman who got stabbed when he caught some drug smugglers, isn't he?' Edward nodded. 'I bet he won't be very proud of a son who's too afraid to walk to Zennor. I reckon he'd be really disappointed in you if he finds out you're that scared. Come on, it'll be fun.'

The fun stopped fairly rapidly as the sea mist rolled in and the rain started. Henry began leading them up a track that he said would take them to the field path. It didn't. 'Let's go back down to the coastal path,' he yelled.

'I don't think we should do that,' said Edward. 'I don't think we should go near the cliff edge again.'

'We'll go this way, then, if you're so afraid,' sneered Henry, heading towards a pile of rocks. 'It looks to me like my dad was right, you are too young for this walk.'

'It looks to me more like we're lost,' said Edward, showing commendable spirit.

Henry ignored him and began climbing over the rocks. Edward followed. He made it to the top but then his foot slipped, and he fell.

David turned inland again, cursing himself for having inadvertently chosen a particularly steep climb off the coastal path. He was a tall man, well over six foot and muscular from years of labouring on the farm. He was only in his early fifties, but today his head ached cruelly, as did his left knee. A few weeks previously, just before Sarah Trehearne had died, he'd had a run-in with the farm's bull, Ferdie. Normally a gentle beast, Ferdie had the hump about something that day. He had charged at

David and tossed him against a barn door, resulting in mild concussion and a badly bruised knee. Everyone said how lucky he was to have escaped with such minor injuries, but with a thumping head and a pronounced limp, he was not feeling particularly lucky right now.

He struggled over a large boulder and stopped to catch his breath. 'Henry, Edward, I've come to rescue you, can you hear me?'

For a moment, there was complete silence. Then, higher up and to the left, David thought he heard something. He tried again. 'Henry, Edward, can you hear me?' he bellowed.

This time it was unmistakable – 'Help!' in a thin, high voice.

'I'm coming,' shouted David. 'Keeping saying "help" so I can find you.'

His aches and pains forgotten, David began scrambling over the rocks and bracken. 'Shout again, shout again!' he kept calling. The cries for help grew louder until David rounded the corner of a pile of rocks to find a small boy sitting on the ground. 'You must be Edward,' he said.

Edward nodded. He was close to tears but fighting them, ferociously rubbing his eyes. His face was filthy and blood had caked down the side of one cheek.

'Are you hurt?' David asked.

'Just my ankle,' Edward replied. He was shivering uncontrollably, which was not surprising as he was only wearing shorts and a T-shirt and so was wet through. David hurriedly stripped off his jacket and wrapped it round the boy's shoulders.

Edward's ankle was badly swollen. David carefully

74

untied his trainer and gently removed the shoe. He felt the ankle, Edward's leg was a mass of cuts and bruises. 'Is it just the ankle that really hurts?'

Edward nodded. 'Yes, I think so. It feels much better now you've taken off my shoe.'

'Well, don't worry. You're safe now. I can carry you up to my car, which is not far. Where's Henry?'

'He's gone down to the cliff path. He's going to walk back to St Ives.'

'To fetch help for you?' David suggested.

'I suppose so, he was very cross with me when he left.' Edward hesitated for a moment. 'I don't like Henry very much but I hope he doesn't fall over the cliff.'

'He'll be alright. Now, before we do anything, we'd better phone your father, hadn't we?'

'What, my real father?' said Edward. 'Does he know we were walking to Zennor?'

'Yes, and your mum too, I expect. They'll be very pleased to know you're safe.'

David rang the police station and asked a very inquisitive Jack Eddy to put him straight on to Louis Peppiatt. 'Chief Inspector, it's David from the Trehearnes, I've found your son and he's alright – a bit battered and bruised with a very sore ankle but I don't think it's broken.'

There was a silence, followed by a ragged sigh, then speaking away from the phone, David heard him say, 'Steph, he's been found and he's OK.' He then returned to the phone. 'David, I don't know what to say, how to thank you enough. Where's Henry?'

'On the cliff path, heading towards St Ives. Hopefully, the coastguards will pick him up. Shall I take Edward straight to West Cornwall Hospital for a check-up, and meet you there?'

'That would be great,' said Louis, 'but can you manage to get off the cliff on your own alright?'

'I'll give Edward a piggyback, my car's at Wicca Farm, not too far away. I'll be very careful.'

'Thank you again, David, I'm so very grateful and we'll head off to Penzance straight away. Could I just speak to Edward?'

David handed over the phone and then stood up, moving away to give father and son a little privacy. As quickly as it had come, the sea mist was starting to curl away. Now, he could see the coastal path beneath him and suddenly he knew exactly where he was. He had walked almost in a full circle. If he continued walking up the cliff, they should reach his car in less than ten minutes.

The walk proved easier than David had expected. Edward, small and slight, weighed very little. David didn't speak as he climbed, reserving all his energy, but his head and knee pain had vanished. *Adrenalin must have kicked in*, he thought. Once in the car, with the heater on full blast, David began telling Edward about how, as a boy, he had become lost on Dartmoor. However, after just a few minutes, looking in the rear-view mirror, he saw Edward was fast asleep.

He smiled, a rare occurrence for David. His life had not been easy in many respects but it always pleased him to know when he'd done something good, when he'd made a difference. Being able to help people gave him a great deal of pleasure.

CHAPTER TWELVE

Louis Peppiatt left home in plenty of time on Sunday morning for his re-scheduled meeting at the Trehearnes' – where he and Jack were due to present themselves at 10 a.m. He'd spent a restless night, reliving the dramas of the previous day, and, in semi-sleep, conjuring up images of his son falling over the cliff, down a mine shaft – even dying of hypothermia, which was a somewhat deranged thought, considering it was July. Still, they were the wild imaginings of a father who loved his son. As dawn was making an appearance, he'd got up, had a long, hot bath and a strong cup of coffee. The idea of breakfast eluded him – the sick feeling in the pit of his stomach was still in evidence.

All things considered, they had been very lucky. The coastguards had found, separately, both Andrew and Henry, cold and wet but otherwise unharmed. But uppermost in his mind was the moment when he and Stephanie had been reunited with their son. Edward was sitting on the side of a hospital bed, draped in a towelling robe, many sizes too big for him. When he saw them, he held out his arms to them both and in seconds, the three of them were in a bear hug – no one ever wanting to let go.

Edward had been told that he must keep the weight off his injured ankle for a few days. Rather than use this as an excuse not to go to school, Edward had asked for crutches, no doubt thinking this would give him hero status among his friends. A kindly nurse had offered to show him how to use them. 'You both look exhausted,' she'd said to Louis and Stephanie. 'Why don't you go and have a coffee and a sit-down, while I teach young sir, here, how to walk with crutches? I'll call you when he's up and running!'

It had been a good opportunity to talk, Louis mused, as he drove on to the A30, heading for St Ives. He'd asked Stephanie whether she thought the incident would damage her relationship with Andrew.

'No,' she'd said immediately. 'It wasn't his fault. His brother, Peter, is a monster and I now understand why Andrew is so unsure of himself, despite his success in business. From what I gather, if we're to assign blame to any one person, then I suppose it's Henry's fault, but only because his father has created him in his own image. I have spoken to Andrew on the phone. He's beside himself with guilt and remorse but I'm sure we can get through it. I'm also hoping that now I have a much better insight into his family background, I'll be able to gradually help him feel more confident. Actually, he did show some spirit where Peter was concerned. When Andrew and Henry were reunited, the coastguards drove them to Andrew's car, where Peter was still asleep, completely oblivious to the drama. Andrew then drove father and son to their hotel. Having deposited them, Andrew told Peter he never wants to see him again. Very strong words for Andrew.'

'He's a good man,' Louis had said.

'Yes, he is,' Stephanie agreed, 'and he's reliable, dependable and safe.' She had laughed a little then, and briefly put an arm round Louis's shoulders. 'Unlike some!'

Louis smiled at the memory of her words. She was right, of course, he was none of those things. In the early years of their marriage, before the children had arrived, they had been very much in love and he loved her still, while recognising they could never live together again. Like many, many women before her, Stephanie was not suited to being a policeman's wife, and who could blame her? As Louis's career had blossomed, and therefore had become more demanding, so he found himself always putting the job before his family. It was not right, nor fair, but he seemed unable to do anything about it.

'I don't think the Trehearnes are going to be best pleased with us, from what I hear,' Jack Eddy said, as they turned off the road onto the lane leading to the farm.

'Where did you hear that?' Louis asked.

'In the pub last night,' said Jack. 'Tom Trehearne had just left when I arrived. He was full of how we'd cancelled the meeting because of the missing boys. I don't think his views on the police were very well received in the pub. When I arrived and explained that it was your son who was missing and his only being nine, I don't think Tom had any supporters left. You're very popular round here, boss, ever since you busted the cocaine smuggling.' There was a pause. 'Well, you and me both, to be honest – me, of course, for saving your life.'

'Of course,' said Louis, 'and thank you again, Eddy.' Louis wondered how many times he had thanked his sergeant over the intervening months, but it was fair enough. His sergeant had indeed saved his life, so there could never be too many opportunities to say thank you.

Tom Trehearne opened the door, a scowl on his face. 'Oh, so you've decided to keep your appointment this time,' he said, by way of greeting.

Louis did not rise to the bait, but produced his warrant card. 'Chief Inspector Peppiatt and this is Sergeant Eddy, who I believe you know.'

They were led through into the kitchen, dominated by a lovely old table around which sat Jago and a women who Louis took to be Gemma. Seeing Jack, she leapt to her feet, rushed over and gave him an enormous hug. Jack looked slightly embarrassed but well pleased. 'Jack, it's been ages since I saw you last. How are you? Jack is my hero,' she announced. 'One summer when I was still quite little, he came to work on the farm. Dad told me to clear out an old barn, which was full of rats. When I said I was afraid of rats, Dad said if I was going to work on a farm, I had to get used to them. Jack overheard and when everyone else had gone back to work, he cleared out the rats for me with the help of our old dog. Dad never knew. Since then, as you can imagine, Jack can do no wrong in my eyes.'

'Merrin has a similar story about Jack rescuing her from a seal when she was pier jumping,' said Jago. He grinned at Jack. 'So I guess you're the Tripconeys' hero as well as Gemma's!'

'So this is clearly the cue for me to say that Jack saved my life a few months ago!' said Louis.

'Let's hope it was worth it,' said Tom savagely.

The convivial atmosphere instantly disappeared. 'Tom!' said Gemma. 'How could you say such a thing.' She turned to Louis. 'I'm so sorry about my brother – that was a dreadful thing to say. We are very angry with the police but there's no excuse to be so rude.' She shot Tom a venomous look.

'I appreciate that tensions are running high at the moment,' said Louis. 'However, can we all please sit down. This won't take long but I have some questions that need answering.' Such was the note of authority in his voice that everyone did as he asked, including Tom, and silence reigned.

Jack took out his notebook. Louis shuffled his notes about. He took his time and then at last he spoke. 'This wasn't how I intended to begin the meeting, but in the circumstances, I think it is probably the right place to start. I didn't want to take on this case; I was in the middle of trying to wrap up a very violent crime. However, I was aware that if I didn't agree to become involved, the investigation was unlikely to get much attention. Philp Trehearne disappeared over thirty years ago. He couldn't be found then, so what chance do I have of finding out what happened to him now? You may well ask – very little chance, I suspect. However, I'm willing to try my very hardest, recognising that you, Tom, and you, Gemma, need some sort of closure. But, I am not prepared to continue with this unless I have your full support and co-operation. I am not the enemy here. I am the man who is trying to help you. So, what shall I do? Walk out of the door now and tell my superintendent that I have studied the file and have nothing to add? Or, are you going to stop sniping and moaning about the police and try your utmost to help me get to the truth? Your call.'

Louis sat back in his chair and waited. Jago had to fight the desire to give him a round of applause. Tom and Gemma looked at one another for what seemed a long time, and then Tom nodded.

'We would like you to help us, Chief Inspector,' said Gemma. 'There will be no more whinging to the press, no more angry posts on social media and no more crass remarks from me or my brother. I realise we've behaved badly but we are so upset and desperately sad. You would have loved our mum, everyone did. She was the kindest person you'd ever be likely to meet and the shock when she took her own life was indescribable. We've been looking for someone to blame other than ourselves, I suppose, and in our eyes, the police were the natural target.'

'I completely understand all of that,' said Louis. 'Shall we draw a double line under everything that's gone before and concentrate one hundred per cent on trying to find out what happened to your dad?'

'Yes, please,' said Gemma.

'Tom?' Louis asked.

'Yes, let's do it,' mumbled Tom, avoiding eye contact with everyone.

CHAPTER THIRTEEN

'So, let's start at the beginning, the day your dad disappeared,' said Louis. 'Tom, tell me what you remember?'

Tom hesitated, then took a deep breath. 'Me and Gemma had been to the cinema with some friends. They dropped us at the end of our drive and we walked back home. It was a very clear night, nearly a full moon, lots of stars. Mum was outside the kitchen door. It was about ten o'clock and she was in a state because she said Dad had gone off to the pub at about seven and had not returned.' He turned to Gemma. 'I don't think we were very worried at that stage, were we, Gem?'

'No,' Gemma agreed. 'I think you said that he had probably met some mates and stayed longer than he meant to. We went inside with Mum and I made us all a hot drink.'

'By the time we'd finished our drinks, it was probably

nearly ten-thirty,' Tom continued. 'Mum suddenly mentioned that Dad was due to meet Jim Ferrell so we suggested she should call the Ferrells, which she was reluctant to do as it was so late.' Tom looked at Louis and almost smiled. 'Ten-thirty is late for farmers!'

'So Mum rang them,' Gemma said, 'and Jim told her that Dad had never turned up at Halsetown Inn. Jim hadn't worried too much, just assuming there had been some crisis on the farm.'

'And that was the moment it all began,' said Tom. 'Mum rang the police, the Ferrells got out of bed and, with our other close neighbours, the Pascoes – the family we'd been to the cinema with – and the proprietors of the pub, we all began searching. Of course, this was before mobile phones, it's hard to imagine now. The police soon joined in – you were there, weren't you, Jack?' Jack nodded. 'And then gradually the news spread, it seemed like the whole town joined in and the coastguards, of course. After the lovely clear night, bad weather set in for several days so we searched in the wind and endless rain. We found nothing, not even a trace of anything that could have belonged to him. He'd literally vanished.'

'Have you anything to add, Gemma?' Louis asked.

'Not really,' said Gemma, 'except what I'm sure you already know. The police checked train and bus services, even airports apparently, though Dad had never been in a plane in his life and he certainly didn't own a passport. They also checked the main Cornish ports to see if he'd gone somewhere by boat. Nothing – but then that didn't surprise us. We all knew he wouldn't have left us of his own free will.'

'Unless he was a very different man from the one we thought we knew,' suggested Tom.

'But you know he wasn't, Tom. You know he wouldn't have just gone; he loved us all and his life here.' Gemma was clearly becoming very distressed and Jago leant forward to take her hand.

'Jim Ferrell is of the same view,' said Louis. 'He says Philip must have been "took", he'd never have left you, unless he had been.'

'He's right,' Tom conceded. 'Yes, of course he is, sorry, Gem.'

'Tell me,' said Louis, 'did your father have any siblings, or other living relatives at the time of his disappearance?'

'His parents were both still alive at the time,' said Tom. 'I'd better start at the beginning with that story. My father had a younger sister, called Celia. She died when she was fifteen of leukaemia. My grandparents never got over it, so as soon as Dad had graduated from college, they handed the farm over to him. They bought a bungalow in Carbis Bay, where I think they were as happy as they could be. However, losing a second child was just too much for them to bear – very soon after Dad disappeared, they died within a few months of one another.'

'Losing two children must have been awful,' Gemma agreed. 'I just can't imagine it. But, oddly, they were never much interested in their grandchildren. They kept themselves to themselves, like their grief was a private thing that they could only share with each other. We saw them at Christmas and birthdays but that was about it.'

'College,' said Louis. 'You said your dad went to college? Where?'

'He went to agricultural college, Seale-Hayne – it's in Devon.'

'I know Seale-Hayne, or rather I did,' said Louis. 'It's closed down now, I understand. I began my career in the police force in Newton Abbot, just down the road. So, he was there for three years, I assume?'

'Yes,' said Gemma. 'It was a bit hard on Mum, I think. She and Dad had been together since their early teens so three years was a long time for her to wait for him. Still, they made it and married soon after Dad left college.'

'At least he was lucky enough to go to college.' The bitterness was back in Tom's voice.

'I gather you left school very soon after you father disappeared. That must have been hard for you, Tom,' Louis said.

'I never went back to school, never mind college,' said Tom. 'I didn't even want to be a farmer, but I had no choice.'

'What would you have liked to have done?' Louis asked.

'I wanted to do business studies or accountancy, maybe IT. I wanted to have my own business – like Jago has done, I guess, only here in West Cornwall. Something unconnected with hospitality so I could offer year-round jobs.'

'It's not unreasonable to suggest that what you have just described is exactly what you already have,' Jago said gently.

'I know,' said Tom, 'but I hate farming – out in all weathers, the mud, the blood, sweat and tears, it's just not for me. You don't know how lucky you are, Jago.'

'That's a stupid thing to say, Tom,' said Gemma, rushing to her husband's defence.

'It's not!' said Tom hotly. 'I'd rather not have the use of my legs than be tied to the sodding farm for another twenty-five years.'

'Tom—' Gemma began.

'It's OK, Gem,' Jago interrupted. 'I understand what Tom is saying. He knows I love my life and I know he hates his. But here's a thought. Now Sarah is no longer with us, you're free to sell the farm. Have you been to see your solicitor about the will?'

'Not yet,' said Tom. 'He's been ill. To be honest, I'm surprised he's still alive, he's so ancient.'

'Well, make an appointment tomorrow, before he completely keels over,' said Jago. 'As I remember it, the farm's been left to you in its entirety, with just a small sum for Gemma. That suits us fine, doesn't it, Gem. We're doing OK, aren't we?'

'You can have the lot so far as I am concerned, Tom, if it helps you set up a new venture,' said Gemma. 'Mum dying is terrible but you are free now to do whatever you want.'

'I think it's probably time we went,' said Louis, standing up. 'I'll keep you informed on any progress and let's arrange another meeting in a week's time. I may well be back before then with more questions.'

Gemma walked out into the yard with Louis and Jack. 'I'm sorry about my brother. He was so rude . . . he's just in such a state at the moment.'

'No worries, I do understand this is a very difficult time for you both,' said Louis. 'Does Tom have anyone – a girlfriend, a wife?'

'He was married years ago, very briefly. Her name was Beth, she was Australian, by coincidence. She was part of a gang of sheep shearers who offer their services to farmers around the country at shearing time. She came to our farm, she and Tom fell in love but the marriage only lasted two years. Tom has always been pretty tense since Dad vanished, she was very laid-back – they were polar opposites. And, of course, she hated the weather. In the end, she went back to Oz and eventually married a nice Australian boy.'

'Poor Tom,' said Louis.

'Yes, indeed.'

'Gemma, while I was here, I was hoping to have a word with David. Is he around? I did thank him at the hospital for finding my son, but it was all extremely hasty. I'd like to thank him again properly and maybe make some sort of gesture – a decent bottle of whisky perhaps? What do you think?'

'He's working up on the top fields today, keeping out of the way as he knew we had this meeting. Also, he's very shy and hates a fuss, oh, and he doesn't really drink. I'm sure an opportunity will present itself for you to thank him, but not today, he won't be back for hours. I am so sorry, none of us have even asked about your son. Is he OK?'

'He's fine, thank you,' said Louis. 'Would you mind just telling David how very grateful I am and that I hope to see him on another occasion?'

'Of course,' said Gemma.

'Well, Jack, what did you make of all that?' Louis asked his sergeant, once they were back in the car.

'Them Trehearnes seem to have had an awful lot of back luck, more than their fair share, I reckon.'

'I agree,' said Louis.

'But there's nothing we can do to help them, though, is there, boss? I did as you asked and made a list of all the things I could think of about the family. But you've covered them all. I don't know any more than you do now.'

'Thanks for trying, Eddy.'

'Everyone is going to have to accept that it's much too late to find out what happened to poor Philip. Don't you agree, boss?'

'On the contrary, Eddy, I think we have some serious work to do.'

CHAPTER FOURTEEN

Louis dropped off Jack at the station. He needed some thinking time and, having had all other duties taken off him, he decided to stay in St Ives. He parked the car, picked up a coffee and found a free bench to sit on, overlooking the harbour. He was instantly reminded of Jago's story of Jack Eddy saving Merrin from a seal. Some children were jumping off Smeaton's Pier, to the backdrop of shrieks of laughter. The tide was in and, a few yards away, a couple of seals were lying on their backs, apparently sunbathing, and taking absolutely no notice of the children. What a wonderful childhood the local children enjoyed, he thought. Yes, there was not much spare money floating about in West Cornwall, and many families were very poor, but compared with life in an inner city, these children were in heaven.

He forced himself away from watching the happy scene

to concentrate on the job in hand. He already had a plan but it all depended on the co-operation of one man – a man who he'd arrested, whose career had been destroyed as a result, who had been sent to prison and so probably hated him. Well, why wouldn't he? And if that wasn't enough, there was a good chance he might not even still be alive.

Everything that he had been told about Philip Trehearne pointed to the fact he had led a blameless life and was loved or liked or, at the very least, admired by all who knew him. So, the only conclusion Louis could reach was that if, as Jim Ferrell suggested, Philip had been 'took', it seemed likely that it must relate to something that had happened during his college days at Seale-Hayne. This was the only period in his life when he had not lived on the farm. If, while living in St Ives, Philip had ever behaved badly, or had acquired a serious enemy, Louis was sure he would know about it by now.

When Louis was a young constable in Newton Abbot, the surrounding farms had suffered from a serious bout of pilfering over a couple of years, with no arrests made. No livestock was involved, nor heavy machinery, but small items like quadbikes, tools and sacks of fertiliser and feed – in other words, things that were easy to move and easy to dispose of. One evening, Louis was in the pub and got talking to an elderly man who was in his last term as a lecturer at Seale-Hayne Agricultural College. The man, whose name was Roger Brooke, having discovered that Louis was a policeman, asked him what progress had been made with discovering who was responsible for the spate of local farm thefts.

Louis had been very pleased with Roger's interest because he had been working on a theory. The farming community kept very much to themselves and unless they were stealing from one another, which seemed extremely unlikely, then he had been looking at the regular visitors to the farms as most likely to be the culprits. There were delivery drivers, of course, and schoolchildren who were taken on farm visits. However, it was the students from the local agricultural college who regularly made day trips to local farms. As a result, Louis's current theory was that a student, or students, could be involved.

He put his theory to Roger, who thought it very unlikely that college students would stoop to stealing from farms, particularly as they were all potential farmers themselves. However, after another couple of beers, he did agree to look up the records of farm visits from the college with a view to enabling Louis to see if there was any correlation between them and the thefts. What followed was a tortuous period with Louis's sergeant accusing him of wasting police time and the principal of the college initially refusing to release any information. However, eventually Roger was able to give Louis two years' worth of records detailing the farm visits by the college students.

After comparing the visits with the thefts, Louis was able to establish a pattern. Five nights running, Louis staked out the farm he reckoned was the next to be targeted, with no back-up help as his sergeant still thought the plan was futile. However, on the sixth night, he got lucky, and caught the culprit in the act of loading a van with stolen goods, only to find that the thief was not a student, as he had suspected, but a lecturer by the name of Donald Coleman. Eventually, after a struggle, he came quietly, almost as if he was relieved to be caught.

The court did not look kindly on Donald Coleman. Not only did his thefts span a lengthy period, rather than a one-off offence, but it was felt that, as a teacher, there had been a serious breach of trust, both towards his students and the wider farming community. Therefore, an example was made of him, in order to try and deter any copycat crimes. He got a prison sentence of four years, and, of course, his teaching career was finished.

However, for Louis, the outcome had been extremely satisfactory. The divisional inspector had complimented him on his 'commendable tenacity' and suggested he put in for his sergeant's exams – which he had passed with flying colours.

Louis had not seen Donald since the trial. However, he was still based in Newton Abbot when Donald was released from prison. Local gossip informed Louis that Donald had returned to the area. His family lived just outside the town and had done so for several generations. If he was still alive, Louis reckoned it shouldn't be too difficult to track him down. The reason for doing so was that he felt there was a good chance Donald might have been teaching at the college during the same period Philip was a student there. It was a tenuous link, but well worth following up. Whether, of course, Donald would be prepared to help him was an entirely different matter. Still, it was worth a try.

Louis stood up, and was just putting his coffee cup in the bin, when he heard his name being called. He turned to see Merrin McKenzie crossing the road to join him.

'Louis, how are you, how's your son? What an awful thing to happen,' said Merrin.

'He's fine, thank you. I spoke to my ex-wife this morning. Edward was still asleep but apart from a sore ankle and a few cuts and bruises, he's relatively unscathed, unlike his poor traumatised parents.'

'I'm not surprised you were shaken up. Can I interest you in a coffee?' Merrin suggested.

Louis knew he should be dashing back to Truro in order to track down Donald Coleman. Also, he'd just had a coffee. 'Yes please,' he said, 'that would be great.'

Having greeted both William and Horatio, Louis sat down at the kitchen table while Merrin made coffee. 'Jack told me about poor Edward's dramas, which means, of course, I have been given every last detail – in fact, I probably know more about it than you or even Edward!'

'Jack is a terrible old gossip,' Louis admitted, 'but his knowledge of this town and its surroundings is quite wonderful and, therefore, invaluable.'

Merrin handed him a coffee and a plate of biscuits. 'Remember, it's a house rule. You have to eat a biscuit so Horatio can have one too.'

'Today, I give in without a struggle. I've just remembered I missed breakfast.'

'Tuck in, then,' said Merrin. 'Honestly, children – they're such a blessing, such a joy but, from time to time, such a bloody worry. Isla's on holiday in Greece with her friend Maggie at the moment. They are both pretty sensible, as you know, but it doesn't stop me fussing.'

'I totally understand,' said Louis. 'I learnt today that Philip's poor parents lost both of their children. A daughter at fifteen and then they were still alive when Philip disappeared. They both died soon after, apparently – hardly surprising.'

'Yes, poor things. I obviously don't remember Celia dying, I'm not sure I was even born, but I do remember Mum talking about it,' said Merrin. 'It sounds awful but I'd actually forgotten all about Celia.'

They sat in silence for a few minutes. 'Jago told me that you had your big meeting at the Trehearnes' planned for this morning,' Merrin said at last. 'How did it go?'

'Not without a few dramas along the way,' Louis admitted. 'However, I think a truce has been agreed – no more public moaning about the police, full co-operation from Tom and Gemma, so long as I come up the goods, of course.'

'And can you come up with the goods? I just cannot see how you can be expected to solve the mystery of Philip's disappearance when no one could do so over thirty years ago.'

'I have a hunch, well, an idea, really, nothing more,' said Louis, smiling at her.

'And I'm sufficiently well trained not to ask what your idea is. However, please indulge me to this extent – it's not going to involve knives and stabbings again, is it?'

'Absolutely not,' said Louis, 'though I suppose there could be the possibility of an odd pitchfork having a role to play.'

'That's not even funny,' said Merrin firmly.

'No, it's not, apologies,' said Louis. 'Hurriedly changing

the subject, what do you know about David, the man who found Edward?'

Merrin considered the question for a moment. 'Not a lot,' she said, 'and I doubt even Jack knows much about him. He is very quiet and shy and he's absolutely devoted to the Trehearne family. When he's not working, he loves tramping about the countryside, which is probably how he knew where to look for Edward. He's a good citizen. If anyone is in trouble, he's always there to help – cattle on the road, broken-down farm machinery, roofs needing mending and, of course, finding lost boys. Why do you ask?'

'Only because I wanted to thank him again for finding my son. We were in such a rush to see Edward in the hospital yesterday evening, it was a very hurried thank-you. I would have liked to have seen him this morning and thanked him properly but he was working some distance away from the farmhouse, apparently.'

'As I said, I don't know much about him but I do know he would hate any fuss. Honestly, leave it. A quick thank you will have been perfect for him.'

'Then I will bow to your superior knowledge, and I must admit, Gemma said much the same thing,' said Louis. 'You must know how I feel, though. He did such a big thing for me – for us – and all he got in return was a hurried and distracted thank-you as we dashed past him to find our son.'

'Of course, I get it,' said Merrin, 'but trust me, all's well.'

'I'd better get going,' said Louis, standing up. 'Thank you for the coffee and biscuits.'

'A pleasure – I should have cooked you breakfast, really.'

'I'm fine, thank you. Goodbye, William, goodbye, Horatio, and take care, Merrin. I will let you know when and if there is any progress to report.'

'Good luck with your hunch,' said Merrin.

CHAPTER FIFTEEN

By mid-afternoon the following day, with the help of the police computer, Louis had discovered that Donald Coleman, at seventy-nine, was still alive. Louis also had his address, which, as predicted, was in Newton Abbot. He pondered the idea of a phone call but decided it would be too easy for Donald to block the call. So instead, Louis booked a room in a hotel in the centre of town, jumped in his car and headed for Devon.

After checking into his hotel, Louis established it was only a ten-minute walk to the street in which Donald lived. The house, when he found it, was not unlike his own, part of a small Victorian terrace in a quiet cul-de-sac. He had not planned what to say, having found over the years that in tricky situations it was often better to be reactive, rather than to go in with all guns blazing. He knocked on the door, which was almost immediately opened by an elderly man.

He was much shorter than Louis remembered and almost bald, but he looked alert and interested, with a friendly smile, as he said, 'Good evening, how can I help you?' His voice was instantly recognisable – rich and Devonian.

'Good evening, Don,' Louis said. 'I don't know if you remember me . . . in some ways I'd rather you didn't.'

'Louis Peppiatt! Well, I certainly remember you; you were pivotal in my life, so to speak. Come in, why don't you?'

Louis was shown straight into the sitting room, where, in an armchair by an open fire, sat a small, cheerful woman, with a book on her lap. The room was stifling.

'This is my wife, Freda,' said Donald. 'Freda, this is the man I've always wanted you to meet – Louis Peppiatt.'

Louis stepped forward and shook Freda's hand. 'I'm very pleased to meet you, Mrs Coleman,' he said.

'He's got nice manners, hasn't he, Don, and he did alright by you, didn't he? Why don't you take him down the pub, I reckon you owe him a pint or two.'

Whatever reception Louis had imagined, it certainly wasn't this. It flashed through his mind that maybe they had mistaken him for someone else.

'If you don't mind, darling, that would be great. I'll put some more logs on the fire to keep you cosy.' Donald began piling logs on the already blazing fire.

Louis must have looked surprised, for Freda explained. 'It's my arthritis, the warmer it is, the less it hurts. I'm sorry it's so hot in here, but you'll like the pub, it's only round the corner.'

The two men said their goodbyes and went out of the

front door. 'I'm sorry about your wife's arthritis,' Louis said, by way of something to say.

'It's very painful, but she never complains. She is one of those marvellous people who, no matter what, always looks on the bright side – a cup half-full sort of person. Actually, no, Freda's cup is always full to the bleeding brim.'

The pub was surprisingly full for a Monday evening and everyone seemed to know Donald and greeted him warmly, which surprised Louis, knowing his background. Drinks were ordered and a table found in a quiet corner.

'Cheers,' said Louis.

'Your good health, sir. Now what can I do for you?'

'Before I answer that, I'm astounded you're even prepared to see me, let alone insist on buying me a drink. You haven't muddled me up with someone else, have you, Don?'

Donald laughed. 'I'm not senile yet and of course I know who you are. But before I tell you my life story, tell me why you're here.'

'I need some information about a student who was at Seal-Hayne, who I'm hoping you will remember from the time you were teaching there. His name was Philip Trehearne. He went missing over thirty years ago but I've been asked to look at his case again.'

'So you're still in the force, then?' said Donald. 'What rank are you now?'

'Chief inspector,' said Louis, almost feeling he should apologise, since catching Donald had undoubtedly helped his career.

'Well done!' said Donald cheerfully. 'The name rings a

bell, what part of the country did this Philip come from and what did he look like?'

'He grew up on the family farm in West Cornwall, just outside St Ives. I have a photo from the police files. It was taken when he was middle-aged, around the time he disappeared. Stupidly, I was with the family yesterday; I should have picked up a photo of when he was younger.' Louis handed the photograph to Donald.

'No problem,' said Donald, 'I recognise him straight away. A tall lad, very pleasant, hard-working but no academic, he was very much a practical farmer in the making. He had a lovely girlfriend, too.'

'So I believe – Sarah, everyone speaks very highly of her,' said Louis.

'No, not Sarah, her name was Mary. Now, she was very studious and probably a good influence on Philip, now I come to think of it. Certainly they worked together a lot.'

'You mean he had a girlfriend here at Seale-Hayne?'

'It was a long time ago, but I particularly remember those two because I taught them during my first year as a very green and nervous lecturer. I'm absolutely certain Philip's girl was called Mary. They were a lovely couple.'

'That's very interesting,' said Louis. 'Do you remember Mary's surname?'

'I'm afraid I don't, but I do keep in touch with one or two old students who now farm locally. I'll ask around. Is it urgent?'

'It is rather,' said Louis. 'It's a complicated family saga but I'm hoping if I can find out what happened to Philip, it might bring them some peace of mind.'

'You say Philip disappeared, I find that extraordinary. I didn't know him well but he seemed such a steady sort of chap.'

'Yes,' said Louis, 'that's what everyone says. Can I get you another drink?'

'No,' said Donald firmly. 'Drinks are on me tonight and when I come back, I'll tell you why.'

Donald returned with two pints and two whisky chasers. 'You're not driving anywhere tonight, are you?' he asked. Louis shook his head. 'Right, then, here I go. Prison was the making of me, which I don't believe can be said of many, but it's thanks to you that I ended up there. I know it sounds mad but I really mean it. I read a lot, thought a lot, made a few friends but the most important thing was, I began to recognise the error of my ways – which I suppose is what prison is for. I was helped by the prison chaplain and the librarian, good men both of them. But it was living with the knowledge of what I'd done, and recognising how wrong it was – that was the biggest help of all. I'd been greedy, selfish and, frankly, downright stupid.'

'So, what did you do when you came out?' Louis asked.

'You're going to have a real laugh at this,' said Donald, 'I started a business selling agricultural machinery.'

'You're joking, a legitimate business?'

'Naturally,' said Donald, smiling.

'But surely, after stealing from so many of the local farmers, no one would want to buy anything from you. How could you possibly have built a local business given your past?'

'Well, it went like this,' said Donald, taking a sip of

his pint. 'I visited every farmer I'd stolen from and, with each of them, we sat down and worked out how much I owed them, and I offered to start paying them back on a monthly basis. It was helped by the fact that I inherited a small sum of money from my father, who sadly died while I was in prison – he provided another incentive for sorting my life out. I discovered I was good at business and, as the sales began to build, I was able to increase my monthly repayments. Once the farmers saw this happening, they naturally bought from me because the more I earned, the more they got back. I paid them all off in nine years.'

'That's amazing, congratulations,' said Louis, really meaning it.

'My criminal activities brought an abrupt end to my first marriage – who could blame her? However, the best bit of all was that at one of the farms I'd stolen from, there was a daughter who was very impressed with what I was trying to do. Her name was Freda. So, as well as paying back the people I'd stolen from, and building a successful business, I was blessed by finding my lovely wife. Oh, and to cap it all, our son, Gerry, now runs the business – Coleman Agricultural Machinery. So what do you think about that, Chief Inspector?'

'I think it's bloody marvellous! And I insist on getting in the next round, Don, or I'll have to arrest you – I'm not quite sure what for, but I'm sure I can think of something!'

CHAPTER SIXTEEN

By ten o'clock the following morning, Donald was able to tell Louis that Philip's girlfriend at college was named Mary Daniels and that the general feeling was that her family came from Somerset. After breakfast at his hotel, by arrangement Louis had returned to the Colemans' house, where he was plied with coffee before he was allowed to leave.

Their parting was surprisingly touching. 'Just remember this, Louis,' Freda had said. 'We have a lovely marriage and two lovely kids. Don and Gerry have built a terrific business and Don is very well respected in the town – and we owe it all to you.'

'I was only doing my job, Freda,' Louis protested.

'I'd been regularly stealing for over two years,' said Donald, 'and no other bugger had got even close to catching me. All I can say is, thank God you did.'

* * *

Before leaving Newton Abbot, Louis had telephoned Constable Colin Haines at Camborne and asked him to try and trace Mary Daniels. By the time he reached home, he had the details. On leaving college, Mary had married a Nigel Anstey and their home was on the outskirts of Ashburton. They'd had two sons – Nigel and Benjamin. Mary had died of cancer in her early forties, just three years before Philip's disappearance. Nigel, though, was alive and still living in the family home. The whereabouts of the sons was still being worked on.

Again, Louis reckoned that a surprise visit in person to Nigel Anstey would be preferable and likely to produce the best results. Having just travelled back from Newton Abbot, he couldn't face turning round and immediately driving to Ashburton. He would leave first thing in the morning. He knew Nigel to be eighty-four. With a bit of luck, if he arrived at an early but respectable hour, Nigel would still be at home.

With an afternoon to kill, Louis suddenly thought of the merits of a flying visit to Falmouth. He could check on Edward and also apologise to everyone for not seeing them over the weekend. Now he'd had time to think through the drama of the lost boys, he realised that if he'd kept his promise to take the children out on Saturday, Edward would never have become lost on the coastal path.

Without prior warning, Louis arrived in Falmouth shortly after the children had come home from school. In fact, they were all there – Andrew as well as Stephanie and the children.

'I hope you don't mind me dropping in unannounced, Steph, only I was passing,' Louis lied. 'I just wanted to check up on the wounded soldier.'

Stephanie smiled. 'As you will soon see, the wounded soldier in question is in high spirits. He's something of a hero at school, sporting his crutches and no doubt embellishing his lost-and-found story. Also, it's only three days until the end of term so everyone is demob happy.'

'Ed is showing off a lot, which is so annoying,' said Daisy, who'd been listening in.

Louis gave her a hug. 'Cut him a bit of slack, darling. He must have been so frightened and he has a mass of cuts and bruises, never mind the ankle.'

Daisy grinned at her father. 'I'll admit I'm glad he's safe, Dad, and I'll even admit he was quite brave at first, but now he's really milking it!'

'Where is the little horror?' Louis asked.

'Well, to confirm Daisy's point, I've sent him up to his bedroom to do his prep,' said Stephanie. 'According to your son, his ankle is too sore to do maths homework. I made the point, not unreasonably I believe, that his ankle is not required for doing sums – or whatever they're called these days. School maths is now a complete mystery to me.'

'I'll go upstairs and beat him soundly, shall I?' said Louis, smiling.

'Absolutely, but before you do so, could you go and talk to Andrew? He's in the study and he needs cheering up.'

Stephanie walked with Louis through the sitting room, towards the study, hopefully leaving Daisy out of earshot. 'What's up?' Louis asked.

'He's beside himself about what happened to Edward,' said Stephanie. 'I'm so glad you turned up today. Andrew

106

says he can never face you again because he put your son in danger. You're not angry with him, are you?'

'No, of course not. I'm not overly keen on Peter and his wretched son, but boys will be boys and these things happen. And remember, Andrew was the one charging about on the cliff path in the mist, while the coastguards confined us to barracks.'

'Will you tell him all that, please, Louis?'

'I'll do my best.' Louis put an arm round her shoulders. 'You really care about him, don't you, Steph?'

Stephanie nodded, uncharacteristically close to tears.

Louis walked into the study to find Andrew sitting at what had once been his old desk and his father's before him. Just for a fleeting moment, it irritated him, which was ridiculous since he and Stephanie had agreed there was absolutely no room for the desk in his house. Andrew leapt to his feet, misinterpreting Louis's momentary look of annoyance.

'I–I wasn't expecting you, Louis,' Andrew said. 'I was going to write to you to try and explain how wretched I feel about putting Edward in danger. I just can't find the words. I can see you're angry.'

'I'm not angry at all. Both Steph and Edward have told me all about Peter and Henry and, forgive me, they also told me how awful they are. Everything you did to try and find the boys was sensible and you walked miles in search of them. As you know, by the time Steph and I arrived, the coastguards wouldn't let us join in the search, which made us feel so helpless but it was comforting to know you were out there looking for them.'

'I should have taken better care of him,' said Andrew.

'And I should have taken the children out for the day on Saturday, as I had promised. If I had done so, none of this would have happened. Honestly, Andrew, there is absolutely no point in going over it again and again. It's not helping you and it's not helping Edward. The boys did a silly thing, you were having to cope with your drunken brother, I'd let everyone down by not taking the children out, and that wretched Henry is a bully and a troublemaker. The fates conspired against us that day, but everyone survived and no one was badly hurt. It's over.'

'But you have entrusted your family to me and look what a hash I made of it.'

'Stop it, Andrew. Honestly, you've got to move on from this. Get a grip. You being so upset is making Stephanie feel miserable and worried, which I believe means she loves you very much. So buck you, you silly sod and count your blessings!' said Louis, smiling.

'And you really don't mind, if she does care about me?' said Andrew.

'We went through all this at the time you decided to marry,' said Louis, failing to hide his exasperation. 'I'm supremely grateful that Steph has chosen a decent, kind, honest, reliable man to spend the rest of her life with. The children think the world of you and so they should. So enough now, right?'

Andrew nodded.

'Good, now I'm just going upstairs to beat Edward until he does his maths prep.'

'What?' said Andrew, aghast.

'A joke,' said Louis. 'I'm going upstairs to give him an enormous hug and then make him do his maths prep. Now, while I do that, you go and give Steph an enormous hug as well, and tell her that you've pulled yourself together and what happened up on the cliff is truly over and done with.'

As Louis drove home later, he tried to sort out his feelings. What he'd said to Andrew was all true. He wasn't jealous of him – apart from anything else, they were two very different men, so comparisons couldn't readily be made. And no, he decided, he genuinely wasn't upset by Andrew's relationship with Stephanie. If he had a problem with Andrew, it was that he appeared to have no sense of humour, while Stephanie was blessed with an excellent one. Would that prove a problem for them, hard to say, but Andrew had reliability on his side, which Louis knew meant a very great deal to his ex-wife. He had nothing to complain about – it was just that he missed terribly no longer being part of a family unit. Other than his visits to Falmouth, there was no one special in his life, and he couldn't imagine how there ever would be again.

CHAPTER SEVENTEEN

The following morning, Merrin picked up her brother from the Trehearnes' in order for them to spend the day together. It also gave Tom and Gemma some privacy. They were going to devote the day to organising their mother's funeral, starting with a visit from the vicar.

'Sis, I would really like to see where you live,' said Jago, as soon as they were in the car. 'I'm pretty good at bouncing my bottom up stairs, if you don't mind carrying my wheelchair?'

'If you're sure, I'd really like that too,' said Merrin. 'It'll feel more like home once you've been in it.'

'But Isla comes home fairly often, doesn't she?'

'Yes,' said Merrin, 'and she's quite reconciled to me leaving Bristol now, and absolutely loves St Ives. How do I explain? I think it's because siblings know one another all their lives. Parents know you for the first half of your life and, if you're lucky, a partner and children know you for the second half. But only siblings are there for the duration. I think I'm trying to say, it will give my little cottage a sense of permanence to have you there.'

They easily managed to negotiate the steps up to Miranda's Cottage, Merrin's little home, which was perched on top of a bakery. Once back in his wheelchair in the kitchen, Jago surveyed his surroundings. 'This is lovely, sis, well done, oh and look who's here!' Jago wheeled himself up to Horatio's cage. 'Hiya, Horatio, do you remember me?' he asked. Horatio let out a squark and climbed straight down to Jago's level for a tummy rub. 'He does!' said Jago, delighted.

'And there's another member of the family I'd like you to meet,' said Merrin.

William was sitting in a chair, trying to make himself look as small as possible. Clearly, he was not at all sure about the wheelchair, never mind its occupant. Encouraged by Merrin, he jumped down, somewhat warily, and came over to Jago for a good sniff around. After some thought, he wagged his tail.

'Who is this and what is he?' Jago asked, clearly not appreciating how honoured he was to receive a greeting so early in their acquaintance. In fact, Jago appeared amused rather than humbly grateful, which would have been a far more appropriate reaction.

'His name is William and, obviously, he's a dog,' said Merrin a little tersely.

'If you insist,' said Jago, now starting to laugh. 'It's hilarious to see how many breeds can be represented in just one small dog, and why is his front half so different

111

from his back half? I'm sorry, sis, but he's not a thing of beauty, is he?'

'He has a beautiful soul and I won't hear a word against him,' said Merrin huffily as she put on the kettle. 'William, ignore Jago, he's always been a brat.'

After some discussion, they managed to reach the balcony. This led out of Merrin's bedroom on the floor above, which involved Jago cheerfully negotiating yet more stairs. When he was finally installed on a balcony chair, brother and sister sat, coffees in hand, and gazed out at the view before them. Immediately in front of them, they could see the slipway and the harbour beach. The tide was now well in, the boats at anchor bobbing about on a slightly choppy sea, which was, nonetheless, deep blue. Below them was Fore Street, already starting to fill up with visitors, as the season was starting to build.

'This place is absolutely perfect, what a find, and just look at the view,' said Jago.

'I can't take any credit for it,' Merrin said. 'When I told Max I wanted to come home, he found it for me. We viewed it together and there was no question of looking at any other property. I already feel I couldn't live anywhere else.'

'How are you – really, I mean?' Jago asked.

Merrin laughed. 'Those are the exact words I was about to ask you.'

'I asked first,' said Jago firmly.

'OK, well, good days and bad days, obviously. I miss Adam terribly but I'm over the shock of his death. In the months following him being killed, I kept forgetting that he was dead. I would turn to ask him something, put out two mugs, two glasses, even lay the table for two, sometimes – and then I'd remember. I was a mess. I don't know what would have happened if I hadn't moved – coming home to St Ives was the best possible thing for me. In Bristol I was reminded of Adam all the time, literally, all the time. Here, there are memories of our childhood, Mum and Dad and, of course, old friends, which, all put together, mercifully interfere with my more maudlin thoughts. I will never get over Adam's death, nor do I want to, but I have reached a sort of contentment, helped, of course, by Horatio and William.'

Jago smiled.

'I mean it,' said Merrin fiercely, 'I couldn't have done it without them. Because I have their needs and quality of life to consider, I don't spend all my time thinking about me, me, me. And then, there's darling Isla. She is a tower of strength. Of course, she misses her dad very much, but she has the resilience of youth on her side, which has enabled her to maintain a real zest for life, thank God. It's a lesson for us all, to get the very best out of every day. Right, enough of me – tell me about you.'

'I'm fine,' said Jago.

Merrin looked at him quizzically. 'The truth now, brother of mine.'

'I am fine, truly. I did a silly thing. It was ridiculous to try and surf those waves, which would have been a challenge even in my twenties, but just madness in my fifties. Still, I could have died, or sustained brain damage.' He grinned. 'And until that bloody wave pulverised me, I was having the surf of my life!'

'You idiot!' Merrin said fondly.

'What I mind most is being a burden to other people, especially my family, which is why I've worked so hard at being independent. If you had given me the key to Miranda's Cottage today, I hope you can see now that I could have ended up on this balcony, in this chair, without any help. I keep life as normal as possible. I can't surf, obviously, but I do swim and also I have a canoe. I have a Jeep, especially adapted for me, and a beach buggy, which I keep in the back of the Jeep and which I can unload myself. This gives me total independence. I can join anyone on the beach with absolutely no help. I go to the gym every day – it's been hard work to get this fit but easier to maintain now.'

Jago hesitated. 'I still feel there is a "but" coming,' said Merrin.

'The business is doing great; Remy loves it and is almost running it single-handed now, obviously with staff. He has great plans. And Suzannah is doing really well at uni – I did tell you she's reading law, like her clever aunt, didn't I?'

'Only about twenty times,' said Merrin. 'Come on, Jago, the "but", please.'

He sighed. 'But things aren't great between Gemma and I, since her mum died. I know it's early days but her resentment seems to go so deep.'

'What exactly is she resentful about?' Merrin asked.

'She now says she hates Australia with a real passion. She blames the country for my accident and for her mother's death. She believes neither would have happened if we'd stayed in Cornwall, which I suppose is correct, at any rate in my case. And, of course, she blames me for luring her out to Oz in the first place. I get it, I really do, but our kids are Australian and they're intent on making their lives out there. What is here for them in the UK, in Cornwall in particular, with so few jobs and such a short season? Hell, we both left Cornwall, didn't we, and for good reason?'

'But as you've just said, it's early days, and Gemma's reaction to the shock of her mum's death is very understandable. Sudden death of a loved one is tough, you go a little mad. Her blaming everything on Australia is just like me laying the table for two. You can't think straight, but it will pass, you just have to be patient. Remember, normally she is a lovely, sensible, sensitive woman who adores you. It's your job to get her through this and you can.'

'It's not just about her mother, though – that was the final straw. It began with my accident – that's what set her off. She worries about Remy, too. She's scared the same thing will happen to him, or he'll be attacked by a shark, or drown.'

'Bad things happen to people all over the word, not just in Australia,' said Merrin. 'Look what happened to Adam.'

'I did mention that to her but she just said it wasn't relevant as he was in a high-risk job, which I guess is a reasonable argument.'

'So, what are you going to do?' asked Merrin.

'Nothing,' said Jago, 'and just hope and pray it will blow over. Come on, sis, enough doom and gloom. We're due at Tristan's Fish Plaice in half an hour. What about giving your big brother a nice glass of wine here on this charming balcony, a stiffener to get us going?'

'Consider it done,' said Merrin, standing up. 'You

know, Jago, when you had your accident and we learnt what the long-term consequences for you would be, guess what Adam said?'

'Tell me,' said Jago.

'He said he could think of no man on God's earth who would cope with a disability better than you. I reckon he's right.'

Jago smiled up at her. 'Thanks, sis. Now where's that bloody wine?'

When Merrin returned with the wine, they raised a glass in silent toast to one another. 'Your Adam was a very fine bloke, and you know what, so is your friendly chief inspector.'

'Heavens above, we've been so busy talking about ourselves, I haven't asked you for your view as to how the meeting went with Tom and Gemma. Louis dropped by for coffee the other day and told me a little about it, but, of course, he had to be very discreet.'

'Game, set and match to Louis really. Tom began by being very rude and aggressive but rather than rise to the bait, Louis handled it brilliantly by simply giving them options. He made a speech really, rather than holding a conversation and, in a nutshell, Tom and Gemma caved in almost immediately. Oh, and Louis did discover that Philip went to agricultural college and so was away from home for three years. There could be something there, I guess.'

They had a delightful lunch with both Max and Clara, who had taken time off work especially. And later, as the wine flowed, they were joined by Tristan once he had finished serving.

Jago had insisted on getting a taxi back to the Trehearnes' so that Merrin could join in the wine-drinking. It was late afternoon by the time she had seen him into the taxi, and she returned home, deep in thought. The tangled web surrounding the Trehearne family seemed to be tightening and now appeared to include the future of Jago and Gemma's marriage. Her instincts told her that if an explanation could be found for Philip's disappearance, it just might solve a lot of problems for everyone. So, it was all down to Louis Peppiatt, and if anyone was able to unpick the past, Merrin believed it might just be him.

CHAPTER EIGHTEEN

Before leaving for Ashburton, Louis rang the chief superintendent's office.

'Is that the fragrant Sally, without whom Devon and Cornwall Police Force would fail to function?' he asked.

'Oh, do be quiet, Louis. What do you want? It's too early in the morning for you and your nonsense.'

Louis could tell from her voice that she was smiling. 'Goodish news, actually, Sal. Is he in?'

'No, he's attending some big meeting up in Bodmin. Can I help?'

'Absolutely. Can you tell him that I've called off the hounds of hell, in other words, there will be no more accusations in the media from the Trehearnes – providing, of course, that I make some progress with the case.'

'That is good news, and are you?' Sally said.

'Am I what?' Louis asked.

'Don't be so maddening, Louis. You know exactly what I mean. Are you making any progress?'

'I might be. To be honest, it's little more than an idea at the moment, but you could big it up for the benefit of sir, if you wouldn't mind.'

'I would mind. Now go away and let me get on with my work,' said Sally firmly.

After a rather dry croissant and a questionable cup of coffee at Exeter Services, Louis made his way to Nigel Anstey's home, which was situated on the outskirts of a delightful village, very close to Dartmoor National Park. The house surprised him – while it was not a stately home, neither was it a country cottage. He judged it to be a small Queen Anne manor house, with an impressive sweep of drive and a beautifully laid-out garden, if a little formal for his liking.

He rang the bell, which could be heard echoing through the house and which was followed by the reassuring sound of footsteps. The woman who answered the door looked to be about sixty, but very well preserved and stylishly dressed in a cashmere sweater, a tweed skirt and an impressive string of pearls. She looked the very quintessence of a lady of the manor, but for the rather coquettish smile she gave him.

'Can I help you?' she asked.

'I was hoping for a quick chat with Mr Nigel Anstey. My name is Chief Inspector Louis Peppiatt.' He produced his warrant card.

'Good heavens, the police, what have we done!' she said in mock horror.

The 'we' gave him the clue, which saved him embarrassment. 'And you are?' he asked with a smile.

'I'm Mrs Anstey, Barbara. Come you in, Chief Inspector, I'll put you in the drawing room and then go and find my husband.'

Drat Colin, Louis thought, *why hadn't he been warned that Nigel had remarried*? It was going to be a lot harder to talk about Nigel's former wife's former boyfriend, with a new wife in residence. But then, she probably wasn't new. Mary had died thirty-three years ago.

The man who entered the room looked extremely good for eighty-four. His gait was steady and energetic and while his complexion did suggest that maybe he enjoyed a drink, he looked generally in good health for his age. 'Good morning, Chief Inspector. This is an unexpected pleasure. May we offer you a cup of coffee?'

'Thank you,' said Louis, 'that would be splendid.'

Barbara Anstey disappeared, presumably in search of coffee, so Louis thought the sooner he explained his visit, the better. 'I am really sorry to trouble you, sir. It's a shot in the dark but I was just wondering whether you could help me.'

'Sit down, sit down, what can I do for you?' said Nigel.

'I believe your former wife, Mary, had a boyfriend at agricultural college, named Philip Trehearne. I wondered if you ever met him, or knew anything about him.'

Louis was looking out for it, of course, and there it was. Just for a second, it was clear the name did indeed mean something to Nigel Anstey.

'I don't think so,' he said. 'My former wife's boyfriend, you say? I didn't meet Mary until she had left college. I farm just over a thousand acres. With my other business interests, at the time I needed a farm manager but couldn't really afford one. Then the idea of a newly graduated student came to mind and Mary was perfect – hard-working, intelligent, resourceful. To be honest, she was quite as good as any farm manager with years of experience. I was very lucky to find her.'

He was talking too much, trying to steer the conversation away from Philip. 'So you married her?' said Louis, smiling.

'Yes, indeed, but believe me, it wasn't for just her management skills. She was a charming girl and once we were working together, our love for one another gradually blossomed.'

At that moment, Barbara Anstey arrived and while she poured out the coffee for the two men, all conversation ceased, creating a slight awkward and tense pause.

'Right,' said Barbara, when she had finished, 'is there anything else I can do for you two gentlemen?'

'No thank you, darling,' said Nigel, 'me, and our friendly policeman here, are just discussing one of my businesses. We don't need to hold you up.'

Barbara smiled slightly and reluctantly left the room.

'I'm sorry, sir,' said Louis, 'am I causing you some embarrassment with my questions?'

'Only slightly,' said Nigel. 'I regret having to lie to her but my wife is a little sensitive about the past. Still, if there's nothing else, let's just enjoy the coffee, shall we?'

'So, you have absolutely no knowledge of Philip Trehearne, then, sir?' Louis persisted.

'I would have said so, if I had,' said Nigel. 'Why are you

asking me about him anyway? It makes no sense.'

'About three years after your wife Mary sadly died, Philip went missing and has never been found. I have been asked to re-open the case, so having learnt of his relationship with your wife, I just came here, on the off chance, to see if you could help me in any way.'

'Good God, man, you're talking about something that must have happened at least thirty years ago. Why on earth are you looking for this Philip now?'

'It's a private family matter, which I'm afraid I can't share with you,' said Louis. 'As I said at the beginning, I know it's unlikely but I was just hoping he might have stayed in touch, become a family friend, perhaps. I gather he and Mary were very close at college.'

'I can't help you in any way.' Louis could tell Nigel's anger was bubbling only just below the surface.

'I believe you and Mary had two sons, Nigel and Benjamin. How are they getting on? They must have been quite young when they lost their mother,' said Louis.

'I don't see either of my sons any more. I have no idea where they are or what they're doing.' Nigel had gone worryingly red in the face.

'Was the rift because they didn't like you re-marrying?' Louis asked, knowing he was chancing his luck.

'As a matter of fact it was, not that it's any business of yours. Still, if I tell you what happened, maybe that will shut you up and you'll go away. I had an affair with Barbara while Mary was still alive, which, when they found out, did not please the boys, as you can imagine. I make no excuses for my behaviour. Mary was ill with cancer for years. I was only in my mid-forties when she became unwell. I'm a normal red-blooded man and there was no way I could be expected to spend years living like a monk.'

Nigel paused to drink his coffee. Louis realised that he was actively starting to dislike this man.

'Anyway, that's the end of the story. Mary died, Barbara and I married, Nigel left home first and then Benjamin. Neither keep in touch. I don't mind, ungrateful boys. I sent them to decent schools, took them on wonderful holidays, clothed and fed them royally and this is how they behave. I'm well rid of them, to be honest, they could be dead for all I know. Benjamin, in particular, he had a serious drug problem.'

Unusually, Louis could think of nothing more to say to this odious man. Fleetingly, he thought of Edward and the terror he had felt when his boy went missing. How could any father speak like that about his child? He stood up. 'I won't trouble you any further, sir. Thank you for your time; I'll find my own way out.'

Nigel Anstey did not reply so Louis left the room to find Barbara hovering in the hall. Louis immediately suspected she had been listening, and he was right.

'He can be a hard man,' she said, 'but he's been good to me, always. He's very bitter about the boys but I'm sure he knows nothing about this Philip you're after. Certainly, he has never mentioned anyone of that name to me and I do believe he tells me everything.' She opened the front door for Louis. 'I am sorry you've had a wasted journey.'

'Thank you for the coffee,' was all Louis could manage.

Back in the car, Louis drove to the end of the driveway and stopped. All round him were Nigel Anstey's rolling acres, which, instinctively Louis felt, brought their landowner no great pleasure, at least not any more. He knew he should feel sorry for this embittered old man who had lost his sons but he couldn't because he knew he had not been told the truth – Nigel Anstey had definitely known, or, at the very least, known of Philip Trehearne. So why should he lie about it?

CHAPTER NINETEEN

Constable Colin Haines became immediately aware that he was not flavour of the month, as soon as the boss entered the room. Tired and dispirited, Louis had come charging into the office and made a beeline for Colin's desk.

'Why didn't you tell me, Constable, that Nigel Anstey had remarried?' Louis demanded.

'I'm sorry, sir. I thought it was Mary Anstey, née Daniels, you were interested in and so having found her husband, I've been concentrating on trying to track down her sons.'

'And have you found them?' Louis asked, a little more graciously, acknowledging, privately, that Haines was probably right.

'The younger of the two sons, Benjamin, died very young, at just twenty-three. He was a drug addict. The older son, Nigel, has completely vanished. I've searched every possible source and the only conclusion I have come to is that he must have emigrated. There really are absolutely no records of him in this country, HMRC have nothing, no bank account or credit cards, no social media presence; he appears to have vanished.'

Louis sat down beside Colin's desk. 'According to their father, both boys left home after he remarried because they did not approve of the new wife. He was having an affair with her before Mary died, so as they had an established relationship, I imagine they married soon after Mary's death. Nigel Junior left first and Benjamin later. I don't know why they didn't leave together.'

'There's a four-year age gap between Nigel and Benjamin,' said Colin. 'Benjamin would only have been fifteen when his mother died, so was really too young to leave home. Nigel would have been nineteen, old enough to strike out on his own.'

'What's really odd, Haines, is that Mr Anstey seems to have no knowledge of Benjamin's death, though, as next of kin, he must have been informed. He told me, very dismissively, that he didn't know if his sons were alive or dead, though he did mention Benjamin's drug problem. Why didn't he just tell me Benjamin had died?'

'Maybe, sir, Benjamin was married, in which case his wife would have been next of kin. I'll see what I can find out – that could be the reason.'

'Good idea, Haines. Also, see if you can find out what happened to Nigel Junior after leaving school, up until you lose track of him. And let's find out about the second Mrs Anstey's background. Her name's Barbara. I can't see any of this will assist us in finding out what happened to

Philip, but you might turn up something that could help. I have to admit I'm struggling with this one.'

'I'll do some digging, sir, and I'm sorry I dropped you in it by not finding out about Barbara Anstey,' said Colin.

'It's me who should apologise, Haines. You're doing a great job and you're right, I did ask you to follow Mary's trail. Just keep at it. I think you're the only person now who is likely to come up with anything useful. Very reluctantly, I have to admit to feeling a dead end coming up fast.'

Jago Tripconey wheeled himself down the farm track leading from the house. He knew he couldn't go far in his wheelchair, the ground was too rough. Still, even a few yards would give him a breather. Following the meeting with Louis Peppiatt, there had been a brief respite when Tom's temper had much improved. However, things had rapidly deteriorated following a meeting with his solicitor. Indeed, the atmosphere in the house was becoming increasingly toxic. Having agreed to stop criticising the police in the media, Tom now had turned his anger towards what remained of his family. He was feeding Gemma's guilt by repeatedly saying how different things would have been if she and Jago had not moved to Australia. He suggested that if they had stayed in Cornwall, then their family – the children, Remy and Suzannah, in particular – would have stopped Sarah from killing herself, by giving her a reason to go on living. Jago had asked Tom several times to stop these accusations. He had tried to explain that Gemma was suffering enough without having salt rubbed in the wounds, but Tom would not listen. Jago had also asked about the meeting with the solicitor, enquiring whether there was any problem with the will. Tom told him that of course there was no problem and to mind his own business. It seemed that every time they were together, another row would break out. It was awful.

Jago was well aware of how lucky he was. He and Merrin had grown up in a close, loving family. Cross words were rare; love and support were plentiful – as, apparently, had been the situation in the Trehearne family, until Philip's disappearance. What would he and Merrin have been like today if their dad, Harry, had done a disappearing act? Jago wondered. Would they be as angry all these years later, as Tom was now? It was hard to tell, but Jago knew himself well enough to recognise he was a relaxed, laid-back sort of chap, which, of course, was why Australia suited him so well. He couldn't imagine maintaining Tom's level of anger and bitterness. Stuff happened, like his accident, like the death of Adam McKenzie. Life was too short to ponder on the 'what ifs'. One just had to get on with it – tomorrow is another day – it was the only way to get through life's difficulties, in Jago's judgement.

With a sigh, he was turning round his chair to begin wheeling back towards the house, when his mobile rang.

'Jago, is that you?' said a voice that at first he did not recognise. 'Sorry to trouble you, it's Louis Peppiatt. I could really do with a chat and some advice. Are you by any chance free this afternoon?'

'Louis, you have just saved me from going mad being cooped up here. Yes, of course, I'm free but I've no transport, I'm afraid.'

'That's no problem. I'm just leaving the Camborne station now so I could come and pick you up.'

'Better not,' said Jago. 'If you come out here, Tom will put you through the third degree. He's a nightmare at the moment. How about I ask Merrin to collect me, that is if you don't mind her being involved in our chat?'

'Actually, it would be great to talk to you both, now I come to think about it.'

'OK,' said Jago. 'I'll get hold of Merrin now and if I don't come back to you immediately, shall we meet at her place?'

'I thought Miranda's Cottage was difficult for you with all those steps,' said Louis.

'That was my sis just being over-protective. We should have a competition – I bet I can shin up those steps on my backside quite as quickly as you can walk up them, Chief Inspector.'

'I very much doubt it,' said Louis. 'I am surprisingly agile for my age.'

'You can boast,' said Jago, 'in the certain knowledge that Merrin would never allow us to behave in such a juvenile manner.'

'Very true,' Louis agreed.

CHAPTER TWENTY

Within the hour, Louis, Jago and Merrin were to be found sitting round Merrin's kitchen table, upon which was a plate of delicious-looking fruit cookies, one of which had already been divided between William and Horatio. It had been decided that as Horatio knew and liked everyone present, he should be allowed out of his cage. He was now sitting on his favourite perch, on top of the wine rack, and enthusiastically joining in the conversation – or rather, one should say, dominating it. There had been riotous cackles of laughter, instructions to 'stop it', a lot of kissing noises and now he was making the very realistic sound of exploding bombs.

'It's like being in a war zone,' said Louis. 'How on earth did he learn to do that?'

'It's Isla's fault. After Bonfire Night one year in Bristol, he started imitating the fireworks and Isla taught him to add an explosion on the end of the screeching noise. I love my daughter very much but it is one of the things for which I can never forgive her. I'll put him in his cage if he doesn't shut up.'

Horatio, who appeared to have understood every word she said, did just that.

'Peace in our time,' said Louis in what sounded like a very passable imitation of Neville Chamberlain.

'And about as likely,' said Jago wisely.

'It's good of you to meet me at such short notice, only I find myself in rather a difficult situation.' said Louis. 'What I'm going to tell you is not really a police matter but, nonetheless, I'm sharing this information with you in the strictest confidence – unless we decide otherwise, and I think the decision should be yours.'

'Intriguing, but of course you can rely on our discretion,' said Jago, and Merrin nodded.

'My starting point was this, but please tell me if I'm wrong. Philip Trehearne comes across as a thoroughly decent bloke, loved and liked by all who knew him. If, during all the years he spent at the farm, he had behaved badly, done something seriously wrong, I would know about it by now, wouldn't I?'

'With dear old Jack as your sergeant, how can you possibly feel you need to ask that question?' said Merrin with a smile. 'Seriously, though, there were no skeletons in Philip's cupboard, were there, Jago?'

'I'm sure absolutely not,' Jago agreed.

'I learnt from Tom that Philip had attended Seale-Hayne Agricultural College. So it seems logical that his disappearance could be linked to the three years he spent at college, which was the only period in his life when he was away from St Ives. Through nefarious means, with which I will not bore you, I discovered that during his period at college, he had a very serious girlfriend named Mary Daniels.'

'That can't be right,' said Merrin. 'He and Sarah were devoted to each other from when they were in their early teens; everyone knows that. Neither of them ever looked at anyone else.'

'I have it on very good authority that Philip did. He and Mary were very close during their years at university. She was very studious apparently, and was good at keeping Philip's nose to the grindstone. He was an excellent practical farmer, but not so good at the academic work.'

'But Sarah waited for him all those years he was away from home,' Merrin protested.

'My sister is an incurable romantic, Louis,' said Jago. 'So let's assume your informant is correct. Why didn't Philip dump Sarah if he was so besotted with Mary?'

'I suspect we all know the answer to that,' said Louis. 'Philip's sister died at fifteen, and according to Gemma, their parents were devasted by the loss. They lost interest in the farm and wanted to retire as soon as Philip had finished college. He would have been under enormous pressure to return to Cornwall.'

'He could have brought Mary with him and they could have run the farm together,' suggested Jago.

'I imagine that wouldn't have made him very popular in St Ives,' said Louis. 'In any event, Mary landed a brilliant job as a farm manager of a thousand acres, just outside Ashburton, and after a while, she married the boss.'

'A farm manager straight out of college, that's insane,' said Merrin. 'I suppose the boss fancied her, which is why he took her on.'

'Maybe, but he went to great pains to assure me that Mary's management skills were exemplary,' said Louis.

'Goodness,' said Merrin, 'so you've met Mary's husband?'

'Yes, we tracked him down and I went to see him yesterday. His name is Nigel Anstey and he lives with his second wife, Barbara, in a truly lovely Queen Anne manor house.'

'So what happened to Mary?' Jago asked.

'She died of cancer, just three years before Philip disappeared but not before she gave Nigel two sons – Nigel Junior and Benjamin.'

'Poor old Mary,' said Merrin. 'She can't have been very old.'

'No, only in her early forties, poor woman. Anyway, the plot thickens. Apparently, Nigel and Barbara were having an affair while Mary was still alive. The boys took exception to this and also their father's subsequent remarriage. So, they left home. Nigel left first, he was four years older than his brother, and Benjamin followed. Benjamin died of a drugs overdose in his early twenties and Nigel Junior has completely disappeared.'

'Nigel Senior must be devastated to have lost both his first wife and his two sons,' said Merrin.

'Not so you'd notice. He's not an easy person to love, is Nigel. He's bitter about his sons leaving home but made it quite clear he didn't care if they were dead or alive.'

'He sounds charming,' said Jago. 'So what are you

saying? Do you think Nigel killed Philip out of jealousy?'

'No,' said Louis, 'because Mary died three years before Philip disappeared. If Nigel was going to murder his rival, surely he would have done it while Mary was still alive and presumably at the beginning of their relationship?'

'But could he be the murdering type?' Merrin asked. 'He certainly doesn't sound very pleasant.'

'He's a typical upper-class landowner, who, I'm sure, went hunting, shooting and fishing with the great and the good, back when he was younger. He's eighty-four now and, I must say, looks very good on it. I believe he's probably a bully but I don't see him as a murderer, though saying that, over the years, I've come across quite a number of very unlikely murderers. Who knows what any of us are capable of, if pushed beyond the limit?'

'There's something about Nigel Senior you haven't told us yet,' said Merrin shrewdly.

'There have been times in our brief acquaintance when I have thought your sister might be far better at my job than I am,' Louis said to Jago.

'It's the lawyer in her,' said Jago. 'She sees stuff that we mere mortals miss entirely. It's very annoying.'

'I am here, you know,' said Merrin. 'Tell them off, Horatio!'

Horatio obliged with a brief but noisy and slightly off-key rendition of 'Mamma Mia', which had them all wincing.

'You're right, Merrin,' said Louis, when peace was restored. 'When I asked Nigel Senior if he knew, or knew of, Philip, he was adamant that he had never heard of him. He was lying. The question is, why?'

'Did you tell him that Philip was Mary's former boyfriend?' Merrin asked.

'I did,' said Louis, 'but he appeared to be entirely disinterested.'

'So what happens now?' Jago asked.

'Well, that's the problem. I don't seem to have anywhere to go from here. I could go back and see Nigel Senior again and try and bully him into admitting he knew Philip. However, I believe he'd be a very difficult nut to crack without any supporting proof. There is a young constable, named Colin Haines, who works out of Camborne Police Station. He's an absolute computer whiz and looks about twelve, of course. He is going to try and find Nigel Junior, or at least try and find out more about him, and he is also going to get the full info on Barbara. He might throw up something but it's hard to imagine what.'

'Definitely the most interesting thing about all of this is the fact that Nigel Senior lied to you,' said Merrin. 'What's the point of not admitting he knew Philip, if he did, unless there is something shady he's covering up – like Philip's disappearance.'

'Which is why I can't let the matter drop,' said Louis.

'Shall I make some more coffee?' said Merrin.

'I'd like to explain first why I asked to see you today,' said Louis.

'Blimey, Louis, I thought you'd already done that,' said Jago.

'No, that was just background. The question I want to ask you is whether you think at this stage I should tell Tom and Gemma what I've found out to date. I'm not obliged to do so, and what worries me is that learning their father had a serious relationship with someone other than their mother might tip them – well, Tom in particular – over the edge. Would it be better to wait and see if I can dig up something useful or positive? They are both so idealistic about their parents' relationship. It feels awful to upset that image, unless, or until, I have something concrete to tell them about what happened to their father. What do you both think?'

'Your call, I think, Jago,' said Merrin. 'We're talking about your wife and your brother-in-law.'

Jago was silent for several moments. 'I think we shouldn't tell them anything at this stage. Everything you have learnt so far, with respect, Louis, is negative and hurtful. If we hit them with this now, I think you're right, Tom will go ballistic and maybe start shouting off to the press again, and Gemma will be enormously upset. Yet, as you say, this information brings us no nearer finding out what happened to Philip. You may not be able to find out anything more but why don't we give it the full week you suggested before having another meeting? If Boy Wonder in Camborne hasn't come up with anything, then you'll have to tell them. What do you both think?'

'I agree,' said Merrin.

'Isn't it going to be difficult for you not telling Gemma about what I've just told you?' Louis asked.

'Not really,' said Jago. 'They don't know I was meeting you today. I said I was going to have lunch with Merrin, so no awkward questions will be asked and, much more importantly, I feel it's right to protect Gemma from all of this at the moment.'

'OK,' said Louis. 'I can promise I will do everything I

can to unravel this sad story as quickly as possible but, I'll admit, at this moment, it is difficult to see how.'

'Good boy, very good boy,' said Horatio.

'I couldn't have put it better myself,' said Jago.

CHAPTER TWENTY-ONE

Merrin was in a tizz. Isla and her friend Maggie were due home early afternoon and she was picking them up from Newquay Airport. Gemma and Jago were coming for supper and she wanted it all to be perfect. Tom had been invited too, of course, but had refused, which was something of a relief. William was sulking because his morning walk had been cut short and Horatio was furious because Merrin couldn't let him out of his cage as she had hot pans all over the stove.

'You wouldn't like burnt claws,' she told him. He didn't consider her observation worthy of a reply, so turned his back and fluffed up his feathers.

Three hours later, a little flustered but with the evening meal prepared, Merrin arrived at the airport. The two girls looked wonderful as they entered the terminal building, waving madly at Merrin. They were deeply tanned and looked both happy and relaxed. It was a relief. They had been friends since they first went up to Oxford University and were in the same college, reading the same subject – history. Both had been through a great deal in their first two years, which was probably responsible for the close bond that existed between them. In their first year, Isla had lost her father. She had adored him. She had only been eighteen at the time and the shock was terrible. Crippled by grief of her own, Merrin had done her best to support her daughter, but it was really Isla's strength of character that had got her through, coupled with Maggie's support. Maggie, too, had lost a parent – her mother when she was only eleven. Her father had remarried and although her stepmother was not unkind, she simply wasn't interested in Maggie, which meant her father became increasingly lost to her as well. Perhaps, looking for a father replacement, at the beginning of the Michaelmas term in their second year, Maggie had fallen in love with their tutor, who was married, a control freak and a heavy cocaine user. Only when he started beating her up had Merrin been able to extract her from the relationship.

However, now after six weeks in Greece, island-hopping, one would have assumed they didn't have a care in the world. There was much whooping, shrieking and hugs once they'd made it through passport control. Packed into the car, the questions came thick and fast. Top of the list, of course, was how were William and Horatio.

'I'm so looking forward to seeing Uncle Jago. How's he coping?' Isla asked.

'Brilliantly, but whatever you do, don't offer to help him with anything or you'll get shouted at,' Merrin said. 'Have you told Maggie about Jago's accident?'

'Yes, she has,' volunteered Maggie. 'I think I'm up to date with all the family dramas including the death of Jago's poor mother-in-law. That sounds awful, how is his wife coping?'

'I'm glad you mentioned that. I need you two to be very tactful tonight. Can you handle that?'

'I can,' said Maggie, smiling, 'but I'm not sure about Isla!'

'I couldn't agree with you more,' said Merrin, which resulted in a great deal of light-hearted banter.

When order was restored, Isla said, 'So give us the gossip, Mum. Why have we got to be on our best behaviour?'

Merrin explained about Tom and Gemma's reaction to their mother's suicide and how necessary it was not to upset them. She then told them about the police involvement and the renewed investigation as to what had happened to Philip.

'But surely that's absurd,' said Isla. 'How can anyone be expected to find out what happened to poor Mr Trehearne after all this time – except perhaps for the talented Inspector P.'

'Funny you should say that,' said Merrin, 'but Inspector P – now officially known as Chief Inspector Peppiatt – is indeed on the case.'

'Brilliant!' both girls said in unison.

'Does that mean we'll see him?' Isla asked.

'Very probably. I'm sure he would be extremely flattered to know two such gorgeous girls were anxious to see him. But seriously, apart from saying to Gemma how sorry you are about the death of her mother, you are not to mention anything concerning police involvement – in fact it's really important that you don't even know they are involved. I've only told you because I didn't want you to ask any awkward questions during supper – just keep right off the subject of Philip, if you can.'

'We'll behave, obviously,' said Isla, 'but do tell us how Chief Inspector P is getting on with the investigation. Has he solved the problem and caught the bad guys – you know, usual Chief Inspector P stuff?'

'No comment!' said Merrin firmly.

The evening was a success. The girls' high spirits were infectious and even Gemma cheered up and genuinely seemed to enjoy their company. Jago was also in good form. There had always been a close bond between him and Isla, which was lovely to see.

Once Jago and Gemma had headed home and, at Merrin's insistence, the girls had been despatched to bed, she slowly began clearing up. Strangely, she liked this part of entertaining, thinking through the evening in peace and quiet as she restored order out of chaos. It was the first time since they had arrived in the UK that Gemma had seemed almost back to normal. After all he had been through in the last few years, Merrin was desperate that Jago's marriage should survive poor Sarah's suicide, and tonight it had seemed possible. Their normal loving and supportive relationship seemed almost restored.

If only Louis could come up with some sort of solution.

At that very moment, Louis Peppiatt was sunk in gloom, only too aware of his responsibilities, but equally aware that he could see no way forward. It was ridiculous to be forced into having to depend entirely on the findings of Constable Haines. While he appreciated that modern policing relied ever more heavily on the IT skills of their officers, he was just not used to sitting about, waiting for something to happen.

He poured himself a second whisky and sat in his chair, staring at the blank television screen. If he went to his chief super, John Dent, right now and told him of his findings to date, there was a slim possibility he would be told he had done a good job and that the case could now be closed. In reality, though, while the threat of Tom Trehearne making more trouble in the media hung over the force, he doubted that John Dent would relent. Tom had the media very much on his side. Police-bashing was a favourite sport at the moment, and the idea that Tom and Gemma had lost both parents through police incompetence made for very good copy.

In any case, regardless of Dent's view, Louis just couldn't leave it – that poor family – and quite apart from his sense of obligation towards them, he had very strong feeling that he was missing something important. And then the phone rang.

'Hi, Louis, it's Don Coleman here. I'm sorry for calling so late – I hope I haven't woken you up.'

'No it's fine, Don, thanks, I'm still wide awake.'

'You don't sound very cheerful,' said Don. 'In fact, I would say you're definitely down in the dumps. Well, I might be able to help with that.'

'What do you mean?' Louis asked, intrigued, 'I must admit I could do with some good news.'

'You remember I told you that I have kept in touch

with a few of the students who went on to become local farmers? I did some research, questioned most of them, and actually landed a few orders for Gerry at the same time. Anyway, I've just left the pub, which is why I'm calling so late. I've come up with something that could be very useful and I thought you should have the information right away. Mary Daniels had a sister. What do you think about that, Chief Inspector?'

Louis sat up straight in his chair, put down his whisky glass and reached for his notebook. 'Is the sister alive?' he asked.

'Very much so. She was born ten years after Mary and is in her early sixties now. She's been married three times, saucy minx, and is now widowed. So watch your step, Louis, she sounds like a right man-eater and from what you told me in the pub the other night, you're now a free man!'

'Do you have any details, Don?' Louis asked firmly.

'Her name now is Teresa Gilbert and she lives in Tavistock. I don't have her exact address but no doubt you guys won't have any difficulty tracing her.'

'But how do you know she's still alive?' said Louis.

'The man I spoke to this evening is a Timothy Gilbert and his older brother was Teresa's last husband. The brother, named Robert, only died about a year ago. Timothy never thought much of Teresa and has made no attempt to keep in touch. However, he is fairly certain that she hasn't moved from their house in Tavistock but you will need to check her up-to-date address to be sure. Will that do you, Louis?'

'It certainly will, Don. Thank you so much. I was really

facing a brick wall with this case – that is until you rang. Why on earth didn't I think of siblings? The trouble is I've been too fixated on Mary's marriage instead of looking at the bigger picture. I'm so grateful.'

'So you caught up with the husband, then?' said Don.

'Yes, I did. I can't tell you the details but the meeting felt like a dead end. Of course, I should have been looking beyond the marriage, which, thinking about it, is obvious.'

'So you'll get in touch with Teresa?'

'I certainly will,' said Louis.

'Well, just watch yourself, lad. She may be older than you but by the sounds of it, she's quite a goer. You don't want to end up as husband number four!'

CHAPTER TWENTY-TWO

By ten o'clock the following morning, Louis had all the information he needed. During another rather sleepless night, the coincidence of Don meeting the brother-in-law of Mary's sister seemed almost too good to be true. Not for one moment did he doubt that Don was telling the truth – it just seemed a bit too neat. It wasn't until the early hours that he realised the link – Timothy Gilbert had been a student of Don's and so had Mary Daniels. They would have known one another and presumably kept in touch, so that at some point during the years that followed, they must have introduced their siblings to one another Admittedly, Teresa had been through two husbands before settling down with Timothy's brother, Robert, but the link was there.

And it was confirmed by Colin. Robert Gilbert had been married to Teresa for eight years but had died thirteen months ago. Robert had a brother named Timothy who still farmed just outside Newton Abbot and Teresa still lived at the same address in Tavistock.

Up until now, Louis had quite deliberately excluded Jack Eddy from his interviews. He had not thought it wise to take him along to meet Donald Coleman because, having sent him to prison, Louis had been very uncertain as to his likely reception – indeed, not knowing if Don would be even be prepared to see him. Likewise, given that Jack was not the most tactful of people, the delicate business of asking Nigel Anstey about his dead wife's missing boyfriend, Louis had felt should best be undertaken alone. However, in the case of the 'saucy minx' Teresa, Louis decided it was time to involve his sergeant.

On the journey to Tavistock, Louis filled in Jack on both previous interviews, just describing Don as 'a friend from the old days' when he'd been a constable in Newton Abbot.

Jack seemed suitably impressed with Louis's progress. 'Well, boss, you might not have solved the case yet but you've found out a lot more than we did back in the day when Philip first went missing.'

'Back then,' said Louis, 'the whole investigation was centred on *where* Philip had gone, not *why*. Without the luxury of searching for Philip, all we have to go on now is why he disappeared. Eddy, I know you can be – how shall I put it – a great communicator. But what I have told you just now must go no further. You must tell no one, not even Mrs Eddy. It's vital we don't advise the Trehearnes of our findings until we have the full story. They've suffered enough. And whatever we find, they must be the first to know.'

'I'll do my best, boss,' said Jack. 'Fancy old Philip having a girlfriend at college.'

'No, Sergeant, doing your best is not good enough,' Louis thundered. 'St Ives is a very small town. If you share any of these details with anyone, I will know about it, and if you do, not only will you be off the case, you might well be looking at early retirement. Have I made myself quite clear?'

'Yes, boss,' said Jack, clearly shocked by the vehemence of Louis's reaction.

Teresa Gilbert's house was charming and so was the occupant. She might be in her sixties but she certainly didn't look it. She was wearing a cream dress, over which she wore a tan jacket, which matched perfectly her tan boots. Her hair was faded blonde and her complexion remarkably unlined. Despite her age, she was stunning and Louis could immediately understand why she'd had no problem acquiring three husbands along life's journey. Jack, who had been sulking ever since Louis's tirade, perked up considerably at the mere sight of her.

Having introduced themselves on the doorstep, Teresa's immediate reaction was to ask if anyone had died. 'No,' Louis assured her, 'we're here to ask for your advice.'

Immediately, she was all smiles. Over the years, Louis had found that asking for advice was a very good way to start an interview, and in this case, it was true. Teresa ushered them into a delightful drawing room, which, of course, was both immaculate and stylish, and called out to someone called Ursula to bring coffee for three.

Teresa gestured for them to sit down, perched neatly

on a chair opposite Louis and fixed him with a radiant smile. 'So, Chief Inspector, what can I do for you?' she said in a husky voice.

Dear God, thought Louis, *Don was right. It's just as well I have Eddy as a chaperone!* 'I hope this isn't going to be too painful for you, Mrs Gilbert,' he said, 'but we want to talk to you about your late sister, Mary.'

'Teresa, please,' she said, crossing and recrossing an excellent pair of legs. 'You had me worried there for a moment, Chief Inspector. I have acquired some very naughty friends over the years, but my sister was certainly not one of them – I don't believe she was ever naughty in her whole life so I have no problem in telling you whatever you would like to know.'

'Did you ever meet, or know of, her boyfriend at Seale-Hayne. His name was—'

'Philip, Philip Trehearne,' Teresa interrupted. 'Yes, I met him several times. Quite a hunk, I was a little jealous of my big sister although I can only have been about eight or nine at the time. Still, I've always had an eye for a good-looking man.' She gave Louis another one of those smiles.

'Did you think they would marry?' Louis asked. 'I understand the relationship was quite serious.'

At that moment, Ursula appeared with the coffee. She looked old and frail and Louis couldn't help feeling that things were the wrong way round – that Ursula was the person who should be sitting in an armchair, being waited on. When she'd left, having spoken not a word, Louis repeated his question.

'So did you think Philip and Mary would marry?'

'Good heavens, how should I know?' said Teresa. 'I was only a child.' She hesitated. 'I believe my parents were very keen on Philip. His parents were going to make over the family farm to him when he finished college. He lived in Cornwall, somewhere. They thought he was a nice boy, with a good future.'

'So, what went wrong?' Louis asked.

'I've no idea,' said Teresa. 'I don't know if they fell out or simply that Mary thought that ghastly man, Nigel Anstey, was a better bet. Have you met him?'

'Yes,' said Louis, 'and his second wife, Barbara.'

'I've never met her. What about the sons, did you see them, or have they at last escaped from under the thumb of their father?'

'When were you last in touch with them?' Louis asked.

'Oh, I haven't seen them for decades, not since Mary's funeral.'

'Even though they're your nephews?' said Louis

'Don't start judging me, Chief Inspector. No one has the right to judge other people's relationships, especially family ones. I have nothing to do with my family and my late husband had nothing to do with his. Our choice, but a good one, I believe, for us, at any rate. Still, what happened to the boys, as a matter of interest?'

Louis felt there was no need to break the news gently. 'The elder boy, Nigel, we've been unable to trace. He may be living abroad but at the moment we can't find him. The younger boy, Benjamin, I am sorry to tell you, died of a drugs overdose when he was twenty-three.'

'I'm not surprised. Nigel wasn't violent but he had a terrible temper, an absolute viper's tongue, and he totally ruled the roost. Also, he loved playing lord of the manor and he's an awful snob. He packed off both boys to boarding school at seven. My parents were horrified and I imagine Mary was none too pleased. Well, you'll understand what I'm saying, having met him. He's not the easiest of people to like, is he, and he's always been very cold when it comes to feelings – I suspect he doesn't care much for anyone but himself. I suppose that's why the boys, each in their own way, made their escape.'

'That's sad,' said Jack. 'I suppose you have no idea where young Nigel might have run away to? Did they have a special place where they went on holiday, or did he ever talk about somewhere he wanted to visit?'

'I'm sorry,' said Teresa, 'but once again, I have no idea. We saw very little of Mary after she married. She was farm manager of Nigel's estate, as well as being a mother, so she was always so busy, poor girl. As for the boys, the conversations I had with them could be counted on the fingers of one hand. Anyway, why are you asking all these questions about Mary and her family?'

'Three years after Mary died, Philip disappeared,' said Louis. 'I have been asked to reopen the case to try and find out what happened to him. I became aware of his relationship with your sister and thought talking to you might throw some light on his disappearance. I know it's unlikely – apart from anything else, it all happened so long ago – but for Philip's family it would mean a very great deal to know what happened to him so I am attempting to leave no stone unturned.'

'But, as you say, Philip's disappearance must have happened at least thirty years ago,' said Teresa. 'I can't imagine you'll find out anything of significance after all this time. Did Philip marry?'

'Yes, and very happily. They had two children and apparently an idyllic life until he vanished.'

'Strange,' said Teresa thoughtfully. 'My parents always described him as a very steady sort of young man. I think that's why they were so keen on the match.'

Louis smiled. 'I cannot tell you the number of times people have described him exactly like that, which, I admit, doesn't make my job any easier.'

'Can I offer you a glass of wine, or sherry, Chief Inspector?' Teresa asked. 'This coffee is frightful; Ursula is completely hopeless at making coffee, and everything else, come to that.'

Louis's sympathy for poor Ursula increased considerably. He shook his head. 'Thank you, but no thank you. We have to drive back to West Cornwall.'

'I'll drive if you like, boss,' Jack suggested.

'No, thanks, Eddy, I'm on duty. Just two more questions, Teresa, and then we'll leave you in peace. Did you and your sister get on well together?'

'Yes,' said Teresa. 'We weren't as close as most sisters, because we were ten years apart in age. By the time I was old enough to be interesting, she was a young adult. We were very different too. Unlike me, Mary was very hard-working and serious, but a thoroughly nice person, if a little dull.'

'And lastly, why do you think she chose to marry a man like Nigel Anstey, particularly when it sounds as if she'd had the chance to marry Philip?'

'God knows,' said Teresa, 'remember, I was only a child.'

'Yes, of course,' said Louis, 'apologies.'

'I've just thought of something we didn't tell you,' said Jack, as the two men stood up to leave. 'The boss told me that Mr Anstey lied about not knowing Mr Trehearne.'

'What do you mean?' Teresa asked.

'What Sergeant Eddy means is that I asked Nigel Anstey if he knew Philip. He insisted that he didn't and had never heard of him. However, it's my view he was lying,' Louis explained.

'Well, Sergeant,' said Teresa, with another dazzling smile, this time directed at Jack. 'I think your observation is the most interesting of the morning. I think if you can discover why Nigel Anstey was lying, you stand a very good chance of finding out what happened to Philip.'

Virtually the same observation as Merrin's, Louis thought, as they walked to the car. Louis was a great believer in female intuition.

CHAPTER TWENTY-THREE

The following morning, adding much to his already considerable frustration, Louis learnt that there had been another post office raid, this time in Bodmin. He immediately called the chief superintendent's office.

Sally answered. 'Is he in? I need to speak to him urgently,' said Louis.

'Goodness, we are grumpy this morning, not even a "good morning, Sally" or a "how are you, Sally". What's up, Louis? No, he isn't in but I am your faithful servant and am happy to take a message.'

'There's been another raid, this time in Bodmin,' said Louis.

'I know,' said Sally, 'but mercifully no one was hurt on this occasion, though they reckon it's the same gang from up country somewhere.'

'They're not from "up country somewhere", they're

from London and when sir took me off the case, I was within a pigeon's fart of arresting the culprits, with the help of the Met.'

'Language please, Louis. I take it you want the case back again? Does that mean you've found out what happened to Philip Trehearne?'

'No, it doesn't. I want the case back because I want those villains caught before they kill someone. Philip's been missing for thirty years – the people running Cornish sub-post offices are in danger right now.'

'When he calls me, I'll tell him all that, but I know what his decision will be. He sees Tom Trehearne as a ticking bomb. On social media, in particular, there have been some awful accusations made against the police and I think, no – I know, he has the top brass breathing down his neck. He's not going to let you focus on anything else until you've resolved the Trehearne case.'

'Sal, I've hit the buffers. I don't see how I can take this any further. It's all too long ago and the principal person who might have been able to help me is dead and her nearest and dearest can offer no assistance. It's hopeless.'

'Louis, you and I have known each other a long time. There are lots of things I love about you, dear boy, but what has always impressed me most is your enormous energy and enthusiasm for your job. I remember a young man who would have positively relished the idea of taking on a case that was considered hopeless. Find that young man inside yourself, and then you'll be able to find out what happened to Philip Trehearne.'

'Oh God, Sal. Why can't you be like a normal secretary

who simply says they'll pass on the message?'

'Stop whinging and get on with it,' was Sally's response.

Knowing that Sally was totally sure-footed when it came to judging John Dent's reactions, Louis sat and stared at the wall for a while, to allow his temper to simmer down. He looked out of the window, saw it promised to be a lovely day and made a decision. He would walk the path that Philip had taken from Trehearne Farm to Halsetown Inn – the scene of the crime, as it were – assuming, of course, there had been a crime at all. If nothing else, the fresh air and exercise might just kickstart his brain and the walk would give him time to think.

He parked his car on the verge, right at the end of the Trehearnes' long drive, and set off on the path across the fields leading to the pub. Part of the way took him over moorland, covered in boulders and bracken, other parts over cultivated fields. Sometimes the path went close to the road, sometimes some distance away. In normal circumstances, the sights and smells along the way would have exhilarated him but not today – his mind seemed to be in a fog.

When he reached Halsetown Inn, he stood outside, wondering what to do next. Should he have lunch at the pub? But he wasn't hungry, he realised. He could walk back to his car along the road, which would be quicker, but that didn't hold much appeal. He would retrace his steps, he decided, and try to focus his mind. Attempting to find his inner young self was far too tall an order, whatever Sally might say.

He was starting to make his way back to the footpath

when a car drew up in front of him and stopped. An arm was waving out of the car window, which, as he drew nearer, he realised belonged to Merrin McKenzie.

'Louis, what are you doing loitering outside a pub?' she asked as he came alongside the car.

'I don't really know,' said Louis. 'I've just walked from Trehearne Farm to here, Philip's last known journey, hoping for inspiration.'

'Any luck?' Merrin asked.

'Absolutely none,' Louis admitted.

'Goodness, you do sound fed up. I know what to do – I'll take you to see someone who will really make you feel more cheerful. 'It won't take long, no more than half an hour. Jump in.'

'I've left my car at the end of the Trehearnes' drive,' said Louis.

'No matter,' said Merrin, 'we're just going into St Ives and then I'll drop you back to the farm. There's no point in you driving into town yourself, now the season is in full swing, you'll never find a parking space.'

Louis did as he was told and climbed into the passenger seat. William, who had been sitting in the back, stood up and, leaning forward, licked Louis's ear, which, for some reason, he found comforting. 'So, who is this wonderful person who is going to make me feel cheerful? Because they've got a tough job ahead of them, believe me.'

'Wait and see,' said Merrin.

CHAPTER TWENTY-FOUR

On the way into St Ives, Louis told Merrin about his visit to Mary's sister, Teresa.

'She plays at being very frivolous but underneath it all, she's no one's fool. In fact, I would say, she's very astute. She summed up our whole meeting by suggesting that if we could find out why Nigel Anstey was lying about not knowing Philip, we could solve the whole mystery. I believe she's right.'

'That's exactly what I suggested,' said Merrin, trying not to sound miffed. 'People don't lie randomly for the hell of it. They lie because they have something to hide.'

'Yes, I know it's what you said, too. What I meant to say was how interesting it is that you both came to the same conclusion. Of course, your observations are only relevant on the assumption that I got it right and Anstey really was lying. I could have imagined it.'

'Oh, for heaven's sake, Louis. You've had years and years of experience interviewing people. If you spotted that he was lying, it means he was doing just that. Come on, buck up!'

St Ives was looking particularly lovely. The three of them, including William, walked from the car park down Bunkers Hill, where nearly every property displayed a wonderful array of flowers. They walked through to the harbour to find the tide was way out, the sand golden, the sea and sky a deep blue.

'It's absolutely perfect,' said Louis.

Merrin nodded. 'When St Ives pulls out all the stops, there's nowhere better. Come on, we're going to Tristan's.'

'Why?' said Louis. 'It's not lunchtime.'

'A little faith, please,' said Merrin.

Clara was laying the tables as they entered. 'Brilliant, Pearl, you managed to track him down. Great, come on through to the kitchen, Louis. You'd better put this on,' she said, brandishing a hairnet, 'and you, William, stay where you are.'

'I'm not wearing that,' said Louis.

'You have to; none of us are allowed into Tristan's holy-of-holies without wearing one,' said Merrin.

'I'm not doing it,' said Louis. 'I'm staying out here with William, who doesn't want to wear a hairnet either.'

Tristan appeared at the kitchen door. 'For heaven's sake, you ladies, stop bullying the poor man. Chief Inspector, come in, there's a very special member of my staff I want you to meet. In fact, he's my only member of my staff.' With a flourish, he opened the kitchen door and Louis walked in.

For a moment, Louis didn't recognise him in his overalls and hairnet. He'd lost weight too, but what made him so very different was his air of confidence as he deftly chopped and sliced the vegetables on his chopping board.

'Steve?' Louis said.

Steve Matthews looked up and his face broke into an enormous grin. 'Mr Inspector! Look, I've got a job and Tristan says I am doing well.'

'And he really is,' said Tristan. 'He began as a kitchen porter, washing up and doing some food prep, but now he's in charge of all the puddings. Honestly, he's well on the way to being my sous chef.'

Steve Matthews suffered from learning difficulties and had become embroiled in the drug-smuggling business that Louis had managed to bust eight months previously. Steve knew nothing about the drugs, believing he was handling fertiliser, and with Merrin's help, Louis had managed the convince the DPP that no charges should be brought against him. Louis had often wondered what had happened to Steve. He should have known. Of course Merrin would have looked after him and found him a job.

He walked over to Steve and shook his hand.

'Congratulations, Steve. It's marvellous you're doing so well. I am very pleased for you. Can you show me some of the puddings you've made?'

As they walked round the kitchen, Steve pointing out his achievements, Clara smiled at Merrin. 'This is really good for Steve, he idolises Louis,' she said in a whisper.

'And believe me,' Merrin whispered back, 'this is really good for Louis, too.'

'I'm very proud to know this young man,' Louis said to Merrin, when they'd finished their inspection.

'I wouldn't have been able to do any of this without you, Mr Inspector, because I'd have been dead,' said Steve, who did not believe in mincing his words.

'You're a clever lad, Steve. Tell me, how's your mum?' said Louis.

'She's very well, Mr Inspector. Can I tell her you came to see me specially?'

'You certainly can, Steve, and please send her my best regards. Hey, it looks like you're needed.'

The restaurant was starting to fill up and Clara had already disappeared to seat people and take orders. Louis raised an arm in farewell and mouthed a *thank you* to Tristan, as he and Merrin hurriedly left the kitchen.

'I'm sorry I didn't tell you about Steve before,' said Merrin, as they walked out onto the Wharf. 'When we had the meeting here with Jago, it wouldn't have been the right moment, particularly when Max arrived. Too many people all at once upsets Steve. And anyway, I didn't want to *tell* you about him, I wanted you to *see* him for yourself. What a transformation, don't you think?'

'It's marvellous, and all down to you, without a doubt. At the end of last year, Clara told me, quite definitely, they couldn't afford to take on any staff. You must have funded Steve's employment.'

'Alright, I admit I helped out with his wages in the beginning,' Merrin said, smiling, 'but since Easter they have been able to afford to pay him. The business is doing brilliantly.'

'Well, thank you for everything,' said Louis, 'and thank

you for reminding me that sometimes we do get things right. When I think Steve could have ended up in prison, it doesn't bear thinking of.'

'It was sheer luck I saw you today,' said Merrin, 'but I'm so glad I did. I know this Trehearne case is really bugging you and maybe you won't be able to solve it. So, you lose some but you also win some – and saving Steve was a big win.'

Suddenly, there was a loud grinding sound behind them. Turning, they saw the lifeboat was coming down the ramp, to be pulled across the sand by the tractor. The boat was manned and the sense of urgency was obvious. This was not a practice.

'God speed,' whispered Merrin, as the lifeboat was pulled across the sand towards the waiting sea.

'The sea seems pretty calm,' Louis said. 'It's hard to imagine there is an emergency today.'

'They've taken the big boat out so it's unlikely to be a swimmer in trouble. It's probably an amateur yachtsman who's got into difficulties. We get a lot of those at this time of year.'

'Brave men and women,' said Louis.

'Yes,' said Merrin. 'When I see the lifeboat go out, I always have such a sense of pride, a thrill really, which is probably the wrong reaction when it means someone is in trouble. When I last lived here permanently, the lifeboat crew were still summoned by rocket. The rocket would go off and all the seagulls would rise in the air squawking with fright. There wouldn't be a person in town who didn't know the boat was going out and they would rush to the Wharf to wish them good luck. Now, they use pagers and the people shopping in Fore Street won't even know about this unfolding drama.'

They stood in silence as the lifeboat was launched at the mouth of the harbour and they continued to watch until it was out of sight.

Louis turned to Merrin. 'Thank you,' he said, 'you've put me back on track.'

'How come?' Merrin asked, although she felt she already knew.

'Seeing Steve, of course, and then this. Most days I push pieces of paper around and interview people. That crew put their lives on the line every time they go out, often in terrible conditions. What right have I to feel sorry for myself when a case isn't going to plan? It's pathetic.'

'Can I remind you that you were stabbed a few months ago and narrowly avoided being killed. And my husband died, doing the same job you do – two brave men. Don't belittle what you do, please, for Adam's sake and your own, just because you're having a bad day.'

'God, I'm sorry,' said Louis, 'I'm such a tactless, self-centred old sod.'

'Occasionally,' agreed Merrin with a smile, 'but the rest of the time you're a relatively decent sort. Come on, I'll drive you back to your car.'

After Merrin had dropped off Louis, he sat in his car for a while thinking about the hour he'd just spent. It was a real pleasure seeing Steve, and Merrin was right, the launching of the lifeboat was a thrill. He felt a new sense of vigour, even a tinge of optimism. Somehow, he was going to find out what happened to Philip.

And then his mobile rang.

It was Constable Colin Haines. 'I think I might have found something of interest, sir,' he said.

'Go on,' said Louis.

'The eldest child of Nigel and Mary Anstey, the one they also called Nigel, was born just three months after they were married, which in turn was soon after Mary left college. I'm just wondering, sir, whether the child might not have been Nigel's – in which case, could he have been Philip's?'

CHAPTER TWENTY-FIVE

They worked it out and Colin was right. The marriage between Mary Daniels and Nigel Anstey took place on 19th October and Nigel Junior was born on 16th January. Assuming Mary had left college the previous July, the only way Nigel Senior could have been the father was if he had known Mary before she left college. This was possible, of course, but he had led Louis to believe that he had met Mary as a result of seeking a college graduate to act as farm manager. Also, he had said that their love had blossomed over time.

Louis had driven straight from the Trehearne Farm to Camborne. He and Colin were now drinking coffee in the canteen and mulling over Colin's findings.

'The thing is, sir, does it really help you solve the case?' said Colin. 'Even if the child is Philip's, it doesn't explain why Philip went missing all those years later, when his son would have been in his late teens.'

'No, I agree, but it gets us closer,' said Louis. 'If Mary did bear Philip's child, we have at last discovered something in Philip's past that could possibly have contributed to his disappearance. Up until now, Philip's entire life has been utterly blameless. Also, I now have the ammunition to interview again both Nigel Anstey and Teresa Gilbert.'

'But also, sir, why did Nigel Anstey give his first-born child his own name, if the child wasn't his?'

'Ah, that's an easy one, which you'd need to meet the man to understand. He's very pompous, very socially aware and likes to play the role of lord of the manor to the hilt. The last thing he would have wanted was to have people think the child wasn't his. By naming the child after himself, it would surely have stopped tongues wagging, if there had been any query about the date of birth. It makes sense, doesn't it?'

'I suppose so,' said Colin, 'but why did he want to marry Mary in the first place when he must have known she was pregnant with someone else's child?'

'Maybe because she was a good farm manager. She was young, attractive and hard-working. It would also have made her beholden to him, which, judging by his character, would have suited him very well. He doesn't seem to have liked his children very much, even Benjamin, who, presumably, was his own son. Maybe he just didn't care too much as long as he had sons to take over the farm, which, of course, in the end, they didn't.'

By the time he reached home, Louis had a plan. He called Jack Eddy and asked him to drive over to Truro the following morning and be outside his house at six-thirty sharp.

'We're going back to Tavistock tomorrow morning to

re-interview Teresa Gilbert, Eddy. I have new information that I believe could be helpful.'

Needless to say, an early start did not appeal to Jack, who didn't seem particularly interested in the new information, but was very anxious to know if they were having breakfast on the way, or whether he should have some at home, before leaving.

Louis suggested both, to be on the safe side.

They arrived outside Teresa Gilbert's house just after eight-thirty.

'It's a bit early to call on someone, isn't it, boss?' suggested Jack.

'If, as I suspect, she has been withholding information about her sister, I don't feel too guilty about cutting short her beauty sleep,' said Louis.

Having brought Jack up to speed on the latest development, Louis had spent the rest of the journey wondering how best to approach Teresa. His thoughts had been uninterrupted, as Jack had slept soundly for most of the journey. Teresa Gilbert was quite manipulative and wasn't afraid to use her undoubted charms. He decided the best approach was to shock her into telling the truth, before she had a chance to think up some avoiding tactics.

Despite the hour, Teresa was not only up and about but again immaculately dressed, with perfect make-up.

'Good heavens, Chief Inspector, have you come for breakfast?'

'No,' said Louis, unsmiling. 'May we come in?'

'Of course,' Teresa said. 'I don't especially want the rozzers on my doorstep at this time of the morning. I think

I entertain the neighbours more than enough as it is.'

She again led them into the drawing room. 'Do sit down,' she said.

Jack did as he was told but Louis remained standing.

'Why didn't you tell us that Mary's first-born was in fact Philip Trehearne's son?' he asked.

'What on earth makes you think that?' said Teresa. Her welcoming smile vanished.

'Because he was born just three months after her marriage to Nigel Anstey, which means the child was conceived while Mary was still at college.'

'So what?' said Teresa. 'There is nothing illegal about Nigel having an affair with a student. It's not as if he was a lecturer at the college. Yes, he was quite a lot older than Mary, but many men marry much younger women. My late husband was much older than me – fifteen years to be precise.'

'Enough!' said Louis. 'This is not a game, Mrs Gilbert. A loving family man disappeared in mysterious circumstances, his family have been left unable to find any closure and his wife killed herself just last month because she couldn't take the uncertainty any longer.'

'That's awful, you didn't tell me about the wife,' said Teresa, looking genuinely shocked.

'Well, I've told you now and so I'm going to ask you again. Was your sister's first-born child, Nigel, actually Philip's son?'

There was a long pause, while Louis and Jack watched her, hardly daring to breathe.

'You do know, Mrs Gilbert,' Jack said, at last, making Louis inwardly wince at what he might be going to say, 'that lying to the police is called *making false statement* and it can result in a two-year prison sentence.'

Amazingly, his timing was impeccable.

'Yes,' said Teresa, clearly close to tears, 'Nigel is Philip's son.'

Quickly, Louis continued before Teresa had a chance to recover herself.

'And did Philip know about the child?' he asked.

'No,' said Teresa. 'Nigel insisted that if he and Mary were going to marry, no one should ever know, especially not Philip. Even my parents believed the baby was Nigel's, although, of course, they realised he had been conceived well before the marriage. Mary had to confide in someone and she chose me but Nigel has no idea that I know, and I'd like to keep it that way, Chief Inspector.'

'That may not be possible but I will try to respect your wishes and I am grateful to you for your co-operation.'

'Co-operation!' said Teresa. 'Co-operation didn't come into it. You bullied me into betraying a confidence – betraying my dead sister's precious secret. I hope you're both pleased with yourselves, and now I would like you to leave.'

'Perhaps we were a bit harsh, boss,' said Jack, as they drove out of Tavistock.

'I don't think so,' said Louis, 'and you did very well, issuing that threat at precisely the right moment. Well done.'

'I feel a bit bad about that, boss. The lady was nearly crying and I don't think she's normally the crying sort. It all happened so long ago. I can't help feeling we should let sleeping dogs lie.'

'It's only just over four weeks since Sarah Trehearne killed herself as a direct result of the mystery surrounding her husband's disappearance. That's not so long ago, is it, Eddy, and the effect on the family has been truly awful. We owe it to them to try and find out what really happened, if we can.'

'So, are we going to see Nigel Anstey?' Jack asked.

'Tomorrow, I think, early like today, I'm afraid. I'm just hoping that Colin might have been able to dredge up something by way of proof so that I don't need to tell Nigel that Teresa is the person who has admitted the truth about Nigel Junior's parentage. Nigel Senior is not a nice man, and I don't like the idea of him possibly bullying Teresa. He's old but not too old to be thoroughly unpleasant. However, hopefully, we may be able to bluff our way through it – it certainly won't be for the want of giving it a damn good try.'

CHAPTER TWENTY-SIX

After a delightful hour spent browsing, Merrin walked out of The Leach Pottery into bright sunshine. During the early spring, she had attended a course there and was toying with the idea of taking up pottery as a serious hobby, maybe even, ultimately, as a small business. Now that she had settled into St Ives life and decorated Miranda's Cottage, the prevarication had to stop. Trying to cope with the awfulness of Adam's death, the move, even the acquisition of William had all taken time to process. Now, she needed to work, rather than just think about it.

Being a potter would mean acquiring a studio, buying equipment, the right sort of clay and glazes and heaven knows what else. A big outlay and, having only completed a short course, she felt impostor syndrome creeping up on her. Was she even good enough to have impostor syndrome? she thought, smiling to herself as she walked down the hill towards the town. And what about Horatio? She could take William to her studio but that would mean leaving Horatio all alone. It was mad to even consider that her future should be governed by the needs of a parrot. However, Horatio would definitely agree that it should, and if she was honest with herself, so did she.

She glanced at her watch – she would have to hurry. She and Clara had arranged to have a quick lunch at noon, before the restaurant became too busy. They had agreed on smoked mackerel pâté and a bottle of Prosecco on Merrin's balcony. It was a perfect day for it, and it would be good to have a catch-up. Isla and Maggie had disappeared off to Polzeath for a few days to stay with some friends from university, who had rented a cottage there.

Settled on the balcony, with glasses filled, a delicious bowl of pâté, made by Tristan, of course, and some warm crusty bread, they were all ready for a gossip.

Merrin tried out her new idea. 'What do you think about me becoming a potter?' she asked.

Clara considered the question. 'I'm not sure, Pearl. I know you enjoyed your pottery course and you've definitely got an arty eye, particularly for colours, but you've worked so hard and have so much experience, it does seem a pity to give up the law completely.'

'I was worn out by it all, even before Adam died. In fact, I was waiting to see Isla settled into uni before having a discussion with him about a possible change of career.'

The thought that no such discussion could now ever take place silenced Merrin for a moment, which Clara picked up on immediately.

'I can't even begin to imagine how tough it must be for you without Adam. But you two knew each other inside out. If you think about it, I bet you'll always know how Adam would feel about any of the major decisions you make.' She grinned, to lighten the mood. 'For example, Adam would have absolutely loved William and now would be so grateful to me for foisting him on you.'

'I would very much like to disagree with you, Clara dearest, but I have to admit that William has been a life-saver so far as I'm concerned and, reluctantly, I owe you a huge debt of gratitude for making the introduction. And yes, Adam would have loved him.'

Merrin topped up their glasses and they made a silent toast to William, who was sitting on Merrin's feet in a nice patch of sun.

'After you and Louis left the restaurant the other day,' said Clara, 'Steve said an odd thing to me. He said that you and Louis were wonderful – that Louis had saved his life and that you had helped him with *bones*. What on earth did he mean by that?'

Merrin frowned. 'I can't imagine – oh, wait a minute, he was probably talking about me helping him pro bono, which means I was advising him for no fee. If someone is not eligible for legal aid, or, as in Steve's case, there wasn't time to apply, then solicitors and barristers can offer legal assistance for no fee, and it's called pro bono. Actually, I didn't offer in Steve's case, I was coerced into it by Louis, but the result was the same! Occasionally, one does get paid. If, for example, Steve had been charged but the court had thrown out the prosecution, then I would have been paid by the other side. If, on the other hand, you manage to keep your client out of court, you earn nothing. As it turned out, I was very glad to be able to help Steve.'

'There you are, good old Steve and his *bones*! That's what you should do – offer pro bono services. Presumably you can pick and choose the people you help. It would be so rewarding – look what you did for Steve – and now and again you might even earn some dosh, in which case, I'm on commission for introducing you to the idea. God, I'm good!'

'I suppose it is something worth thinking about, particularly if I could work locally. I really don't want to start charging round the country. I want to stay settled and focused in St Ives, or at least in Cornwall. As for your commission, sod that.'

'Honestly, Pearl, you're so ungrateful, but because I am such a generous and forgiving soul, here's another idea for free. Surely Louis would be able to put some work your way, if not directly, then through other cases he hears about in the area? And talking about Louis, how's he getting on with finding out what happened to Philip?'

'He's made some progress, but I'm not allowed to tell you about it. He's spoken to me and Jago but that's it for the moment. Sorry, but I have promised.'

'He must have told Jack Eddy about what he's up to since Jack is supposed to be helping him. I'll ask Jack; he won't be as toffee-nosed, as you, darling Pearl.'

'Please don't, seriously don't,' said Merrin. 'The thing is, all the information he has found out so far is bad news, really. We have decided it is better that Tom and Gemma are not kept informed until he has completed his investigation. It would be absolutely terrible if the news got out ahead of them being told. You must see that, Clara, it's really important.'

'Of course I do, silly old Pearl; don't fret, my lips are sealed. Good luck to Louis with keeping Jack quiet, though.'

'I expect Louis will have made it quite clear that Jack will lose his job if he blabs.'

'That possibly might just be enough!' said Clara.

Merrin was about to offer coffee, when there was a call on her mobile. 'It's Gemma,' she mouthed at Clara as she answered the call. There was then a long silence while Merrin listened and said nothing. Finally, she thanked Gemma and ended the call.

'What was all that about?' Clara asked. 'That is if I'm allowed to know.'

'It's about Sarah's funeral. It's taking place this Friday at 11 a.m.'

'Where?' Clara asked.

'In town, at St Ia's Church, which I imagine will be full to bursting. Actually, it sounds particularly sad – there's going to be no wake and Sarah is going to be buried in the cemetery at Carbis Bay but only family are invited. I'm included but that means there will only be four of us at the burial, unless Isla is back in time. It just seems so awfully bleak.'

'Back in the day, you had to be buried outside the cemetery walls if you had killed yourself, so things have improved,' said Clara. 'Still, no wake, that really is awfully sad – Philip and Sarah loved a party and threw some marvellous ones. I suppose Tom and Gemma just don't feel there is anything to celebrate, understandably.'

'Also,' said Merrin, 'Tom and his anger – there's a good chance he'd have got very drunk and caused an awful scene, so maybe it's just as well.'

'Poor old Sarah, not much of a send-off,' said Clara.

'Poor Sarah, poor family,' said Merrin.

CHAPTER TWENTY-SEVEN

'Don, it's Louis Peppiatt, so sorry to trouble you yet again.'

'No problem, Chief Inspector. How are things going? Are you making any progress?'

'Not a lot, I think, would be the correct answer. Don, were you ever aware of a chap called Nigel Anstey visiting the college? He was interested in employing a graduate as a farm manager.'

'Rather ambitious,' said Don.

'But cheap,' said Louis. 'I mention him because, in the end, he selected Mary Daniels to be his manager and, ultimately, his wife.'

'Good Lord, poor old Philip. The trouble is, after you very efficiently tackled me to the ground, I was forbidden to go near the college or communicate with the staff. I don't remember a Nigel Anstey and I have totally lost touch with members of staff who might have been able to help.'

'Digressing,' said Louis, 'the question you never really answered at the time was why.'

'Why what?' Don asked.

'Why did you start stealing in the first place? It makes no sense. You had a good job, with excellent prospects, and while no teaching salary is great, it is enough to live on.'

'It began when I was young and very stupid. I graduated from the Royal Agricultural College in Cirencester, which a lot of rich kids attend, many of whom go on to inherit thousands of acres from daddy. I got a taste for their lifestyle. It was pathetic. I bought an over-priced sports car, if I took a girl out for the evening, we always kicked off with a decent bottle of champagne. My suits and shoes were handmade. I never touched drugs, I didn't gamble and I drank no more than the average young man, but I was addicted to a way of life I could never financially maintain and so I got into huge debt. I could never earn enough to straighten out my finances, and over the years, I got myself deeper and deeper into debt. At the time, stealing seemed the only way to avoid bankruptcy.'

'I can't remember the details now, but when I efficiently tackled you to the ground, I hope you weren't wearing one of your handmade suits?' said Louis.

'Mercifully, no, farmer's overalls in order to blend in!'

'I suppose you don't have any contacts among the teaching staff who might know if Nigel Anstey ever appeared on the scene?' Louis asked.

'Unfortunately, no. Most are probably dead by now,

anyway. However, following my spell in the clink, I have remained *persona non grata*, so far as they were concerned. I'm very sorry I can't help'

Louis and Jack drove up to Ashburton by appointment the following day. Nigel Anstey had been very reluctant to see Louis again.

'Surely whatever questions you still have to ask me can be dealt with over the phone. It's an appalling waste of taxpayers' money to drive up here yet again,' he had said.

But Louis had insisted, so now they found themselves parked up outside the Ansteys' beautiful manor house.

'Just look at that,' said Jack, 'nice pad! I'm not looking forward to this, boss. From what you've told me, he sounds a disagreeable sort of chap and I can't see that he's likely to spill the beans about his elder son.'

'I tend to agree, Eddy, but I have to try. You just take notes and keep quiet, however tricky it gets. Alright?'

'Roger that, boss.'

Once again, the door was opened by Barbara Anstey, only today she was far less friendly. 'I can't imagine why you're back again, Chief Inspector, and who's this?' she said, nodding at Jack.

Jack dutifully produced his warrant card. 'I'm Sergeant Jack Eddy, madam.'

'So you'd better both come in, though heaven knows why it's necessary for two policemen to interview my husband. This time, I'm going to be present. I'm not having an old man of eighty-four being bullied by the two of you.'

'The subject I wish to discuss with Mr Anstey is rather delicate. He might prefer to talk to me alone,' said Louis.

'Certainly not,' said Barbara. 'As I've already told you, Nigel and I have no secrets from one another, and if I feel your questioning is too much for him, I will ask you to leave. I hope that's understood.'

'Perfectly,' said Louis.

Nigel Anstey was sitting in an armchair, by an open window. It was another beautiful day and the smell of roses was intoxicating as it wafted through the window from the flower bed outside. 'You've got five minutes,' he said belligerently.

Louis wasted no time. 'I've come to understand that the natural father of your elder son, Nigel, is not in fact you, sir, but Philip Trehearne. Would you confirm this, please?'

There was a stunned silence. Louis caught the glance Barbara gave her husband, which suggested she certainly did not know all his secrets.

'How dare you!' shouted Nigel, standing up and going very red in the face. 'How dare you!' he spluttered again. 'Of course I can't confirm any such thing. Nigel is my son.'

'Legally, I agree, sir,' Louis persisted, 'but at the time Nigel was conceived, not only were you and your first wife, Mary, not married, you hadn't even met.'

'And your proof that we hadn't met? I would be most interested to hear about that,' said Nigel, more composed now and returning to his seat.

'At the time of Nigel's conception, Mary was still in a relationship with Philip and still an undergraduate, yet to complete her finals. It was a brave decision to employ a graduate as a farm manager, but an undergraduate unable to provide the results of her finals, that is surely madness? Also, you told me that you employed Mary for her managerial skills and that your relationship developed later. However, if you're really Nigel's father, then the dates suggest that Mary was already pregnant with your child before she even sat her finals – in the spring, in fact, which does mean that by then, you were very well acquainted, very well acquainted indeed.'

'I hardly think that when Mary and I became *well acquainted* is a police matter,' said Nigel.

'I absolutely agree, sir, unless Nigel's parentage contributed to Philip's disappearance and probable death,' said Louis.

'So, are you now suggesting that I killed Philip? Can I remind you that from what you've told me, Philip disappeared three years after Mary died, when I was already happily married to Barbara. What possible reason could there be for killing him then – or ever, come to that? You have absolutely no proof of any of this, Chief Inspector; you're just fumbling about in the dark.'

'Enough of this rubbish,' said Barbara. 'You're to leave at once and stop upsetting my husband. It's disgraceful.'

Louis stood up to go, followed by Jack. 'Well, sir, I suppose we will just have to wait until we are able to find young Nigel and then we can run DNA tests to see which of us is right.'

'If you ever do find Nigel.'

'Are you suggesting, sir, that you have information concerning Nigel's whereabouts that you are not prepared to share with us?'

'Go to hell!' was the reply.

CHAPTER TWENTY-EIGHT

Louis's appointment with Chief Superintendent John Dent was fixed for ten o'clock the following morning. He arrived in Sally's office ten minutes early and collapsed in the chair opposite her desk.

'Dear me, Louis,' she said, 'what on earth's wrong with you now? It's not often we see you so consistently miserable. Would a coffee help?'

'It might,' Louis said ungraciously. He remained slumped in the chair until Sally returned with a mug of black coffee. 'Sorry, Sal,' he said, accepting the coffee.

'I should think so, too,' she said. 'I assume, from the bleakness of your expression, that all is not well with the Trehearne case?'

'I can do no more. I would like the case closed down. What sort of mood is sir in?'

'Equally bleak, it's not a good moment, Louis. There's

been yet another sub-post office raid, no injuries again, thankfully.'

'Not another! If he'd just left me in charge, we'd have the villains behind bars by now,' said Louis morosely.

'Now that's something I would strongly advise you don't say to sir. I agree, it might well be true, but trust me, Louis dear, this is not the right time to criticise his decisions.'

'Even when they're wrong?' Louis asked.

'Especially when they're wrong.'

Chief Superintendent John Dent was sitting behind his desk, his impressive eyebrows already bristling. He motioned Louis into the chair in front of his desk. Not a good sign, this was not going to be a cosy chat.

'Well?' he said.

'I don't think I can progress the Trehearne case any further. Sir, it really isn't a police matter any more.'

'Are you questioning my judgement, Peppiatt?'

'No, sir, of course not. But obviously, after thirty years, there's no physical evidence to pursue. I have therefore been trying to unpick relationships from the past to try and find out some sort of reason or motive for Trehearne's disappearance. I've made a little progress in discovering what Philip got up to at college but none of it leads, in any obvious way, to explaining his disappearance.'

'Can I suggest, Peppiatt, that if there was an obvious explanation, the original team would have found it. That's why I brought you in – to track down the less than obvious.'

'I appreciate that, sir, but I honestly don't think I am going to be able to unravel this one. There are two people who might have been able to help – Philip's former girlfriend, Mary, and a possible son, conceived while he and Mary were still at college. Mary died thirty-three years ago and the son, Nigel, has disappeared, without trace.'

'And because you can't find this Nigel, you're giving up?' The eyebrows were now extremely impressive.

'I have Constable Colin Haines working on the case. If anyone can find Nigel, it's Haines and, so far, he can find no trace,' said Louis.

'It's all very well relying on these young so-called whiz kids, working their magic on computers. I believe in good old-fashioned police work and I know you do, too. Shoe leather, talking face to face with real people, instinct, listening, asking the right questions, searching, thinking, looking for a way through what often seems unsolvable. If this son hasn't been declared dead, then presumably he is still alive, in which case he's somewhere. You're not thinking hard enough, Peppiatt – relive all the conversations you've had, see what you've missed and, in my experience, you will find you have overlooked something significant. Use your policeman's nose. Haines is simply a tool – you are the man who is going to find out what happened to Philip Trehearne. Oh, and the answer is no.'

'What was the question, sir?' said Louis.

'No, we're not closing the Trehearne case and you, Louis, are still on it. Keep searching and you will find.'

Louis closed the door to John Dent's office, and let out a theatrical sigh.

'I did warn you,' Sally said. 'Look, I suspect sir is not going to make any demands on me for at least half an hour; he has quite a number of calls to make. Take me through it.'

'Take you through what?' Louis asked.

'Oh, for heaven's sake, Louis, just tell me what you've found out so far and why you feel you've ground to a halt.'

So, Louis detailed all the twists and turns of his investigation so far. When he'd finished, he said, 'So you must see, Sal, this is not police work. Mary and Nigel chose not to tell anyone that the baby was Philip's, including even Philip himself. That may be morally wrong, but it's not illegal. I'm wading about in the cesspit of some young people's messy relationships that took place decades ago. It's, frankly, none of my business.'

'But what definitely is your business is to find out what happened to Philip,' said Sally. 'I've looked at the file – the search was meticulous, his motives for leaving home were nil. Someone stopped him from going home, which in my view means someone killed him. Sir is right, you have to find that son, assuming you're confident that Mary's sister, Teresa, was telling you the truth about baby Nigel?'

'Yes, I am,' said Louis.

'Then ask her for some photographs of Mary, when she was at college and then later, before the poor woman died. More importantly, ask her if she has any photographs of young Nigel, even if it's only as a boy. I don't know how that will help you but it just might. From what you tell me, Philip led a blameless life in Cornwall. Therefore, his disappearance has to be linked to this son, conceived while he was at college and who, according to Teresa, he never knew even existed.'

Louis smiled at Sally. 'OK, Sal, I'll go back to the drawing board. I'll pull myself together and do as you say. Basically, I do believe in what sir says. I do still think that good old-fashioned police work normally brings in the best results. However, when one is dealing with something that happened decades ago, I think the computer is probably king. The other trouble is I'm used to working with a team, which is why I'm so very grateful to be able to talk things through with you, I really am. However, the fact remains, when I started this case I had one missing man. Now I have two.'

CHAPTER TWENTY-NINE

Although, in passing, Louis Peppiatt had often looked appreciatively at the architecture of St Ia's Parish Church, in St Ives, he had never before been inside it. He was immediately spellbound; history seemed to be seeping out of its very walls. Although not a deeply religious man, he loved churches and he had read up at little about St Ia's. He knew there had been a chapel of ease on the site since the 1400s but even the current building dated back to the reign of Henry V. The church itself was dedicated to a fifth-to-sixth-century Irish saint called St Ia the Virgin. He found it astonishing to find all this history in the church of a fishing village, even though St Ives had once been a small, but relatively important, fishing port. And for all its ancient history, Louis was pleased to find in the Lady Chapel a statue by Barbara Hepworth, whose work he greatly admired.

He had arrived early for the funeral of Sarah Trehearne but members of the congregation were already starting to trickle in. How it would help him, he didn't know, but he wanted to study who attended the service. He settled himself in a corner of the back row of seating, which gave him a good view but, hopefully, he would remain fairly inconspicuous. It soon became obvious that the whole town had turned out to pay their respects to Sarah. There were faces he knew. Steve Matthews and his mum, Brenda, were among the first to arrive. Steve spotted Louis and waved frantically, then nudging his mum to join in – so much for trying to attend the service incognito. Then, much to his amusement, Jack Eddy arrived, preceded by a large lady who marched down the aisle ahead of him, like a ship in full sail. On her head she wore what appeared to be a navy blue knitted tea cosy. Having found a row of seats to her liking, she pushed Jack in first as if he was a naughty child. So that was Mrs Eddy – no wonder Jack was not in a hurry to retire!

Clare and Tristan arrived with Max, followed shortly afterwards by Merrin. She spotted him, too, but had the good sense to recognise that he wanted to play a low profile. There was no sign of Jago, but then Louis realised he would probably be following the coffin with Gemma. Soon the church was full to bursting, with standing room only. If Louis had needed proof, it was there for all to see – the Trehearne family were much loved and respected in the town.

The little troop who walked up the aisle was very poignant. Tom, immediately behind the coffin, was accompanied by a collie dog – no lead needed – he walked in step with his master, his head hanging as if he understood the sadness of the day, which he almost certainly did. Behind him came Gemma, walking beside Jago in his wheelchair. *I have to find some answers for these poor people*, Louis thought, the sadness of the day hanging as heavily upon him as it appeared to be upon the poor dog following the coffin.

It was a short service. Louis remained seated as everyone filed out of the church. He met the vicar at the door as he left. 'You did a very good job, in very difficult circumstances,' said Louis.

The two men shook hands. 'One wonders why some people, some families, have more than their fair share of grief,' said the vicar. 'Are you a friend of the Trehearnes?'

'Sort of,' said Louis.

Outside the church, Louis saw Merrin helping Jago into her car. Presumably, Tom and Gemma had gone ahead in the hearse. He sprinted over.

'Shall I put the wheelchair in the boot for you?' he said.

Merrin lifted her head and Louis could see she'd been crying. 'Thank you, Louis, that's very kind.'

'A miserable day, I'm so sorry,' he said.

Walking along the Wharf, Louis could see that many of the mourners were stopping off at various bars to presumably drown their sorrows. There was a notice on the door of Tristan's Fish Plaice. Louis stopped to read it – *We are closed today as a mark of respect for the life and death of Sarah Trehearne.*

Louis drove out of St Ives in a sombre mood. He decided that he would telephone Teresa Gilbert as soon as he was home. As Sally had suggested, he would attempt to obtain some photographs of Mary, and, more importantly, of young Nigel. He was decidedly sceptical as to his likely reception, given that Teresa had ordered him and Eddy out of her house on the last visit. And who could blame her.

As it turned out, he need not have worried. In response to his introduction, Teresa's reaction was delightfully unexpected.

'Good afternoon, Chief Inspector,' she said. 'I'm so glad you called. I was plucking up the courage to contact you and apologise for my over-reaction the other day. I was positively hysterical, which was ridiculous. You and your sergeant were only doing your job.'

'That's most kind of you,' said Louis, 'but there's really no need to apologise. I think, on reflection, we were a little heavy-handed. It's very understandable that you should feel protective towards your sister's memory.'

'Actually, I've come to realise that the very best way to honour my sister's memory is to help you solve the riddle of both missing Philip and missing young Nigel,' said Teresa.

'I'm obviously delighted to hear that,' said Louis. 'Any help you can give us would be gratefully received.'

'Nigel Anstey, the elder, made Mary's life a misery,' said Teresa. 'He worked her to death, even when she was pregnant and when she was up half the night with small babies. He treated her like dirt, because he thought he was entitled to do so. He had *saved* her reputation by marrying her and he never let her forget it. No one knows what triggers breast cancer but Mary was under stress from the moment she began working for Nigel and I bet that was a contributary factor to her becoming ill.'

'I have to admit that Nigel's behaviour towards your

sister doesn't surprise me but I still don't see where you're going with this,' said Louis.

'Revenge, Chief Inspector, that's where I'm going with this. If you can find Philip's son, then the story is bound to come out and that will really upset Nigel, who puts himself about as a pillar of the establishment.'

'Teresa, I'm attempting to find out what happened to Philip Trehearne to help a grieving family and, hopefully, finding young Nigel is a part of that. I'm not in the business of trying to discredit anyone, including Nigel Anstey, however odious you think him to be. I've just returned home from Sarah Trehearne's funeral. I know I mentioned to you that Philip's wife killed herself a month ago because she could no longer cope with the uncertainty surrounding Philip's disappearance. If you had witnessed the funeral today, I think you'd understand where my priorities lie.'

'Of course, I understand that,' said Teresa, 'but the fallout from you solving the mystery could easily make Nigel Anstey look like the monster he is.'

'So, how would you go about doing that? Go to the press, put the story on social media? How do you think the Trehearne family would feel? Nigel Anstey isn't the only potential victim here. Just think for a moment. If this story gets out, Philip's children will have to accept that their father, who they idolised, was unfaithful to their mother.'

'Oh, for heaven's sake, Louis. These "children" must be middle-aged by now. Surely to God it's not going to upset them to hear their father had a fling while he was at college? I think if I was them, I would be more concerned if my father hadn't sowed his wild oats while he was a student. Now that really would be a worry.'

'Teresa.' Louis paused. 'How do I put this? You have led a far more colourful life than most of us and that's not intended as a criticism. But the way you have lived your life is massively different from a tight-knit farming family in West Cornwall, whose world has fallen apart.'

'Changing the subject since it's obvious we're not going to agree about this, why were you calling me, anyway?' Teresa asked.

'I was going to ask whether you could let me have some photographs of Mary, when she was a student and maybe later in life. I also wondered whether you have any photos of young Nigel, even if they are only of when he was a child.'

'And do you still want the photographs after what I've said?'

Louis sighed. 'I suppose I do, but I am now extremely worried about the Trehearnes. Until I have a fuller picture, I was planning not to tell them anything about Philip and Mary.'

'OK,' said Teresa, surprisingly. 'I'll hunt out some photos for you. Text me over your email address and also your home address. If there aren't many, it would be quicker if I photograph the photographs and email them over. I'll just see what I've got. Also, I take your point about the Trehearnes, I won't personally tell Mary's story to the press nor put it on social media. It's true that revenge is something of a poisoned chalice. You have my word.'

'Can I really rely on that?' Louis asked.

'An insulting question, Chief Inspector,' said Teresa. 'I've been a naughty girl over the years on many, many occasions, but if I make a promise, I never break it, so yes, you can rely on me keeping my word.'

'Why the sudden change of heart?' Louis asked.

'Because I've just realised that if you solve this thirty-year-old mystery, I won't need to do a thing – the publicity will be unstoppable and Nigel Anstey will have nowhere to hide.'

CHAPTER THIRTY

Merrin was feeling very despondent. She had just spoken to Isla. She and Maggie had decided to go back to Oxford for a few days. There were a couple of parties the following weekend. Also, from the beginning of July, they had started paying the rent for their new flat so they wanted to have a proper look at it and see what needed doing.

'We'll be back before term starts,' Isla assured her mother, which didn't sound as if they were going to be in Oxford *for a few days* – more like a few weeks.

Prior to her conversation with Isla, Merrin had also called Jago to see if she could take him and Gemma out to lunch.

'Tom's refusing to work on the farm at the moment and so Gemma is having to help David,' was Jago's reply to the invitation. 'Obviously, everyone is feeling very raw after Sarah's funeral but Tom is being particularly difficult. It is moments like this when I really mind my disability. All I can do to make myself useful is tidy up and cook a few meals, that sort of thing. Apologies, sis, I'd love a jolly lunch with you. It's deeply depressing here and I just can't find any more original words of comfort to give them – nothing that I haven't already said over and over again.'

'I'm so sorry, Jago. I'm sure you're being a big help by just being there,' said Merrin. 'Give me a call if there is anything I can do.'

'Presumably we'll be meeting Louis over the next few days, as his time is running out?' said Louis. 'Tom is certainly not in the mood to be patient. I presume you've heard nothing from our chief inspector?'

'No,' said Merrin. 'I saw him briefly yesterday at the funeral but obviously it wasn't the moment to talk about his investigation.'

After the phone calls, Merrin sat sadly in Adam's chair with William on her lap, wondering what to do. It was raining. From her window, she could see the visitors walking up and down Fore Street, umbrellas crashing into one another, looking rather like she felt. It was certainly not a beach day.

Until Adam died, her years in Bristol had been a juggling act of trying to fit in the demands of work and family life. Back then, she would have relished a day to herself when she could do whatever she liked, or indeed, nothing at all. Now, she found the lack of calls on her time extremely depressing. Clara was right – she would talk to Louis about the possibility of pro bono work, but not now, when he was struggling so hard to unravel the Trehearnes.

'Come on, William,' she said. 'Let's have a walk in the rain. You'll love it, really, we both will.'

William gave her a look that could have stunned a charging rhino, and then, magically, the phone rang.

'Merrin, it's Louis. I have some photos I want to show you. Are you free? I thought I might take you out to lunch to cheer you up.'

Merrin perked up immediately. 'That's really kind of you. How did you know I needed cheering up?'

'Yesterday's funeral? It was a particularly sad occasion but I imagine the burial must have been especially difficult.'

'It was very bleak,' Merrin agreed. 'How very kind of you to think of that. Shall I book lunch? What time and any preferences?'

'Say twelve-thirty. This sounds rather ill-mannered, but could it be somewhere other than Tristan's? There are just some details I need to go through with you . . .'

'In peace?' Merrin suggested.

Despite being the height of the season, Merrin managed to reserve them a table at Porthminster Kitchen, even one by the window – not that much could be seen through the rain and mist.

'This weather is very reminiscent of the day Edward went missing,' said Louis as he joined Merrin at the table. 'At the very least the little horror could have chosen a better day to disappear but, no, he had to go for a thick sea mist, followed by torrential rain. Bless.'

'Is he OK?' Merrin asked. 'No ill effects?'

'None whatsoever. I'm going to order a bottle of wine, provided you promise to drink most of it as I have to drive. Agreed?'

'Reluctantly,' said Merrin, definitely feeling more cheerful.

'Let's order and then I'll bring you up to date. I imagine Tom will want a meeting early next week and I have to decide what to do – things have moved on rather.'

Food and wine ordered, Louis sat back in his chair and stared at Merrin for a moment. 'I have reason to believe that Philip and Mary, his girlfriend from college, had a child together, a son, who was brought up as young Nigel Anstey.'

'Good Lord,' said Merrin, 'are you sure?'

'As sure as I can be without a DNA test, which is proving rather difficult because, as I think I mentioned to you and Jago, the eldest son of Nigel Senior has completely disappeared.'

'How do you know all this?' Merrin asked.

'Come on, now,' said Louis, 'you know better than to ask me that, but my sources do seem very reliable. The search began when Colin, our IT Boy Wonder, realised that their first-born baby arrived just three months after Nigel and Mary were married. I can't say more than that at this stage.'

The wine arrived and when the waiter had left, they raised their glasses. 'To Sarah Trehearne, by all accounts a brave and much-loved woman,' said Louis.

'Sarah,' Merrin murmured. 'But just because the baby was conceived before the wedding, it doesn't mean a thing. It happens all the time these days. I don't see why it's a reason for supposing that Nigel Senior isn't the father.'

'Because Nigel Senior himself told me that he didn't meet Mary until she had graduated. She must have become pregnant during her last term at college, when she didn't even know Nigel. Mary also confided to a third party that the child was Philip's.'

'So, if you're right, it means Tom and Gemma have a half-brother. Goodness knows what Tom will make of that!'

'Let's eat and then I would like to show you some photographs of Mary and I also have one of young Nigel.'

'So what are you going to tell Tom and Gemma?' Merrin asked.

'I'll have to tell them everything but I would so like to have first found out the fate of their half-brother, as well as their father. If young Nigel is still alive, it would have been good to have DNA proof. This is so not a police matter; I shouldn't have allowed myself to become involved in delving so deep into their personal lives. I was hoping to make things better, instead I've made them much, much worse. I will have to expose Philip's affair with Mary, the probable existence of a half-brother, and, to cap it all, I have so far totally failed in my main objective – to find out what happened to Philip.'

'But, Louis, there has to be a link. If Philip had ever been involved in any serious disputes here in St Ives, it would be a different matter. But we both know how much the locals cared about him. The only person who had cause to dislike him is Nigel Anstey, or maybe Mary, if he dumped her when she was pregnant, I suppose.'

'But if Nigel was ever going to do Philip any harm, it would have been right at the beginning when he discovered that Mary was carrying Philip's child.'

'And knowing what an old softie Philip was, I simply

cannot believe he would abandon a woman who was carrying his child. It is totally out of character.'

'I can explain that,' said Louis. 'According to my source, Philip never knew that Mary was pregnant.'

They finished their meal and ordered coffee. Then Louis produced from his wallet three photographs. 'These first two are of Mary – this one, when she was at college, at the time she must have known Philip.'

Merrin looked at the photograph of a beautiful young woman. Her blonde hair was in a long bob, and although she was wearing a pair of muddy dungarees, it was possible to see she had long legs and a marvellous figure. 'She's stunning,' said Merrin.

'Yes,' said Louis. 'You can quite see why Philip fell for her. And here she is in her late thirties, a few years before her death.'

'She's still incredibly beautiful but so careworn, old before her time,' said Merrin.

'Obviously, that maybe due to the cancer that was going to kill her, but I understand she worked terribly hard all her married life.' He turned over the final photograph. 'And here is a photo of her little boy, Nigel. He looks about nine, I think, about Edward's age.'

Merrin studied the photographs for some moments, and it seemed to Louis that she had gone suddenly very pale. 'Does the boy remind you of someone?' Louis asked. 'Philip maybe, or Tom at a similar age?'

'I'm not sure,' she said, clearly worried. 'Louis, can I keep these? I will be very careful with them and not show them around or anything.'

'Yes, of course,' said Louis. 'I have them on my laptop,

but you've spotted something, haven't you? What is it, you seem upset?'

'Maybe, maybe not. I could be imagining things. Look, I'm so sorry, I need to go now, there's something I need to check. Thank you so much for lunch; I'll be in touch, at the very latest, by tomorrow morning.'

Merrin's coffee was untouched, her wine glass half full and she almost ran out of the restaurant.

Louis stared after her. He was fairly sure it was the photo of the boy that had disturbed her so much. He contemplated running after her and then thought better of it. Whatever it was that had spooked her, it was best he let her work it out.

Above all, he trusted her.

CHAPTER THIRTY-ONE

'Jago, Jago, is that you?'

'Yes, of course it's me, sis. Are you OK? You sound weird.'

Merrin took a deep breath. 'No, I'm not OK, I need to speak to you urgently, but alone. Can I come and collect you now – I really mean now?'

'Of course come now, sis, but we don't need to go anywhere. Gemma and Tom have gone to choose a headstone for Sarah's grave. The place they're going to is in Truro and they said they would probably get some lunch on the way. They've only just left so they won't be back for at least a couple of hours. What's up that's so urgent? You're worrying me.'

'I'll explain when I arrive. I'm just collecting William and then I'll come straight over.'

* * *

Louis paid the restaurant bill and walked round to the station, where Jack Eddy was dealing with the after-effects of a lost dog. An elderly woman, in floods of tears, was clutching a chihuahua to her ample bosom – so tightly Louis feared that the dog would be either crushed to death, or suffocate. Certainly, it looked fairly desperate, as did his sergeant.

'Everything alright, Eddy?' Louis asked, failing to suppress a smile.

'All's well, boss. I've found this lady's dog for her and I think she is very relieved.'

The tear-stained woman turned to Louis. 'Boss? Are you this gentleman's boss?'

'I am, madam. I trust he's looking after you.'

'He's been marvellous. He deserves a medal. He found Jemima so quickly, it was wonderful. I thought I'd lost her for ever.' This brought on a fresh bout of tears.

'I'm sure Sergeant Eddy would be pleased to make you a cup of tea, to help with the shock,' said Louis, not daring to look at Jack.

'Oh thank you, but I must go. I've left my husband sitting on a bench. He'll be worried sick. I need to tell him Jemima is safe. Thank you both so much.'

She swept out of the office and Jack collapsed in his chair.

'Well,' said Louis, 'you've done it again, Eddy. Another heroic deed.'

'This one really was heroic, boss,' Jack agreed. 'It only took me five minutes to find the dreadful little dog, which incidentally bit me for my trouble, but a good half an hour to be thanked. I'm exhausted, with a sore ankle.'

'Go and get yourself a cup of tea and a plaster and then come and look at some photographs,' said Louis.

By the time Jack returned, Louis had set up his laptop. 'Look carefully at these photographs. Is there anything about them that is familiar?'

Jack fetched his reading glasses and sat down in Louis's chair.

'Well, boss, the first two photographs seem to be of the same lady. She's lovely but looks a bit sad and much older in the second photo. As for the boy, he's a little smasher. I think he must be the lady's son – same blonde hair, and their eyes are alike.'

'Full marks so far, Eddy. Do you recognise either the woman or the child?'

'I really don't think so, boss, but I wouldn't mind clapping my eyes on that lovely lady.'

'What's it worth not to tell Mrs Eddy what you've just said, Sergeant?'

'My life's savings,' said Jack without hesitation. Louis could well believe it.

'I met Mrs McKenzie just now and showed her the same photographs,' said Louis. 'She didn't recognise the woman, but seemed – how shall I put it – upset, I think, when she saw the photograph of the child. Are you sure this isn't a local boy? You know everyone.'

Jack peered at the photograph again and, after a moment, shook his head. 'Honestly, boss, I've never seen the lad before in my life.'

Merrin leapt out of the car, followed by William. Jago was waiting for her by the open door of the farmhouse. 'What on earth's happened? You look very fraught. Are you ill?'

'No, can we come in quickly so I can explain everything in case Gemma and Tom come home?'

Merrin went straight to the kitchen table and laid out the three photographs Louis had given her.

'Who are these people?' Jago asked, wheeling his chair up to the table.

'Since Louis saw us last, he has discovered that Philip and Mary, his girlfriend at college, had a child, a boy.'

'Blimey, what happened to the boy? Was he adopted?' asked Jago.

'In a way,' said Merrin. 'He was brought up as Nigel Anstey, Mary's husband's eldest son.'

'The one who disappeared?'

'Exactly,' said Merrin. 'These are two different photographs of Mary, taken at different times, and this one is of her son, Nigel Anstey.'

'What a lovely looking girl,' said Jago, 'but the years were not so kind to her, were they? A nice-looking boy, too, and you say Louis reckons he's actually Philip's son?'

'Does he look familiar to you, Jago?' Merrin asked. She sounded nervous.

'Not really. He's got long legs for his age, which probably means he's going to be tall, like Tom, and Philip was very tall too – unusual for a Cornishman. The boy has his mother's thick fair hair. No, sis, he could be anyone's child and I can't see an obvious Trehearne family likeness. Apart from his possible height in later life, he favours his mother much more than the Trehearnes. How does Louis know that this child is Philip's?'

'He wouldn't tell me, but he seemed to be very sure of his

source. As he said, without a DNA test, nothing is certain. Jago, I want to check out something in the farm office. Would you keep a watch for me in case the Trehearnes come back early?'

'That's a bit cheeky, sis. I really don't think you should go poking about in their office. If you are going to do such a thing, at least tell me what you're looking for and what this is all about.'

'I will, I promise but I need to find something first – I could be completely wrong about all this,' said Merrin.

'If you'd just tell me what it is you're looking for, I could help you,' said Jago, exasperated.

'No, now you don't recognise him from the photograph, I'm starting to think I might be making a complete fool of myself. I won't be long. Could you let William into the garden? He must be dying for a pee.'

Jago did as he was told and wheeled himself out of the back door, obediently followed by William. The rain had stopped, the air felt fresh and full of the scent of the honeysuckle that trailed over the porch. A weak sun was making a strenuous attempt to be seen. Leaving William to his ablutions, Jago returned to the kitchen, picked up the photograph of the boy and wheeled over to the window for a better light.

He stared at the photograph, trying to envisage what his sister thought she had seen, which he had failed to recognise. And then he saw it too, at the very same moment as Merrin burst out of the office.

'I know who Nigel is and where he is,' she cried out.

'So do I,' said Jago.

CHAPTER THIRTY-TWO

'Louis, where are you? Are you still in St Ives?' The urgency in Merrin's voice was unmistakeable.

'I was just driving out of town but I can drive straight back in again, if it's important, which it rather sounds like it is,' he said.

'It really is,' said Merrin. 'Jago and I are in the car now, on our way into St Ives. My cottage in ten?'

'I'll be there, Merrin, but put me out of my misery. Is it good news?' Louis asked.

'Sort of, though it's rather mixed. We'll explain all when we see you.'

Louis pulled off the road, turned round in the fire station car park and headed back into town. What did she mean? he wondered. She'd recognised the boy, yet he did not look especially like the Trehearnes. Still, she and Jago had obviously discovered something but whatever it was, it didn't seem to suggest a particularly happy outcome – which pretty much mirrored the whole case. Sadness seemed to reign where the Trehearnes were concerned.

By the time Louis had parked his car and walked down to Miranda's Cottage, Jago had successfully shuffled his way up the steps and was levering his way into his wheelchair.

'Louis, come and sit down,' said Merrin. 'I think you're going to need to do so for this one.'

Louis did as he was told and took out his notebook. 'Go on, then,' he said.

Merrin took a deep breath. 'I'm sorry I left you so abruptly at lunchtime but I suddenly thought I recognised the little boy in the photograph, but not because I'd known him as a boy, which confused me. I dashed straight over to Jago, who initially thought I was mad, until without any prompting from me, I promise you, he saw it too.'

'So what did you both see?' said Louis, unable to control his impatience.

'Nigel Anstey Junior has changed his name to David Reed,' Merrin said, with more than a hint of triumph.

'Who the hell is David Reed?' Louis asked.

'David who works for the Trehearnes,' Jago said, as patiently as he could. 'David, the man who found your boy when he was lost on the cliff. That David.'

'Sorry,' said Louis, clearly very shocked. 'I didn't know his surname. But surely it can't be him? He's worked for the Trehearnes for years; he would have told them, wouldn't he? Are you absolutely certain about this? It just seems so unlikely.'

'I couldn't believe it either when I first recognised the

photograph,' said Merrin. 'It's why I left the table so quickly because I didn't want to suggest to you that it might be David without being absolutely sure I was right. So, having discovered from Jago that the Trehearnes were out, I rushed over to the farm. Much against Jago's wishes, I went into the farm office looking for the employment records, and David's details in particular. I found them easily, Sarah was so neat and organised with her paperwork. David Reed's birthday is shown as 16th January 1971, which I expect you'll find will also be Nigel's.'

'But what does that prove, even if it's true?' said Louis. 'I'll admit the date does sound familiar, but even so, there must be thousands of babies born on that day.'

'Louis, will you please just let me finish,' said Merrin, becoming increasingly agitated. 'His employment records also showed his full name, which is David Daniels Reed – Daniels, if I remember correctly, is Mary's maiden name. It's not exactly an obvious middle name, is it, unless, of course, it happens to have belonged to your poor dead mother?'

'That's extraordinary but, if David really is Nigel, I wonder what prompted him to change his name?' Louis said.

'Changing names is not as unusual as one might think,' said Jago. 'In David's case, from what you've said, he probably wanted to distance himself from Nigel Anstey senior, who sounds a fairly odious chap. While Merrin was driving over here, I checked out the mechanics for changing your name. If you just do it by deed poll – you can actually apply online these days – it's fairly difficult to trace a name change. It's only if you enrol the change through the courts that the details can be found.'

'I can quite believe that he didn't want the same name as his father, well, his stepfather, I suppose,' said Louis. 'But if this is all true, what on earth brought him to his birth father's farm? It can't be a coincidence.'

'Oh Louis, of course it's not a coincidence,' said Merrin. 'You're right to be cautious and I do understand why you've not totally bought in to what Jago and I are saying. Nonetheless, surely there has to be a link to Philip's disappearance? Five weeks after Philip vanishes off the face of the earth, the son he never knew existed turns up at the farm wanting a job.'

'If we've got this right and all of it is true, then it's an awful situation,' said Jago. 'Tom has been working with his half-brother, without knowing it, for over thirty years. And why hasn't David told anyone who he really is? Possibly, it was to spare Sarah's feelings, I suppose, but Sarah had a big heart. I think she would have welcomed Philip's boy, once she'd got over the shock – she might even have found it a comfort. Instead, he's been living this sort of half-life for decades, working himself to death for the family – no friends, no girlfriends, no family of his own – tramping alone on the cliffs being his only recreation. Something about him isn't right. It's just because he is so good at his job and so reliable that no one has ever taken the time to consider why he's living the way he does. You don't know him well enough, Louis, but he's wonderfully kind and helpful to everyone, except himself. Please believe me – when one thinks about it, David has just been existing. He must have been leading this insular life for a reason.'

Louis was already on the phone. 'Could you put me through to Constable Haines,' he said. 'Haines, can you tell me the date of Nigel Anstey Junior's birth, please.'

Louis put his phone on loudspeaker. '16th January 1971,' was the reply. 'Sir, I'm sorry, I still don't seem to be able to track him down but I have established that Benjamin was married to a girl called Nancy, née Bates, hence why Nigel Anstey senior wasn't informed of his death, as he wasn't the next of kin. I imagine Nancy didn't contact Nigel with the news because she had been told by Benjamin just how awful his father was. She may well have held Nigel responsible for her husband's drug addiction.'

'Well done, Constable,' said Louis. 'I don't think you need to worry about trying to find Nigel Junior any more – it looks like we may have just done it. I'll fill you in with the details later.'

There was silence in the room for a while, as all three of them considered the implications of David being Philip's son. Eventually, Louis broke the silence. 'Well done, the pair of you, you've been marvellous. I've only seen David once, at the hospital after he'd found Edward. We were so anxious to see our boy, I thanked David, of course, but the whole thing is a bit of a blur. I'm not sure I'd even recognise him in the street, let alone as an nine-year-old, in a slightly faded photograph. Thank you both so much.'

'So, what happens now?' asked Merrin.

'I'll have to take David in for questioning in the morning. He has every right to change his name and, as you say, Jago, he has an obvious motive for doing so. But turning up at his birth father's farm so soon after Philip's disappearance – he really needs to explain that.'

'It's going to be damned awkward,' said Jago. 'What on earth are you going to say to Tom when you collect David?'

'That's one of the very few advantages of being a policeman. I genuinely don't have to say anything. If asked, I just say it's a confidential police matter,' said Louis.

'And if David does admit to being Nigel Anstey, who's going to tell Tom and Gemma that they have a half-brother?' Merrin said, looking increasingly unhappy.

The three of them looked at one another in ill-disguised discomfort. 'If my findings involve the law in any way, then it's down to me,' said Louis. 'If David has a plausible reason for turning up at the farm when he did, and for disguising his true identity, then, obviously, it's his story to tell so ideally he should tell it. If he is involved in any way with Philip's disappearance, or he cannot face telling the Trehearnes who he really is, that's another matter. Let's not pre-judge this. Jack and I will pick up David at 8 a.m. tomorrow and see what he has to say.'

'I've just realised, Louis, this can't be easy for you either,' said Merrin. 'David is the man who rescued your son.'

Louis looked grim. 'Yes, I'm very much aware of that,' he said.

CHAPTER THIRTY-THREE

On the way to the farm the following morning, Louis briefed Jack on all that had been discovered the previous day.

Jack was clearly deeply shocked. 'Are you sure about this, boss? I know those Tripconeys are a couple of bright sparks, but I don't know how they could have recognised David from that photograph. I certainly didn't. And just because his middle name is Daniels, I don't see what that proves.'

'Don't forget Nigel and David have the same date of birth as well, Eddy. I agree it all seems improbable but the facts add up. I'm as certain as I can be, without a DNA test, that David is Philip's son.'

'But why are we arresting him, boss?' Jack asked.

'We're not,' said Louis, exasperated. 'We're taking him in for questioning. We need to know why he turned up at the farm when he did, and why he told no one in the family who he really was. Underlying all that is the big question – did he have anything to do with his father's disappearance?'

'I don't believe he'd have done anything to hurt Philip,' said Jack. 'He's such a kind, gentle soul, always ready to help – look how he found your Edward.'

'Sergeant, as I have said many times, I have lost count of how often I have been told someone couldn't possibly be a murderer, a thief, a blackmailer, an embezzler, a wife-beater, or whatever. No one really knows what they are capable of until faced with a situation where a terrible crime is apparently the only way out.'

'Well, I'm certain I couldn't murder anyone, whatever the circumstances,' said Jack stoutly.

Just for a fleeting moment, Louis was tempted to ask how Jack would react to someone who had murdered Mrs Eddy. Swiftly, he abandoned the idea.

The yard was empty when they arrived, except for a tractor and the family Land Rover.

'Everyone's here by the look of it,' said Louis, with a sigh. 'Come on, Eddy, let's get this over with.'

'Shall we go to the house, boss?' said Jack.

'No, let's look in the barn first – the door's open.'

The darkness inside the barn contrasted strongly with the July sunshine outside. Louis stared around him, his eyes slowly adjusting to the gloom, but he could see no one. 'Hello,' he called, 'is anyone here?'

A figure detached itself from a dark corner and came towards them. 'Can I help?'

It was David, without a doubt. Louis recognised him now from their brief encounter at the hospital. 'I don't know if you remember me,' Louis began.

'Yes, of course, Chief Inspector Peppiatt,' said David. 'How is Edward?'

Louis hesitated. *This was even more awkward than he had imagined,* Louis thought. 'He's absolutely fine now, thanks to you, David. Look, we'd like you to come down to the police station to answer a few questions.'

'What on earth for?' David asked.

Louis studied him carefully. He looked perplexed, as anyone would on being unexpectedly asked to come into a police station for questioning. He also appeared neither fearful, nor particularly worried.

'It's a slightly delicate personal matter, which I'd rather discuss with you at the station,' said Louis.

'We've a lot to catch up on the farm, having lost last Friday because of the funeral,' he said. 'Couldn't you just ask your questions here to save time?'

'No,' said Louis firmly, 'but we'll be as quick as we can.'

'I'll have to tell Tom; he won't be too happy. He's in the house – I won't be a moment.'

Here we go, thought Louis, *this isn't going to be fun.* Sure enough, within a couple of minutes, Tom came roaring out of the house, followed by David.

'What's the meaning of this?' Tom yelled at Louis. 'As if we haven't got enough troubles. You're supposed to be finding out what happened to my father, not interrupting our day's work. What on earth can you want with David?'

'It's a private matter,' said Louis, 'which I'm afraid I can't discuss with you. Jack, could you escort Mr Reed to the car.'

'You're crazy, Chief Inspector, and today is the day you

are supposed to be reporting back to me on what progress you've made. I'm afraid our deal is off – I'm going to report this to your superiors and I'm sure the press will be very interested in your so-called progress.'

'I really wouldn't do that, Tom,' said Louis. 'It could badly rebound on you. I'll talk to David and hopefully the issue can be resolved, in which case I will be able to bring you up to date on our investigation.'

Without waiting for a reply, Louis climbed into his car and drove off. In his rear-view mirror, he could see Tom, still standing in the yard, presumably cursing him. Hopefully he wouldn't carry out his threat – not yet, at any rate.

The journey to the station passed in an awkward silence. Once there, Jack showed David into the interview room and offered him a coffee or tea, which he declined.

'David's ready to be interviewed,' Jack said to Louis, who was waiting outside in the corridor. 'I'm still not happy about this, boss. I'm really not sure about it at all.'

'I know you're not, Eddy, and for that reason I would prefer that you are not present at the interview. Send in one of the constables, instead. While I appreciate we are all entitled to our own view, this interview is tricky enough without you tut tutting in the corner.'

Louis decided the occasion did not call for a subtle approach. 'David, I believe that several decades ago, you changed your name from Nigel Anstey to David Daniels Reed. Is that so?'

'Can I ask what business it is of yours what I call myself?' David said.

'Ordinarily, I would absolutely agree with you, but the

implications surrounding your change of name do need investigating.'

'Why?' challenged David.

'Alright,' said Louis, 'I'll start from the beginning. I believe you are the son of Mary Daniels and Philip Trehearne and that Nigel Anstey married your mother, Mary, and raised you as his own son. You left home after your mother died, having discovered that Nigel had been conducting an affair with a lady named Barbara, while your mother was still alive. Nigel subsequently married Barbara and neither you nor your younger half-brother Benjamin thought much of the arrangement, so you left.'

Louis paused but David said nothing, so he continued. 'At some point, before her death, your mother must have told you of your true parentage and therefore you tracked down the whereabouts of Philip Trehearne. There are three questions that I have to ask you. Firstly, on the day you arrived at the farm, did you expect to find Philip there? Or, secondly, did you already know he had disappeared? Thirdly, are you responsible for his disappearance?'

'You've certainly been very busy, Chief Inspector. Why on earth do you believe me to be this Nigel Anstey?'

'You have the same date of birth as Nigel, your new identity includes the middle name of Daniels, your mother's maiden name, and your aunt Teresa gave us this photograph, which both Jago and Merrin recognised as being you. Finally, your aunt told us that Mary had confided in her that she was pregnant with Philip's child – you – but asked her to tell no one else. Your mother had either decided herself never to tell Philip, or had been instructed not to do so by Mr Anstey.' Louis pushed the photograph across the table towards David. He studied it in silence for some time.

'Do you want me to repeat anything I've just said?' Louis asked gently.

'No, Chief Inspector. Many, many years ago, I was the boy in this photograph and my name was Nigel Anstey.'

CHAPTER THIRTY-FOUR

There was a prolonged silence, followed by a tentative knock on the door on the interview room.

Curiosity had obviously got the better of Jack Eddy. 'Would you like some tea, boss?' he asked.

'Three teas, please Eddy, but take your time making them,' said Louis.

Just for a moment, as Jack left the room, Louis and David's eyes met and the ghost of amusement hovered between them. 'He's a good man,' said Louis, 'but he likes to know what's going on. In his defence, he is the most honest man I have ever met which, in my job, I find deeply refreshing – as opposed to the lies and cover-ups that I normally have to deal with.'

His words immediately turned the atmosphere a little chilly, so Louis thought it best to move swiftly on. 'So, what brought you to Trehearne Farm, just five weeks after Philip's disappearance?' he asked.

'You're right, my mother did tell me, almost on her deathbed, who my birth father was. Strangely, it didn't come as a huge shock – it was almost as if I'd always known that I didn't quite fit in. If you've met him, you'll know that Nigel, my stepfather, as it turns out, is not a particularly pleasant character. He was pretty hard on me, and strangely, he was equally tough on his own son, my younger brother, Benjamin. I don't know if you're aware, but Benjamin became a drug addict very young and, ultimately, the drugs killed him.'

Louis nodded. 'Yes, I do know about that. I'm so sorry. Were you two close?'

'Not really. I suppose we were co-voyagers on the sea of Nigel's bullying and ill-temper. I was very sad to hear that Benjamin had died but we had drifted apart by then.'

'So, you found out where your birth father lived,' Louis coaxed.

'Yes, it wasn't difficult. My mother said he had a family farm just outside St Ives.'

'But you didn't go and see him for over three years after your mother's death. Why was that?' Louis asked.

'If you have Nigel as a father, you don't get to have much self-esteem, which was what killed Benjamin, really. I was working as Nigel's farm manager, having taken over from my mother. It was helpful in a way, as it gave me good experience and she had already taught me a great deal about farming. I was worried about being rejected by my birth father, of course, that was my main fear. I kept putting off making contact. Then, my relationship with Nigel began to deteriorate. As I grew more confident regarding my farming skills, I would come up with the odd good idea and, as a matter of principle, he would reject it. Working for him became increasingly intolerable. Then one day, I saw an advertisement in *Farmers Weekly*. A family farm, requiring a farm manager, and the name Trehearne leapt off the page at me. It seemed like fate beckoning me – the perfect opportunity to meet my father at last. If I was granted an interview and we didn't get on, I reckoned he need never know who I was.'

The tea arrived, and Jack settled himself quietly in a corner. David took a sip of tea, and Louis noticed his hand was trembling. Was this a story he'd ever told anyone before now? Louis wondered. He expected not. 'So, you went for the interview,' Louis encouraged.

For the first time, David seemed reluctant to go on. He stared down at his teacup, which he was now holding in both hands in order to steady it.

At last he spoke. 'When I arrived, the scene I'd dreamt about so often could not have been more different. The family were in chaos, in a state of shock and grief. Tom was only seventeen and Gemma was fifteen. Tom had been forced to leave school to try and run the farm but his heart wasn't really in it. Philip had been missing for five weeks; all searches had been called off. Trehearne Farm was a place of despair.'

'So you stayed,' said Louis.

'Yes, I stayed and gradually sorted out the farm. I didn't even have a formal interview, I just got stuck in. Initially, I slept upstairs in the spare room but after a year or two, we converted one of the small barns so I have my own home.'

'But you never told them who you were?'

'No, in the early days, I was so busy and then when I'd got on top of things, it just seemed too late. Also, I was worried about the effect it would have on Sarah. I really grew to love Sarah, she was so warm and kind. I loved my mother too, but she worked so hard and was deeply depressed during most of my childhood, I now realise. Also, Sarah used to tell me a lot about Philip and what a wonderful man he was. How they had become teenage sweethearts and neither of them had ever looked at anyone else. How could I break her heart by telling her that wasn't true? I was in too deep. I couldn't possibly tell her who I really was.'

'And the name change?' Louis asked.

'When I applied for the interview, I thought up the name David Reed. I didn't know whether Philip knew about Nigel Anstey, so I thought I'd better meet him under a pseudonym. My wages were paid in cash in those days and after a few months, I changed my name by deed poll.'

'Adding Daniels as a nod to your mum?' Louis said.

David smiled. 'Yes, of course. And that's my story, Chief Inspector.'

'So, you had nothing whatsoever to do with the disappearance of Philp Trehearne?' said Louis.

For the first time, David appeared irritated. 'I've already told you, the first day I visited the farm was five weeks after Philip had gone missing.'

'You're still not answering the question,' persisted Louis.

'No, Chief Inspector, I did not have anything to do with Philip's disappearance,' said David, his tone was now decidedly frosty.

'And finally,' said Louis, 'this is the question I have asked everyone, and living so long and closely with the family, you are more qualified than most to give an opinion – what is your view as to what happened to Philip?'

'How should I know? I wasn't there, was I?' was all David was prepared to say.

For most of the interview, it seemed as if the two men had liked one another and David had seemed relieved to be able to talk to someone about his background. There was the added element of David having found Louis's son, which possibly made Louis's interrogation gentler than it might otherwise have been. Now, however, the atmosphere had changed and it seemed, Louis thought, to have occurred at the moment when he'd asked if David knew anything about Philip's disappearance. Did he just feel insulted, or did he know more than he was saying? It was hard to tell.

'So, what happens now?' said David, still sounding hostile.

'It's up to you,' said Louis. 'Your background is not a police matter. You have to decide whether to tell Tom and Gemma that you are their half-brother, or whether that secret remains yours. All I would say is that Jago and Merrin know who you are, which is going to make things difficult for Jago, in particular. It doesn't seem to be the sort of information he should keep from his wife. Also, maybe you might feel better for getting things out into the open. After all, you don't have Sarah's feelings to consider any more, sadly.'

'This mess is all your fault,' David said, standing up. 'Why on earth did you involve Jago and Merrin in this?

Why meddle in my past and share it with others? It isn't your story to tell.'

Louis remained seated and spoke calmly. 'I'm trying to find out what happened to your father – that was my brief. In doing so, I have to look at every aspect of his life. You must see that an affair at college, which led to the birth of a child Philip never knew existed, did need investigating. You've told me what happened, I have to accept that. However, you have to accept that it isn't my fault you decided not to tell the Trehearne family of your true identity. That was your decision and yours alone. How you deal with it is up to you.'

'But I understand you have a meeting with the Trehearnes this week. Tom is going to want to know what progress you've made. How are you going to deal with that?'

'I'm going to fix the meeting for Thursday, to give you time to decide whether you're going to explain your relationship. At that meeting, if you have decided not to divulge your true identity, I will be simply telling Tom and Gemma that as yet I have made little progress in finding out what happened to their father – unless, of course, I have a breakthrough in the meantime. As I've said, your parentage is not a police matter.'

'Thank you,' said David. 'I'll let you know what I decide to do.'

'Don't thank me,' said Louis. 'I'm just doing my job, but there is one thing of which I'm absolutely sure. Now I know he has three children to mourn him, I will not rest until I find out what really happened to Philip Trehearne.'

CHAPTER THIRTY-FIVE

While Jack drove David back to Trehearne Farm, Louis left the station and walked over to Porthmeor Beach. The tide was way out and the day was damp and cloudy, so there were very few people on the sand. He thought longingly of a coffee in the Tate Gallery café, but he needed some fresh air to clear his head and so took the steps down onto the beach and began walking out to sea.

It had been an extremely awkward interview with David. Louis was aware that he had not pushed him hard enough. Partly, this was because, in different circumstances, this was a man who, instinctively, he felt sure he would like. Also, of course, there was the elephant in the room – it was hard to separate David the possible suspect from David the man who had saved his son.

Most of David's answers had been plausible and extremely sad. There was no doubt that his life had

223

not been easy, both as a child and as a young man. As an adult, he had made the extraordinary decision to withhold his true identity from his own birth family. This decision, without doubt, had coloured his whole adult life. As Merrin had indicated, it made sense now that he had few friends and, apparently, had made no attempt at marriage, or even a serious girlfriend. How could he have a meaningful relationship with anyone, while keeping the truth of his identity to himself? How could he share it with anyone when he had not shared it with his family?

Yet for all his apparent candour, Louis still felt David was holding something back. Was it that he was carrying the burden of recognising the time had come to tell Tom and Gemma who he really was, now he did not need to protect Sarah? Was it something to do with his obviously close relationship with Sarah? From the moment he had first read up on the case, Louis had speculated on the timing of Sarah's suicide. Why had she chosen now, after so many years without Philip? Had the loss of him built up to a crescendo, or had there been some sort of trigger that had precipitated her decision? Was David that trigger? Despite what he'd said in his interview, maybe he had confided his true identity to Sarah and for that reason, she could not bear to go on living. Her doctor had been a witness at the inquest. *I'll talk to her*, Louis thought, wondering why on earth he had not done so before getting tangled up with the Ansteys.

So, all Louis's instincts suggested he should have pressed David harder, delved deeper. Without doubt, Louis accepted that he had been too soft on the man, and that the reasons for doing so offered no excuse for a poor interview technique.

Louis was retracing his steps back towards the Tate when it occurred to him that he would be betraying no secrets if he told Merrin that David had confessed to being Nigel Anstey. It would at least provide her and Jago with a reason for talking things through with David, and hopefully persuading him to tell his half-brother and half-sister the truth.

Mercifully, Merrin was at home. 'Come in, Louis. Heavens, it looks like you have the world on your shoulders. Coffee?'

Once installed at the kitchen table, Merrin asked for an explanation for his obvious gloom.

'You and Jago were correct,' said Louis. 'David is, was, Nigel Anstey.'

'Goodness,' said Merrin, 'so what happens now? Is he going to tell Tom and Gemma?'

'He's thinking about it. That's the reason I'm here. I had to tell him that you and Jago recognised him from the photograph, and I suggested perhaps it was the moment he should come clean with his half-siblings. I made the point that it was a bit much to expect Jago not to tell his wife, and, of course, if Gemma knows, Tom has to be told. I was hoping you and Jago might persuade David to own up. Apart from anything else, I think he might find it a big relief, having lived a lie all these years.'

'I know I can speak for Jago in saying we'll definitely have a go at persuading him,' Merrin said. 'Did David explain why he ended up at Trehearne?'

'Yes, hopefully he'll tell you all the details but he saw an advertisement for a farm manager at the Trehearne Farm. He already knew he was Philip's son; his mother had told him shortly before she died. He didn't realise when he went for the interview that Philip was missing. He'd thought up a new identity at the time of applying for the interview because he thought Philip might know the name Nigel Anstey.'

'Interviewing David can't have been easy for you,' suggested Merrin.

'No,' agreed Louis. 'To be honest, I made a bit of a hash of it, I didn't go in hard enough.' He sighed. 'There's something I'm missing, I just can't work out what it is. Also, I'll have to fix up a meeting with Tom and Gemma; I promised them some answers this week.'

'So you're going to have to tell them about David, if he won't?' said Merrin.

'No, I've explained that to David. His change of name is not a police matter. What he has done is totally lawful, so I've given him until Thursday to decide what he wants to do. If he decides to keep his identity secret, I'll just have to tell Tom and Gemma about whatever progress I have made by then, excluding David's true identity.'

'It still feels to me that everything has to be connected,' said Merrin.

'I agree, the question is how.'

As soon as Louis left, Merrin rang her brother, who managed to wheel himself into a bathroom for some privacy. Merrin explained what had happened and what Louis wanted them to do.

'I might have an opportunity to talk to David this evening,' said Jago. 'Gemma is going to see her friend Annie for a drink tonight and Tom has taken to shutting himself in the snug with a bottle of whisky, once supper is over.'

'That doesn't sound too good,' said Merrin.

'It's not. Leave it with me, sis, and I'll come back to you.'

Jago called a few hours later. 'I spoke to David. I don't know him all that well but whatever domestic or farm-related drama is going on, he's normally calm and affable. Tonight, he was anything but. He is very upset that we know his former name. He said Louis had no right to have told us of his true identity, to which I replied that Louis didn't tell us – we told him. Also, Tom has been giving him a hard time, wanting to know why the police had interviewed him. David said it was a traffic offence but, of course, Tom doesn't believe him. I promised, if asked, we would tell Tom that we didn't know why the police had interviewed David, but it made no difference. He says he won't discuss with us what he is going to do, and that it is none of our business.'

'Well, you did your best,' said Merrin, 'though heaven knows what happens now.'

CHAPTER THIRTY-SIX

Annie Pascoe and Gemma Tripconey had been friends since nursery school, much like Merrin and Clara, but, of course, Annie and Gemma were nearly ten years younger. Like Merrin and Clara, though, there had been many periods in their lives when they had seen very little of one another. Certainly, Gemma making her home the other side of the world hadn't helped. Nonetheless, it was one of those relationships where it didn't matter how long it had been since they last met, they were immediately at ease with one another, slipping back, seamlessly, into the old banter, jokes and, of course, gossip.

While Jago was having his unsuccessful conversation with David, Annie and Gemma had polished off a bottle of pinot grigio and had embarked on a second.

'I'm too old for all this boozing,' Annie complained. 'I blame you, coming back here with your Aussie ways and leading me astray. It's a good thing you only have to walk home.'

The Pascoes' land joined onto the Trehearnes'. Annie's elder brother, Geoff, who was four years her senior, had taken over the farm from their parents. She also had a little brother, Dan, who was three years younger than her. Growing up, the Pascoe and Trehearne children were in and out of each other's houses and their parents were good friends, too. On the night of Philip's disappearance, the Pascoe family were first on the scene to help with the search.

Annie had never married. There had been the odd boyfriend, but the only real love of her life was Tom Trehearne. Both families longed for the two of them to get together but it had never happened. Although Annie was a nice-looking girl, and a delightful person, Tom showed absolutely no interest in her and, instead, unwisely married Beth, the sheep sheerer – a marriage doomed to fail. Gemma, of course, knew of Annie's feelings for her brother, but it was an unwritten rule between them that Tom was never discussed.

So, it was unusual that Gemma mentioned him now. 'Our boozing is nothing compared with Tom's,' she said. 'He's getting through the best part of a bottle of whisky a day at the moment, and he is so angry – all the time.'

'I never thought of Tom as being much of a drinker,' said Annie cautiously.

'No, he wasn't. It's Mum dying that has tipped him over the edge. He's blaming the police for both her death and Dad's disappearance.'

'I know,' said Annie, 'I've seen the press coverage. Do you feel the same?'

'I did,' said Gemma. 'I do feel very guilty about not being here for Mum. I should never had moved to Australia, when, underneath it all, she must have been so fragile. I thought she was OK but I realise now I was selfishly thinking only of my own happiness.'

'You're wrong there,' said Annie. 'She adored Jago and couldn't have been happier than when you two got married. Yes, of course she missed you and watching your children growing up, but she was so delighted for you and your new exciting life in Australia with the man you loved – honestly, Gem, I know it's true.'

'It's nice of you to say so but the guilt lingers on, and it was that that made me join in Tom's rant initially. However, the police have put a very senior man in charge of the new investigation into Dad's disappearance. His name is Chief Inspector Louis Peppiatt and I really believe he cares and is trying his best to find some new evidence concerning Dad's disappearance. But thirty years on, it's a tall order.'

'But the caring chief inspector hasn't been able to calm down Tom?' Annie asked.

'Briefly, about a week ago, he did manage to get Tom to co-operate, but there has been no news from him since and Tom is really losing the plot, although another meeting is planned shortly. Honestly, Annie, I just don't know what to do with him and neither does Jago. We're all desperately sad about Mum, we loved her to pieces, as you know, but what we should be doing at this time is supporting each other. Instead Tom seems to hate us all, not just the police. I know he can be pretty volatile but I've never known him to be as vile as this. He seems to have a different agenda from the rest of us but what that is, heaven only knows.'

'The trouble is with his parents both dead and you living in Australia, he has no family left and no partner. I suppose he does have David, who, presumably, will always be around – Tom and David do work well together, don't they?'

'Well, that's another thing. The police collected David yesterday and took him in for questioning. Tom's furious about that as well, and David has been monosyllabic ever since he got back from the station. He told Tom it was about a traffic offence, but I think that's very unlikely. He was collected by two policemen, one of whom was the chief inspector himself.'

'So what do you think David's been up to, then?' Annie asked.

'I've no idea, but it can't be anything serious,' said Gemma. 'You know David probably better than me but I can't imagine him being in any sort of serious trouble. He's so calm, a bit on the bland side really, but kind and helpful. It is slightly odd, though, the police wanting to see him.'

'I hadn't realised that the police had launched a new investigation into your dad's disappearance. Do you think David might have been questioned about that?' suggested Annie.

'I can't believe that's the case,' said Gemma. 'David didn't appear in our lives until some weeks after Dad vanished. It was probably just a traffic offence, like he said.'

After Gemma had left, Annie went and sat on the bench outside the back door. It was a beautiful starlit night, much like the one on which Philip had vanished. The pattern of fields, drenched in moonlight, lay out before her. It was magic, but her mind was far away.

A new investigation raised all the old anxieties in Annie. She shivered, despite the warmth of the night. She tried to quieten her mind. She had drunk too much, now was not the moment to make decisions. She would see how she felt in the morning.

After a restless night, Annie rose just before 5 a.m. and went down to the kitchen she shared with Geoff and his family. No one else was up as yet. She made herself a coffee, then went outside and sat on the same bench as the night before. This morning, it was wet with dew but she barely noticed. Thirty years ago, she had said nothing, told no one. Why? Well, although only fifteen, she was already hopelessly in love with Tom Trehearne, and her best friend in all the world was his sister, Gemma. If someone had asked her, maybe it would have been different – but no one ever did.

CHAPTER THIRTY-SEVEN

The following morning, Louis presented himself at the doctor's surgery at nine sharp. After waving his warrant card around and generally making a fuss, he was given five minutes with Sarah Trehearne's former doctor, a Dr Elizabeth Andrews.

Dr Andrews was not in her first youth and was immediately uncompromising. 'Chief Inspector, you cannot have reached your exalted position in the police force without learning that we medics do not discuss our patients' details, even with their nearest and dearest, never mind the police.'

'Your patient has sadly died. I am not asking for details of her treatment and I know she killed herself with an overdose of sleeping pills. There is just one question I want to ask you – why do you think, after thirty years of being without her husband, did she choose to kill herself now?'

'I'm not a psychiatrist, Chief Inspector. I'm a humble GP.'

'But I suspect you've known Sarah a long time? This is not idle curiosity, Dr Andrews. Her children desperately want to know what happened to their father and why their mother killed herself when she did. The family have been living under a cloud for decades; I'm just trying to give them some sort of closure.'

Dr Andrews was silent for several minutes, apparently deep in thought. Finally, she spoke. 'For a policeman, I'll grudgingly admit, you are showing a surprising degree of sensitivity. I can't really help you and certainly I can't give you a professional opinion. You're right, I have been Sarah's doctor since before Philip vanished. She had to keep going immediately after his disappearance for the children's sake. Of course, they haven't been children for a long time now but once they didn't need her any more, she transferred her emotional energy into believing Philip would come back to her one day. Over the years, the longing for his return exhausted her. I don't believe she killed herself because of any outside influence. I think she did it because finally she gave up hope, and as we all know, without hope, life isn't worth living.'

'Poor woman,' said Louis. 'I agree, being without hope must be one of the saddest of human conditions.'

'Yes, indeed,' said Dr Andrews, frowning at him. 'You're an odd sort, Chief Inspector. Now be off with you, I have a very busy morning ahead.'

Louis was just leaving the surgery when his mobile rang. It was Jack Eddy. 'Sorry to disturb you, boss, but I thought you should know straight away,' he said.

'Know what, Eddy?' Louis said patiently.

'I've just had Annie Pascoe on the phone and she wants to talk to you about Philip Trehearne.'

Louis was suddenly very alert. 'Who is Annie Pascoe? Her name's familiar. I'd like a complete bio on her right now, please, Eddy. I know I can rely on you.'

'Well,' said Jack, with obvious relish. 'Annie is a spinster lady. I think you'll remember her name from the file. Her family went to the cinema with the Trehearnes that night. Anyway, she lives on the family farm, which is now run by her elder brother, Geoff. She lives with Geoff's family and I believe it is a happy arrangement. She gets on well with her sister-in-law, Cath, and used to help with babysitting and nowadays helps out on the farm.'

'How old is she?'

'I'm not sure exactly. Oh, wait a moment, she is best friends with Gemma Trehearne so they will be the same age – mid-forties.'

'And where is the family farm?'

'It backs onto the Trehearnes'. The two families have always been close friends – the kiddies and the parents. Rumour has it that Annie was in love with Tom Trehearne but nothing came of it. Shame really, it might have been the making of him. She's a lovely lady.'

'Did she give you any details as to why she wanted to see me?'

'No, she just said she would like to come to the station and suggested ten o'clock this morning. Can you make it in time, boss, or shall I ask her to come later?'

'No, it's fine, I'm already in St Ives so I'll be with you in a few minutes. Don't go wandering off anywhere I'd like you to be present at the interview.'

Louis climbed into his car and, instead of driving off, sat staring out of the window, wondering what Annie Pascoe had to say for herself. Could this be the breakthrough he'd been looking for – a close family friend with a story to tell? It seemed too good to be true but then, Louis thought, he was certainly due some good luck with this case.

At first glance, Annie Pascoe was not particularly memorable. She was of medium height, of slim build, with short brown hair, neat regular features and dressed in jeans and a rather faded tartan shirt. But then she smiled, as Louis walked across the room to shake hands, and her face was transformed. She was not a beauty but she was a nice-looking woman and there was something warm and approachable about her. At this particular moment, though, she was clearly very nervous.

Introductions made, they settled down. 'Would you like tea or coffee?' Louis asked.

Annie shook her head. 'No, I'd rather get this over with as quickly as possible,' she said.

Louis smiled reassuringly at her. 'You tell me why you're here and I will try not to interrupt you, I promise.'

There was a pause while Annie collected herself. Jack, sitting in a corner of the office, opened his notebook, pen poised.

'You probably know that it was my family who went with the Trehearnes to the cinema on the night that their father disappeared?'

'Sorry,' said Louis, 'but I'm going to interrupt straight away. Can you tell me exactly who was in the party?'

'Yes,' said Annie. 'Tom and Gemma, of course, me and my younger brother, Dan. He was twelve at the time. My older brother, Geoff, drove us there – he didn't stay for the film but did collect us at the end and take us home. The film was *Home Alone*, which I imagine wasn't his thing – he was in his late teens.'

Annie paused for a moment; it seemed to Louis as if she needed all her strength to continue. 'When we were queueing to buy our tickets, Tom suddenly said that he didn't want to see the film either, that it was childish. "Tell Geoff I'll walk home or hitch a lift," he said.

'Gemma tried to get him to stay, saying that the film would cheer him up, but he wouldn't. He seemed very angry and upset. Gemma told me, while we waited for the film to start, that Tom and his dad had badly fallen out that afternoon. His dad was in the middle of a difficult calving and had asked for Tom's help. Tom had refused, said he hated farming and had stormed off.'

Annie seemed unable to go on. 'Please take your time, Miss Pascoe,' said Louis gently. 'Shall we have a tea break?'

'No, no,' said Annie desperately, 'or I'll never get this out.' She took a deep breath. 'When the film was finished, Geoff collected us and dropped off Gemma at the end of the lane leading up to the Trehearne Farm. Much to our surprise, Tom was waiting for us there and seemed very agitated. Gemma immediately asked him if he had made it up with their dad and Tom said he hadn't seen him. It's difficult to explain but the Trehearnes were such a happy family so this falling-out between father and son was a big thing and very unusual.'

'Are you saying that you think Tom might have been involved in his father's disappearance?'

'I don't know!' said Annie, bursting into tears. 'I don't know what I'm saying. It's just I've kept this information to myself all these years and now I know you're investigating Philip's disappearance again, I just couldn't keep it to myself a moment longer. Do you understand?'

'Of course I understand,' said Louis. 'You were fifteen years old, Gemma was your best friend, and I understand you were very fond of Tom. Of course you didn't want to make trouble for them.'

'Jack, did you tell the chief inspector about me and Tom?' Annie asked, turning to face him and looking none too pleased.

'I did, my girl,' said Jack, 'and I'm very sorry but I thought I ought to.'

'Did you and Gemma ever discuss what Tom might have been doing while you were in the cinema?' Louis asked.

Annie shook her head, then blew her nose and wiped her eyes. 'No, Gemma and I never discuss Tom because it's awkward. She knows I've always loved him – yes, really loved him, even when I was still only a child. She also knows how much it hurt me that Tom didn't reciprocate my feelings, and I know how much she would have liked Tom and I to get together. What finally made me come and see you today was that last night, for the first time ever, she did talk to me about Tom.'

'Before you tell me about what Gemma said, I didn't

find anything about all of this in the original file. Apart from mentioning the trip to the cinema, there is nothing else. Did no one interview any of you about what actually happened that evening?'

'No, they just assumed that everyone had seen the film, except, of course, for Geoff, who went home to help our dad with some paperwork.'

Louis shook his head in disbelief. 'The perfect alibi by default,' he said. 'So, can you tell me what happened last night, Miss Pascoe?'

'Gem and I hadn't seen each other since she and Jago came home for Adam McKenzie's funeral. We drank rather a lot of wine and suddenly Gemma started talking about Tom and about how angry and upset he is. He never was a drinker but he's now on a bottle of whisky a day, apparently, and is being absolutely horrible to everyone. I suddenly thought that if he had been involved in some way with his dad's disappearance, he would now probably also feel responsible for his mum's death. In other words, he linked the two deaths together in order to blame the police. Maybe he's drinking so much and being so horrible because really he's blaming himself.' Annie burst into tears again. 'I can't believe I saying this about Tom, I just can't believe it.'

The two men were propelled into action. Jack immediately put on the kettle and fetched a glass of water. Louis produced a handkerchief and held Annie's hand while she cried her heart out.

Eventually, after a cup of tea, heavily laced with sugar, Annie calmed down. 'I know you must think I should have talked to the police at the time, and come to that, so should Gemma, Dan and Geoff, who all knew Tom hadn't been at the cinema. It wasn't' – she paused – 'a conspiracy of silence. It was just that as the police didn't ask us, I suppose we kidded ourselves that it wasn't important. To the best of my knowledge, no one has ever talked about Tom's absence that evening' – she wiped her eyes – 'which could, of course, have been entirely innocent.'

'Yes, indeed,' said Louis, 'I am very aware of that. However, I am going to have to bring him in for questioning. You do understand, don't you?'

Annie nodded. 'But will he have to know that it was me who told you about him going missing? I just can't bear it if he and Gemma find out.'

'I'll be honest with you. It depends so much on how the interview goes. If he admits he wasn't at the cinema, then hopefully I can avoid telling him who provided the information. If he denies it, then it will be difficult, but I do promise I will try and keep your name out of it. For all we know, he may have a legitimate explanation as to where he was that evening; he might even have a witness to prove it. So, I'm not going to jump to any conclusions, I promise you that, and I am very grateful to you for coming in to see us.'

'I hated all of that,' said Jack, when Annie had left. 'Dear little Annie, she was so brave to come and see us. She absolutely loves Tom, it's why the poor dear lady never married. It is so sad and now she's had to tell us such terrible news.'

'*Terrible news* is going way too far, Eddy,' said Louis. 'There may be a completely innocent explanation for Tom going missing. Maybe he was meeting some mates, or even a girl, which he didn't want to mention in front of Annie. As for a quarrel with his father, what father and son don't fall out now and again, particularly when the son is a teenager? I am not particularly looking forward to Edward's teenage years, I don't mind admitting.'

'I suppose so,' said Jack, 'I just don't have a good feeling about all this.'

'Well, one thing's for sure, we need to bring Tom in for questioning under caution. Tomorrow morning at eight, I'll pick you up. There definitely needs to be two of us – I can't imagine Tom is going to be very pleased with this development.'

CHAPTER THIRTY-EIGHT

Tom Trehearne woke up with a terrible hangover. His head ached, his mouth was dry, he felt sick and when he tried to move, his limbs felt unnaturally heavy. He staggered to the bathroom – while he couldn't remember how much he'd drunk the previous day, he certainly remembered the cause. Tom was angry with David on so many levels, he couldn't bear to even look at him, let alone speak to him. In order to avoid him, Tom had not gone to work yesterday and had left all the farm's chores to David. As a result, Tom had started drinking at midday and had continued until he'd crashed out in his bed, fully clothed, sometime during the late evening. God, he'd had a skinful.

He splashed his face with cold water and stumbled down the stairs. In the kitchen, he found Gemma and Jago having breakfast.

'Tom, you look dreadful,' Gemma said. 'You've got to

stop all this drinking, it's solving nothing and making you ill.'

'Don't start, I'm not in the mood,' said Tom.

'Sit down, old lad,' Jago said, wheeling himself over to the Aga. 'I'll get you a mug of coffee and, sis, could you fetch him some water and painkillers?'

Gemma stood up reluctantly. 'He should be getting them himself. He did absolutely nothing at all yesterday except drink. Poor David had a very long day.'

'Please, darling, just fetch the pills,' said Jago. 'He's in pain, in all sorts of ways.'

'Oh, so you're a psychiatrist now, are you?' said Tom nastily. 'Let's hope you make a better job of it than you did as a surfer.'

'Tom!' shouted Gemma, slamming the pills and water on the table beside her brother. 'How dare you speak to Jago like that! You're turning into such a bastard, you really are.'

'It's OK,' said Jago. 'Tom, why have you suddenly started drinking like this? I know it's terribly sad that Sarah has died but she wouldn't want to see you in such a state. As we briefly discussed the other day, you are free now to do whatever you want for the rest of your life. You really can follow your dream now.'

'Don't be ridiculous – *follow my dream* – you sound like something out of an awful pop song. I've wasted my life. The day Dad walked out on us, my life was effectively over.'

'It's you who's being ridiculous, and pathetically sorry for yourself,' said Gemma. 'You're only in your mid-forties. You've time to start a new career, get married, maybe even have a family. Jago's right, you can do whatever you want – it's exciting, thrilling – you don't realise how lucky you really are.'

'And getting married means I have to give in and marry Annie Pascoe, I suppose?'

'No chance of that,' Gemma lied. 'She'd never have you now.'

At that moment, there was the sound of car wheels crunching on the gravel outside.

'Who's that?' demanded Tom, 'I can't cope with visitors right now.'

Gemma went to the window. 'Goodness, the police are back again – both the chief inspector and Jack. What on earth has David done to have them come here again?'

There was a knock on the door and Gemma went to answer it.

'Good morning, Chief Inspector, hello, Jack, would you like some coffee?' she said, as she ushered them into the room.

'No, thank you,' said Louis.

'Now look,' said Tom, rising unsteadily to his feet. 'Whatever it is that David has done, we have a right to know. He lives and works with us – for all we know, he might be dangerous. He lied and told us you wanted to talk to him about a traffic offence. We're not so stupid as to think the police would send a chief inspector to interrogate a suspect over a traffic offence. I want to know exactly what he's done wrong.'

'I'm afraid I cannot disclose the details of the conversation I had with David Reed – not with you, Tom, nor with anyone else, without his express permission,' said Louis.

'At least we have Jack as a witness to your lack of concern, if David murders us all in our beds,' said Tom grumpily.

'I think you can be confident, Tom, that David is not going to murder you in your bed, or anywhere else,' said Louis, privately thinking, *I wouldn't blame him if he did!*

'Anyway, assuming you want to interview him again, I have no idea where he is,' said Tom.

'It's not David I want to take in for questioning, it's you, Tom,' said Louis.

Gemma gasped, Jago looked astounded, Tom exploded.

'Oh brilliant!' he shouted. 'You can't find out what happened to my father, so you're picking us off, one by one, in the hopes of being able to pin the blame on someone other than the police. Well, I'm not coming with you, Chief Inspector.'

'I am hoping we can do this the easy way, Tom, with your co-operation,' said Louis. 'Jack, please take Mr Trehearne to the car and read him his rights.'

Jack moved to take Tom's arm but Tom lashed out, missing Jack completely and falling on the ground. Louis and Jack got him to his feet, cuffed him and Jack led him away.

Louis turned to Gemma and Jago. 'I'm really sorry about this but I do need to talk to him to clarify one or two things.'

'He's in no fit state to be interviewed and he hasn't had anything to eat since yesterday morning,' said Gemma.

'I'm well aware of the state he's in and I appreciate that it would be very unfair and pointless to try and interview him now,' said Louis. 'I'm going to take him to Camborne, see he has breakfast and then give him the chance to have a sleep in one of the cells for a few hours, until he's sobered up. Don't worry, we'll look after him and hopefully he will be back with you this evening. Do you have a coat for him?'

After the car had driven off, Gemma sat down and stared at her husband.

'You don't believe Tom had anything to do with Dad's disappearance, do you Jago?' she said.

'No, of course not,' said Jago soothingly. 'We don't even know that these two interviews with David and Tom are anything to do with your dad. It may well be about something else entirely.'

'Of course it's about Dad!' said Gemma, close to tears.

'How can you possibly say that?' Jago asked.

'Because there's something I've never told you, or anyone else.' Gemma took a deep breath. 'That evening that Dad disappeared, we went to the cinema.'

'I know that,' said Jago.

'But what you don't know is that Tom came to the cinema, but he didn't stay to watch the film.'

CHAPTER THIRTY-NINE

By early afternoon, Louis decided Tom was ready to be interviewed. He'd had a large breakfast, plenty of water and coffee and several hours' sleep. However, the most telling sign that Tom was ready for interview was the constant banging on his cell door, demanding to see the chief inspector, accompanied by enough swearing to make a sailor blush.

While Tom was being shown to the interview room, Louis and Jack met in the corridor. 'Thinking about it, I really don't believe Tom had anything to do with his dad's disappearance. This is just us going through the motions, after Annie's visit to the station. That's right, isn't it, boss?' Jack asked.

'He'd had a row with his dad and he wasn't in the cinema. I agree, it's hard to imagine but it has to be a possibility, Eddy. We must keep an open mind.'

'But they were such a loving family. As you said earlier, Tom behaved like a normal grumpy teenager who couldn't be arsed to help with the calving, but that doesn't mean he's a killer, does it, boss?'

'Tom's feelings about farming go much deeper than that. I think he was under a degree of pressure to join the family business, but it's not what he wanted to do. Anyway, let's see what he has to say for himself.'

Apart from his rumpled clothes, his unruly hair and the fact he needed a shave, Tom looked a whole lot better than he had done earlier. His mood, however, did not appear to have improved.

'What right do you have to shut me in a cell, Chief Inspector? You haven't charged me with anything, you haven't even interviewed me. This country is turning into a police state.'

'I did it as much for your sake as mine, Tom,' said Louis firmly. 'You were in no fit state to be interviewed. I hope the meal and a sleep have made you feel a little better. So, let's get straight down to business. On the night your father disappeared, where did you go? We know you were dropped at the cinema with everyone else, but you didn't stay to see the film. The next time the party saw you was at the end of the driveway to your farm, which was where Geoff Pascoe dropped off your sister. By my calculations, that means you were missing for at least three and a half hours, probably nearer four. Where were you, Tom?'

'It's none of your sodding business. I'm not staying here to listen to this rubbish.' He went to stand up but Jack, surprisingly light on his feet, jumped forward, put a heavy hand on Tom's shoulder and pushed him back into his seat.

'Come on, Tom, don't make a fool of yourself. Just tell the boss the truth and then we can all go home.' Jack continued to stand over him, and miraculously Tom sat back into his seat.

There was a very long silence. Over the years, Louis had come to view silence as his friend, even a tool. Sooner or later, someone, usually the interviewee, can stand it no longer and starts to talk. The wait for Tom was longer than most but eventually he began to speak.

'I went to meet a girl. Her name was Jenny, she was a visitor.'

'Do you know her surname? Have you kept in touch?' Louis asked.

'No, of course not, she was just down here on holiday with her parents for a few days. She was a bit older than me, so she bought a bottle of wine and I bought some chips and we just sat on the beach and talked.'

'Which beach?' Louis asked.

'Oh, for God's sake, it was thirty years ago and why does it matter anyway?'

'A pretty girl, no doubt, a bit more worldly-wise than you,' said Louis. 'You were just seventeen, and in those days, you probably hadn't yet done much dating. Don't tell me you can't remember where you sat and talked – of course you do!'

'OK, yes, we sat in Kitty's Corner.'

'Where's that?' Louis asked.

'Far end of Harbour Beach, boss,' said Jack, 'just by Smeaton's Pier. It's named after an old girl called Kitty. She had a black cat and did her washing in the sea. It's a very sheltered spot. I did much of my courting with Mrs

Eddy there, I have to admit – though, of course, it wasn't named after Kitty then. She must have been alive but I don't remember her – mind on other things, I suppose.'

'Thank you, Sergeant, most helpful.' Louis looked at Tom and just for a moment he spotted a small smile. Jack was a man of many unusual talents.

'So, when you were drinking the wine and eating your chips in Kitty's Corner, did you see any of your local friends – just to wave at, or say hello?'

'I don't think so,' said Tom. 'I suppose, like Jack, I had my mind on other things. Why are you asking these questions, anyway? What's the point?'

'I'm trying to find you an alibi for the night your father disappeared,' said Louis.

'Great, so I'm a suspect now, am I? So what do you think I did – killed my own father and dumped his body in the sea?'

'That wouldn't work,' said Jack. 'If you're going to dump a body in these parts, you have to put it in a boat and take it to the other side of Seal Island, then it's likely to end up in Padstow, if it doesn't get eaten by crabs. Put it in the sea here, even throw it off Man's Head, and it will come back into St Ives on the next tide. Funny, that.'

'Sergeant, much as we appreciate your fund of local knowledge, could you please not interrupt again.' Louis turned to Tom. 'No, Tom, I don't find it easy to believe you killed your father but now I know you weren't at the cinema, I do need to find a way to eliminate you from my enquiries. Did you see anyone during that period, when the others were in the cinema – apart from Jenny, of course?'

'No. I suppose Jenny and I were on the beach for over

an hour but then she had to meet her parents. So, we said goodnight and I walked home.'

'Why did you wait at the end of the drive for the cinema party to return? You must have had to hang around quite a while for them.'

'It was a beautiful starry night,' said Tom.

'Come off it, Tom, I've had enough of this,' said Louis. 'No teenage boy spends his time staring at the stars. Was it because you didn't want to go home on your own?'

'Alright, yes,' said Tom. 'I'd had a row with Dad. Also, Mum and Dad were hoping I would start dating Annie Pascoe. I know they had this idea of joining the two farms together. They would not have been pleased to learn that instead of going to the cinema with Annie, I'd gone off with someone else. It was ridiculous, trying to plan a future based around a non-existent teenage romance. Because Mum and Dad got together at about fifteen, they assumed that was the way things are done, but by the time Gemma and I were teenagers, life was very different, of course.'

'Why are you drinking so much?' said Louis.

'Now that really isn't any of your business, unless I drink and drive, which I don't.'

'Everything connected to your family is my business if you want me to find out what happened to your father. I don't have you down as being much of a drinker. When did this all start?'

'Only in the last few days, so I don't think that suggests I'm an alcoholic, do you?'

'What has caused the drinking?'

'As I said, none of your business.'

'Don't be daft, Tom,' said Jack. 'He's clever, my boss,

he'll find out what's ailing you. Better to tell him and get it over with. Better out than in.'

'I've had some bad news concerning my mother's will.' Tom hesitated. 'I hadn't bothered going to our solicitor when she died because I knew the farm was left to me with Gemma being given a modest share. Mum had drawn up the will when Dad, at long last, had been registered as missing, presumed dead. We were all happy with the arrangement and discussed it together. Our family solicitor is elderly. He'd been ill for some weeks but once back in the office, he called me up immediately. My mother had made a new will, shortly before she died. The farm is to be divided in half, between me and a third party. Gemma's share is to come out of my half. I just can't believe it.'

'And the third party is?' asked Louis, already fearing he knew the answer.

'David,' said Tom. 'David Reed, our farm manager.'

CHAPTER FORTY

Merrin had made a decision about her future. She had telephoned her old law firm in Bristol and spoken to the senior partner, who had always been something of a mentor. He thought the idea of her doing pro bono work was an excellent one and said he would be pleased to pass work her way, recognising she did not want to do too much travelling. Fired up by this, she had then enrolled in a year's course of pottery classes, based in Penzance. So, she had a part-time job, and a hobby that might well develop into a little business one day.

She was surprised as to how much relief she felt now she had a plan. Of course, after Adam's death, making the decision to move back to St Ives was major. However, once she had settled in, renewed old friendships and begun to feel part of the community again, she found she had lost her sense of direction. While everyone around her seemed to be getting on with their lives, she had stagnated. It was depressing and increasingly she was starting to live in the past, which she knew was not healthy. Now she had a plan, one of which she knew Adam would approve wholeheartedly.

Bamaluz Beach is the only beach in St Ives where dogs are allowed all day, even in the season. The tide was well out and Merrin decided she would have a swim, accompanied by William, of course. William did not approve of her swimming, in fact, it worried him a great deal. He would sit at the water's edge as she swam – not barking, nor running off, nor making a nuisance of himself in any way. But he wore an extremely worried expression, which did dampen Merrin's enjoyment and often shortened the length of time she spent in the sea because she felt so guilty about making him unhappy.

This was the case today. The beach was crowded and William was having difficulty picking out her head amongst all the others bobbing about in the sea. He was becoming increasingly anxious, so after a short swim she came out of the water to a joyous reunion. She was just drying off when her phone rang. It was Jago.

'Where are you, sis? Can you talk?' he asked.

'I'm on the beach, I've just had a swim but I can perch myself on a rock. Hang on a moment.' Merrin wrapped herself in a towel, climbed onto a rock and settled down. 'What's up? Are you OK?'

'Louis has taken Tom in for questioning, under caution. Gemma's in bits. I've just wheeled myself down the drive in order to talk to you privately. Have you heard anything from Louis?'

'Heavens!' said Merrin. 'I wonder what he wants with Tom. No, I haven't heard from Louis since he asked us to try and persuade David to talk to Tom and Gemma. It's all rather odd, isn't it?'

'I'm not so sure,' said Jago. 'You may remember that the night Philip went missing, his kids and some neighbours went to the cinema?'

'Vaguely, yes, yes, I think so, now you mention it.'

'Well,' Jago continued, 'Gemma has told me just this morning that Tom didn't go to the cinema that night. He had a lift into town with everyone else but then left and went off without saying where he was going. They didn't see him again until Gemma was dropped off, after the film, at the end of the Trehearne drive. Tom was waiting there. Somehow, Louis must have sniffed out that Tom didn't see the film.'

'Surely no one is suggesting Tom is responsible for his dad's disappearance?' said Merrin. 'That would be madness. I'm sure Gemma can't believe her brother was involved.'

'Apparently, Tom and Philip had a row during that afternoon. I don't think any of us can believe Tom is involved, but he has been behaving in an extraordinary way just recently – boozing and shouting at everyone.'

'That's as may be,' said Merrin, 'but I refuse to believe Tom had anything whatsoever to do with his dad's disappearance. I know he's not the easiest man in the world, but not this. Louis can't believe he's guilty of anything, can he?'

'There was a frightful scene when Louis and Jack came to take Tom in for questioning. In the end they had to handcuff him because he tried to hit Jack. He was still drunk from the day before and very abusive.'

'Trying to hit a policeman! Blimey, is Jack going to press charges?'

'Of course he won't,' said Jago. 'You surely know Jack better than that.'

That evening, Louis took his customary whisky into the tiny garden behind his house. He sat down on the solitary garden chair, placed his glass onto the table, and stared at the garden. It was a mess, now totally out of control. Even the small patch of lawn had run away with itself.

'Rewilding,' said Louis, by way of explaining the situation to the magpie sitting on his fence, with a rather critical expression. 'Anyway,' he added, 'mind your own business, I have bigger problems to think about than gardening.' He shook his head in disbelief, this case was definitely getting to him – talking to a magpie, with a view to seeking its approval, was surely not a good sign!

He had kept Tom in the cells overnight, partly to see if being incarcerated would encourage him to reveal anything more, and also to keep him off the booze. The web seemed to be increasingly entangled. Although David had insisted otherwise, it now seemed possible that Sarah might have learnt of David's true identity – what other reason could there be for changing her will? And why had she not told her children what she'd done? It seemed so cruel leaving Tom and Gemma to find out about details of the new will after her death, and from what he'd learnt about Sarah, such apparent callousness seemed so very out of character. Something was very wrong there.

Two men; Tom, with no alibi for the period during which his father went missing, who'd had a row with his father on the day he'd disappeared, who had a well-known nasty temper and today had shown his violent streak in trying to hit Jack; and David, who had never even met his father at the time Philip had disappeared off the face of the earth, who was normally gentle and kind and happy to help anyone who needed it – but who was also leading a half-life and had proved weak and cowardly in his dealings with the Trehearne family.

Up until now, the deeper he dug and delved, it seemed to Louis that he had simply uncovered more and more family secrets, which were going to cause a great deal of pain, and yet had brought him no nearer finding out what actually happened to Philip. But sitting in the calm quiet of his garden, he suddenly felt he could see a glimmer of light, which might show him the way ahead. It brought him no pleasure, though, no pleasure at all.

Why had Sarah disinherited her son of half the farm without telling him anything? It was definitely not the sort of thing a caring mother would do to a beloved son unless he had done something truly awful to upset her. That had to be significant. Louis sighed and finished off his whisky. With all the evidence stacking up against Tom, he felt he was almost in a position to charge him in the morning – but with what, exactly?

CHAPTER FORTY-ONE

The following morning, David had a late start. He had slept hardly at all, his mind whirling round what seemed to be the insurmountable decisions that lay ahead. He checked on the calves, let out the chickens and filled the water butts. Bleary-eyed and with an aching head, he decided, for speed's sake, to go up to the farmhouse for a coffee instead of to his own home, which was a converted barn right at the end of the lane.

So tired was he that it took him a moment to register the scene before him. Gemma was sitting at kitchen table, crying. Jago was trying to reach the kettle from his wheelchair, without much success.

'Oh, sod it, David. Help me with this kettle, please. I need to comfort to my wife.' Jago, normally such a cheerful man, looked racked with worry, and something else – it looked to David like grief.

David hurried over and reached for the kettle. 'What's wrong? What on earth has happened?'

Nobody answered, so David filled the kettle and put it on the Aga. He was about to ask the question again when Gemma spoke. 'They've arrested Tom, they think he murdered Dad.'

Jago, back beside his wife, put an arm round her. 'That's not what the police said, darling. They simply said they were arresting Tom under caution. They didn't say why.'

'When did this happen?' David asked.

'Yesterday morning,' said Jago. 'We were just having breakfast. They took him to Camborne and have kept him in the cells overnight.'

'They took him to a station where there are cells because they're going to charge him with killing Dad, I just know it,' said Gemma, beginning to cry again.

'So, they haven't charged him yet?' asked David.

'Not as far as we know,' said Jago. 'Louis and Jack came to fetch him. Unfortunately, Tom was still drunk from the night before and took a swing at Jack. It wasn't the best of starts for being interviewed by the police.'

'The idea of my brother killing our father, it's just awful. It can't be possible,' said Gemma, 'but then maybe that's why Tom has been making such a fuss, blaming the police, being so angry, getting drunk. If he did something to Dad, he'll blame himself for Mum's death, too. I just can't bear it.'

David stared at Gemma, tears pouring down her face, now ravaged by grief. 'I have to go,' he said. 'Can I take the Land Rover? My car's in for a service.'

'Where are you going?' Jago asked.

But David had already taken the car keys off the hook and was sprinting across the yard towards the Land Rover.

At the sound of the car engine, husband and wife stared at one another.

'Why's he dashed off like that?' Gemma's voice was still muffled with tears.

'I have absolutely no idea,' said Jago.

The kettle began to whistle on the Aga, but it was some time before either of them thought to do anything about it.

By ten o'clock, both Louis and Tom Trehearne were exhausted. Quite apart from the interview going round in circles, both men had endured a virtually sleepless night. Louis left Tom alone in the interview room with a mug of tea, and sat down in the office with Jack Eddy to compare notes.

'I don't think he did it, boss,' said Jack, handing Louis a much-needed black coffee.

'By *it*, I assume you mean Tom being responsible for his father's disappearance?' Louis said wearily. 'What about our old friends – *motive, means and opportunity* – he has those in spades.'

'He doesn't, boss. *Opportunity*, yes, *motive*, yes – if you accept not wanting to be a farmer as a good enough motive for killing your father – but *means* just doesn't work. How could he have got rid of the body, if he'd killed Philip? He didn't have a car and he hadn't even started to learn to drive.'

'Reluctantly, I have to admit that you're probably right about that, Eddy. He could never have disposed of the body – well, anyway, not without help. We come back again and again to the heart of this mystery. How could Philip have just vanished?'

'There's another thing, boss. As you know, I was quite close to Tom, when he was a boy, and I was working on the farm. I know he's a bit of a hothead, but I can't believe he would kill his own father, who he worshipped. He's got the tongue of a viper, I grant you, but he's not a violent man.'

'There's two things wrong with that statement, Eddy,' said Louis. 'He tried to punch you, someone who is supposed to be a good friend – and he would have succeeded but for the fact he was so drunk. Secondly, he can't have been all that devoted to his father – he felt under considerable pressure to take on the farm and he wouldn't even help his father with the calving. People change, Sergeant. I've seen it many times when life hands someone what they perceive to be a raw deal. The bright young man becomes an angry middle-aged man and ultimately an embittered old man. I'm sure, if you're honest with yourself, the Tom you knew as a boy is very different from the man in the interview room.'

'OK, boss, but I still don't agree with you. You said yourself, the other day, that a teenager having a row with their dad didn't mean much,' said Jack. 'Tell me this – what half-decent teenage boy would want to stick his arm up a cow's arse when he was shortly due to go out on what was probably his first proper date with a gorgeous young lady?'

Louis smiled. 'You do have a way with you, Sergeant, of getting straight to the nub of the problem. We'd better go back in. I'll have one more go.'

'Are you going to charge him?' Jack asked.

'With what?' said Louis. 'Unlike you, I still believe he might be responsible, in some way, for whatever happened to Philip but without a confession, I have absolutely nothing to go on.'

As they re-entered the interview room, Louis was aware that Tom looked as exhausted as he himself felt, and, momentarily, he felt sorry for the man – whatever he may or may not have done. Then he pulled himself together.

'Tom, I have listened very carefully to everything you've said but you have failed to convince me that you were not involved in some way with whatever happened to your father. You were very young and there are bound to be some mitigating circumstances – just tell us what really happened that night.'

'I've told you, over and over, what happened that night,' said Tom wearily – his normal go-to behaviour of shouting and anger had completely disappeared. 'I met a girl on the beach, we talked, drank a bottle of wine, did a little bit of very innocent kissing and then I walked home. I didn't want to face Mum and Dad on my own, so I waited for Gemma. Look, are you going to charge me and if so, with what? I'd asked for my solicitor to be present but, as I've mentioned, he's about one hundred and five and fairly useless. Just let me go, there's nothing else for us to say to one another. I'm telling the truth, you don't believe me and neither of us have any proof to help resolve the matter.'

Louis took a deep breath and prepared to wade in one more time, when there was a loud knock. Jack stood up and opened the door. 'What is it, Constable? We're busy, I said we were not to be disturbed.'

The young constable looked past Jack to Louis. 'Chief Inspector, I'm sorry to interrupt but there's someone here you really need to see, as a matter of urgency.'

'Can't it wait?' Louis asked.

'No, sir, sorry, sir, I don't think it can. It's about this case.' He nodded in the direction of Tom.

'Alright,' said Louis, standing up. 'Jack, you stay here and try and talk some sense into Tom, for all our sakes.'

The man standing at reception had his back towards Louis, and it wasn't until he turned round that Louis realised it was David Reed. 'Hello, David,' said Louis, 'what can we do for you?'

David looked pale and strained. 'Is it true that you've arrested Tom?' he asked.

'He's in here for questioning,' said Louis.

'Have you charged him with anything yet?'

'No,' said Louis.

'Can I ask why you're holding him in custody?'

'You must know I can't answer that,' said Louis.

David was silent for a moment. There was tension in the air, he seemed to be struggling with something. 'Jago has told me that you came to the farm to collect Tom yesterday morning and he and Gemma both think it must be in connection with Philip's disappearance.' Louis said nothing and after a moment's hesitation, David continued. 'If you think Tom was involved with that in any way, Chief Inspector, you're wrong.'

'Why are you so sure, David?' Louis asked.

'Because I'm responsible for what happened to Philip.'

CHAPTER FORTY-TWO

Louis took David into the empty office and gestured to
him to sit down.

'David, before you say anything more, I just hope
this isn't some cack-handed way of trying to protect the
Trehearnes because I'm not in the mood for being messed
about.'

'Why do you think I'm trying to protect the Trehearnes?'

'Because it's obvious you've been doing just that for
the last thirty-odd years. After Philip disappeared and
you began working for them, you seem to have been on
a one-man mission to make life as comfortable for them
as possible. With Gemma in Australia for much of that
time, there has just been the three of you – you, Tom and
Sarah. Tom hates farming so you must have done the lion's
share of the work. You were obviously very fond of Sarah,
and she of you. I imagine you were easier company than

poor old Tom. You have filled the place left by Philip to such an extent that you've had no life of your own. You've sacrificed yourself on the altar of the Trehearnes because they are your birth father's family, therefore your family. So, naturally, now Tom is in trouble, you're here to protect him, whatever the cost. I did not have the privilege of knowing Philip but I am absolutely certain he would not want you to ruin the rest of your life in order to save Tom, assuming he is even guilty.'

'I am very sorry but I lied to you the other day – I was just too much of a coward to tell you the whole truth in one go. As a result, you've got it all wrong,' said David. 'I'm here to protect Tom, not from his own folly, but to save him from a possible miscarriage of justice. I killed Philip. I didn't mean to, it was a tragic accident, but Philip is nonetheless dead because of me. You're right, I have sacrificed a normal life in order to help the Trehearnes, but you've misjudged my primary motive. I have done everything I can for them because I am responsible for Philip's absence from the family during the last thirty years.'

'Hi, sis, it's me, can you talk?'

'Yes, of course, Jago,' said Merrin. 'What's up? You sound stressed.'

'Gemma asked me to call to see if you can help. Tom was kept in the cells overnight so Louis must at least be thinking of charging him with something. Gemma is starting to believe that Tom really may be guilty, but I still don't think he is. We wondered if you could have a word with Louis and find out what's going on. Sorry to ask but Gem's going mad here.'

'Oh, Jago, that's awful,' said Merrin. 'For what it's worth, my immediate reaction is to agree with you. I can't believe Tom was involved in any way. I wonder why on earth Louis thinks he is – and why Gemma does, come to that. I suppose it's all to do with him not going to the cinema with everyone on the fateful evening?'

'That, and also he's just been so odd lately,' said Jago. 'We all know Tom, he's not the easiest, but something has really upset him, and I don't just mean his mother's death, which, God knows, is bad enough. Anyway, do you think you can find out what's going on?'

Merrin thought for a moment. 'I'm family, I suppose, so Louis may be able to tell me something. I think my best bet is to leave it until this afternoon. If Tom is going to be charged, I imagine it will be this morning, after a night in the cells. If not, then I think he will have to be released. Certainly, tell Gemma I'll have a go but hopefully, with a bit of luck, the matter will be cleared up and Tom will be home by this evening.'

'The other thing that's odd is that David went rushing off the moment he heard about Tom. He asked if Tom had been charged yet and when we said we didn't know, he grabbed the Land Rover and left, without any explanation. We don't know why or where he went. I tried his mobile but it's still sitting here on the kitchen table.'

'That is peculiar. Is Gemma with you?' Merrin asked.

'No,' said Jago, 'I sent her upstairs for a lie-down. She is so upset, sis.'

'Of course she is, poor lamb. So, am I right in thinking that Tom and Gemma still don't know that David is their half-brother? I assume he hasn't told them?'

'No, he hasn't but I imagine the reason he left in such a hurry was in order to try and help Tom, in some way – brotherly solidarity, sort of thing. It's so awkward not being able to tell Gemma. Assuming Tom is released and this is just a police over-reaction, we are going to have to tell Tom and Gemma about David, even if he won't. You know me, I am a very straightforward sort of chap and I hate keeping such a big secret from my wife. It's become much harder now all this police activity has kicked off.'

'Of course, it's awfully difficult for you, I do see that. Send Gemma my love, tell her I don't believe Tom has done anything wrong and that I will call Louis later this afternoon. Obviously, let me know if Tom is released in the meantime. Love you, Jago.'

'Love you too, sis. Haven't we been lucky? Losing Mum and Dad was tough, but we Tripconeys were such a happy uncomplicated bunch, weren't we?'

'We really were, but remember, so were the Trehearnes until Philip vanished.'

'Stay here,' Louis said to David.

He walked through to the front desk. 'Constable, see if Tom Trehearne wants anything to eat or drink but he is to remain in custody for the time being. Tell Sergeant Eddy he can get on with other duties. I'm interviewing in the office and I don't want to be disturbed under any circumstances.'

Louis returned to the office, firmly closed the door and drew up a chair beside David. He studied him in silence for some time.

'David, believe me, I do understand your desire to protect the Trehearne family. Since your mother and brother died and your birth father went missing, presumed dead, the Trehearnes have been your only blood relatives. Tom is your half-brother; of course you want to help him, but not to the extent of taking the rap for him. Anyway, I don't see how you can make the logistics work. You didn't come down to St Ives until five weeks after Philip's disappearance.'

'But that's just it, I did,' said David.

'Go on,' said Louis.

'You can probably tell, I'm not a very confident person and that was particularly so when I was young. It took me a while to pluck up the courage to even seriously contemplate a meeting with my birth father, although, obviously, I had known who he was for several years. Because my mother had told me, I also knew that Philip had no idea that I even existed. She told me he was a very kind man, but I still found it a daunting prospect having to tell him he had a son he knew nothing about. I thought he might not believe me. I'm not very good at dealing with emotional situations; I haven't had much experience.'

'I understand,' said Louis. 'Go on.'

'I didn't go to university or college, I simply went straight from school to working on Nigel's farm. He treated me more as an employee than a son. I didn't like him, I didn't like the way he had treated my mother, and he made it perfectly clear he didn't like me either. That apart, we worked together well enough at the beginning until, as I told you, things began to deteriorate.'

David paused.

'I appreciate this is hard,' said Louis, 'but please believe me, I have a great deal of sympathy for your position.'

David took a deep breath. 'That summer, the summer I was nineteen, Nigel gave me a few days off. It was unlike him, but things were quiet on the farm and it was in lieu of paying me the overtime he owed me. I told him I was going to stay with an old school friend in Ashburton. Instead I drove down to West Cornwall. I had looked up the Trehearne farm on a map many times and I knew it was just outside St Ives, and that the nearest pub was Halsetown Inn. I drove to the inn and parked up in their car park. I was about to go inside when I spotted a girl clearing the outside tables so I asked her the way to Trehearne Farm. She told me the way by car and then said, as it was a lovely evening, I could walk there and showed me where to join the path. I thanked her and was walking away when she called after me and said that if it was Philip I wanted to see, he'd likely be in the pub later as it was Friday.'

David looked at Louis. 'I don't know how I can tell you the next bit. Obviously, I've never told a living soul until now. You would think after all these years, it would fade, that I could almost forget all about it, but it is still so clear in my mind, so terribly, horribly clear.'

'Stay there,' said Louis. 'I'm going to fetch us both a cup of tea. Try and relax. I know it's hard but I believe you may find it a huge relief to speak at last about what happened. You're in safe hands with me, we'll unravel this together.'

CHAPTER FORTY-THREE

The two men drank their tea in silence. Louis could feel the tension in David mounting by the moment.

'Right, David,' he said at last, 'it's time to tell me everything. You owe it to the family and you owe it to yourself. Take your time, but I need to know every last detail.'

David put down his mug and took a deep breath. 'I waited in the car for a while. It was an old covered Jeep that belonged to the farm. Nigel had let me borrow it, which was surprising. I can't remember what time it was when I started on the path. I know the pub was filling up and the sun was low in the sky. I walked along the path and I can't have been walking for more than a few minutes before I saw a figure coming towards me. I knew immediately, even in the gathering dusk, that it was Philip, that it was my father. It was extraordinary; he looked so familiar, like I'd always known him.

'The path was narrow, we were almost upon one another, when Philip smiled and said something like, "Good evening, what a beautiful one."' David stopped speaking and pulled out a handkerchief, blowing his nose and wiping his eyes. He looked at Louis. 'I can't even remember the only kind words my father ever said to me. Isn't that awful? I was so fixated on what I should say to him, I couldn't concentrate.'

'So what did you say?' Louis asked gently.

'I said, "Good evening, Mr Trehearne. I'm sorry if this comes as a shock, but I'm your son and my name is David. I've been wanting to meet you for so long."'

'And he replied?' Louis encouraged.

'Philip looked me up and down. He wasn't angry but he clearly thought I was delusional, basically off my trolley. When he spoke, his voice was gentle but firm. "Don't be daft, lad," he said. "You're not my son. I already have one of those and his name is Tom."

'He went to walk round me, which meant coming off the path and onto the grass verge. I put out an arm to stop him. I've been over it a million times in my mind – I didn't hit him, obviously, and I didn't push him either. I just wanted to stop him walking away and out of my life. He must have slipped on the grass because he lost his footing and fell backwards. His head struck one of those big boulders that are scattered about these parts. He was very still and his eyes were wide open. I thought he would get up but he just lay there. I found my torch and turned it on, I felt for a pulse, but couldn't find one . . . and then I panicked.'

At this point, David began to sob. Louis sat with him

for a while and then quietly left the room. He walked down the corridor to the interview room. Tom was still sitting in his chair, staring blankly at the wall. He looked even more exhausted.

'You're free to go now, Tom,' said Louis. 'No arrest, no charges. The enquiries are finished so far as you're concerned. I'll arrange for Jack to take you home.'

Tom stood up and reached for his coat. 'So, you believe me at last and I trust, therefore, you're prepared to admit you were wrong, Chief Inspector?'

'That's about the size of it, and I apologise for taking up so much of your time.'

'And I suppose you are no nearer finding out what happened to my father?' said Tom, with a rather unpleasant sneer.

'I think it's fair to say we have mounting evidence to suggest we know some details as to what happened to your father,' said Louis carefully.

'So who the devil is responsible?' said Tom.

'I'm afraid I am not at liberty to say at this stage,' said Louis, as calmly as he was able.

'God, you people!' shouted Tom, obviously back on form, as he slammed his way out of the door.

David was back in control of himself when Louis re-entered the room, carrying, this time, two mugs of coffee. He handed one to David.

'Are you fit to go on now, David?' Louis asked.

David nodded.

'So, at this point, did you realise that Philip was dead?' Louis asked.

'I thought so, yes. On a farm, you are used to dealing

with life and death. The light had gone out of his eyes. It was terrible.'

'What did you do next?'

'As I said, I panicked,' said David. 'My immediate thought was to move him. I couldn't leave him there on his own, for a stranger to find him. I stood up and saw we were close by the hedge that bordered the coach road. Looking on the hedge with my torch, I could see there was a lay-by very close.'

'I know the one,' said Louis.

'I ran back to the pub, fetched the Jeep and drove to the lay-by. The hedge was very thin there, I managed to pull him through without hurting him and I lifted him into the back of the Jeep.'

'And no one saw you?' asked Louis.

'No, it was dark by then. There was no one on the path and no cars passed while I was putting him in the Jeep. It was terrible, he was very heavy and I couldn't look at his face. I'd killed him, my own father. It felt unreal, I could hardly believe what I was doing.'

'What did you do next?'

'I started to drive out on the coach road. I needed to think. I turned off at Trencrom and drove through to the woods, where I stopped the Jeep. I could hardly breathe, I was sweating profusely and my heart was doing somersaults. After a while, I went to the back of the Jeep and looked again at my father. I wasn't imagining it – he was quite dead. I closed his eyes and covered him with some old sacking that was in the back of the Jeep. Then I sat in the Jeep for some time while I tried to decide what to do.'

'The only sensible thing to do would have been to telephone the police from the pub and to have left Philip where he was. Why didn't you do that?'

'As I said, I panicked. I'd done this awful thing and I suppose I couldn't face the reality of it,' said David, starting to become distressed again.

'What did you decide to do then, while you were in Trencrom woods?'

'I decided to go back up to Dartmoor and bury my father there, where no one would ever find him.'

'Why Dartmoor? I just don't understand, David. I do hope this isn't some fantasy of yours. As I've already said, I am not in the mood for being messed around, I'm really not.'

'It's not a fantasy; I wish it was. I know Dartmoor very well. I grew up on the edge of the moor and as I drove there, I realised I knew just the place to bury him, where he would be safe and no one would ever find him.'

'And do you know where the place is, thirty years later?' asked Louis, feeling increasingly sceptical.

'Oh yes, definitely. It's by a large rock that is mostly surrounded by bracken. I dug the hole really deep and then dug the bracken back in on top of the grave. I finished just as the dawn came up. I said prayers, I said "sorry" again and again. Then I left and I have never returned there.'

'Despite the time lag, if I send you up to Dartmoor tomorrow morning, would you be able to take a team of policemen straight to the exact spot of the burial site?'

'Yes, I would. When I was a child on a school outing, I got lost on Dartmoor. My mum and a teacher found me. I was sitting on that same rock. My mum's face when she found me, I've never forgotten. It's why I went looking for Edward because I knew how your family would be feeling.'

The mention of Edward silenced Louis for some moments. Then he rallied. 'I'm going to keep you in the cells overnight without charge. In the morning, you, Jack and a constable can travel up to Dartmoor to meet a specialist team who can start digging where you direct them to do so. It won't be pleasant for you but then it hasn't been very pleasant for the Trehearnes to be kept in ignorance for over thirty years, has it, David?'

'No,' murmured David.

Louis's frustration boiled over. 'I just don't understand you. The death of your father, as you describe it, was an accident. I doubt very much if you would have been prosecuted with anything. How old were you, did you say?'

'Nineteen,' said David.

'As I thought,' said Louis. 'You're a mild sort of chap now. Were you any different as a young man – perhaps you were a hothead like Tom?'

'No, no, I was very shy and unsure of myself.'

'The whole situation is just madness, David. You've stood by, all these years, and watched, at first hand, the effect that Philip's disappearance has had on the family – Tom's mounting anger and frustration, Sarah's suicide, Gemma's guilt. At a stroke you could have put them all out of their misery. Why, in God's name, didn't you tell them what had happened?'

'What I told you about applying for the job at Trehearne Farm was completely true. They all made me hugely welcome and were so grateful for my help, I just couldn't bear to tell them who I was and what I'd done, particularly Sarah, for obvious reasons. I realise it was very weak of me.'

'*Weak* doesn't begin to cover it,' said Louis. 'That poor family.'

CHAPTER FORTY-FOUR

Louis was in his small, but oddly comfortable, sitting room. The room was almost in darkness, except for one small table lamp. Louis sat in his armchair, a whisky in hand, deep in thought. As a policeman, even though a degree of compassion was necessary at times, his job required him to be impartial. His role was to see that the law was upheld, to keep a firm hand on the tiller and steer through the inevitable emotions that accompanied many of the cases with which he had to deal.

This case, he felt in many ways, was more a job for social services than the police. Although it appeared he had solved the mystery of Philip's disappearance, in all other respects, he felt he had spectacularly failed. In his first interview with David, he had been too lenient because he liked the man and above all because David had rescued Edward. With Tom, he had perhaps been too harsh. He hadn't listened to him enough, had allowed Tom's anger, rudeness and frustration to mask his view of the man underneath. If he was honest with himself, he didn't like Tom very much and perhaps, as a result, he had been too ready to jump to conclusions. And now, he was giving David a hard time – judging him for keeping the secret of Philip's demise to himself and causing the Trehearne family so much grief. David had only been nineteen when he made the worst decision of his life.

How would Adam McKenzie have dealt with it all? he wondered. He wished he knew the answer to that one. And then, as if on cue, his mobile rang.

'Hello, Louis, I'm so sorry to disturb you. It's Merrin here.'

'That's a coincidence,' said Louis. 'I was just thinking about Adam and assuming he would have made a much better job of the Trehearne case than I have. He really understood people, didn't he?'

'Yes, he did,' agreed Merrin, 'but so do you. I know Adam didn't always get things right. I assume your gloomy introspection is the result of beating yourself up about something you regret having done, or said, or come to that, not done, or not said?'

'You really do understand the tortuous meanderings of a policeman's mind,' said Louis.

'I jolly well should do, after all these years. Listen, I'm sorry to disturb you but Gemma had asked me to call you this evening about Tom, but I gather he has been released without charge. Is that right?'

'Yes, it is. Actually, I'm glad you called. I was going to ring you in the morning to call in a favour.'

'Go on,' said Merrin.

'I believe the reason Tom has been behaving so oddly – the drinking, the extreme bad temper – is not directly related to either his father vanishing, nor his mother killed herself, although both must have considerably contributed to his state of mind. Shortly before her death, Sarah changed her will. In the original will, she left the farm to Tom, in its entirety, with a small share for Gemma. Both her children were happy with this as Jago and Gemma are very comfortable financially. However, her new will leaves half the farm to Tom and half to David. Gemma's share is to come out of Tom's half, as things stand, which means that David is the majority shareholder.'

'That's extraordinary,' said Merrin. 'Does that mean Sarah knew David was Philip's son?'

'That's exactly what I thought, initially, but David assures me that he never told Sarah who he was because he knew how much it would upset her.'

'Tom must be devastated because there was talk of him selling up and doing his own thing at last,' said Merrin. 'That won't be so easy if he's only got half a farm to sell. No wonder he's taken to drink, I don't blame him, and, of course, he still doesn't know who David is, so he must be very confused.'

'This is where you come in,' said Louis. 'I have spent the day with David. He wants to return his share of the farm to Tom. He's absolutely insistent on it. I wondered if you could put together the necessary paperwork for him. You can liaise with Tom's solicitor, who has the new will, but apparently he is ancient, so you may have to do most of the work so that David can sign the farm over to Tom.

I'd like to get this done as soon as possible.'

'Why, do you think David might change his mind?' Merrin asked.

'Not a chance,' said Louis. 'I just want to rush it through for Tom's sake.'

'There you are!' said Merrin. 'You really are a nice, kind people person. Email me over the details and I'll be straight on it in the morning. I will need David to instruct me, of course, and I assume, once again, no fees are involved.'

'I'd like you to prepare the paperwork with Tom's solicitor without any contact with David tomorrow. He won't be available all day. On Friday, he will be appearing in Truro Crown Court at ten in the morning. It will be a very short hearing but I'm hoping you can pick him up from the court and take him straight round to Tom's solicitor, who is based in Truro. Just to add to your chores, I was also hoping you might drop him back to collect his car, which is in for service, in Hayle. It's on your way home, but if that's not convenient, Jack can do it.'

'I suppose there is absolutely no point in me asking why he's been summoned to the Crown Court?'

'Absolutely no point, but you could attend the hearing if you wish and then you'll find out. Also, depending on how tomorrow goes, I'll be needing to speak to the family tomorrow evening, before the hearing. If that's the case, I think it would be very helpful if you could be there, too, mainly so you can reassure Tom about his inheritance and possibly help keep the peace.'

'A bit of a tall order. I'm still concerned about taking instructions from you rather than my client. Are you sure I can't see him at all tomorrow?' said Merrin, a little tersely.

'Trust me, you absolutely can't, and when you learn why, you will understand completely,' said Louis. 'As for gifting the farm back to Tom, David won't change his mind. He's desperate to get it done. I'll email over to you details of the Trehearne solicitor and he's expecting to hear from you.'

'Oh, so you were anticipating that I would say "yes" to sorting out this will? That was a little bit presumptuous of you, Chief Inspector!'

'Of course it was, and I apologise, but everything has moved so quickly and, after all, Tom is your brother-in-law,' said Louis.

'Only teasing – of course I'll help,' said Merrin.

'Thank you, I should have known,' said Louis. 'The only possible spanner in the works with these arrangements is the very slight chance that bail will be refused at the hearing. I'm going to recommend it should be granted and David has enough savings to cover security, so I don't envisage a problem – but with these judges, one never knows for sure. Still, I don't have to tell you about that, do I?'

'You certainly don't,' said Merrin. 'Louis, can I ask just one thing to put me out of my misery? If tomorrow and the next day go as you hope they will, could this mean an end to the mystery of what happened to Philip Trehearne?'

'Yes,' said Louis.

'I'm very proud of you,' said Merrin, meaning it.

'Thank you, though it's a bit too soon to claim success. Still, your encouragement means a lot – I'm grateful, truly.'

CHAPTER FORTY-FIVE

Louis had decided he would not join the party travelling up to Dartmoor. There was the paperwork to sort and also he needed to talk to the chief super. He had taken the decision to press ahead with arranging for David to appear at the Crown Court, although they would not have DNA evidence to confirm that the remains were Philip's for at least another week – and that assumed the remains could be found. The Trehearne family was a bubbling cauldron of anger, misery, guilt and sadness. Urgent closure was essential – and David had confessed.

Still, Louis was a bag of nerves. David's desire to protect the Trehearne family potentially made his story less credible in Louis's eyes. He would do anything for them, anything at all – including, perhaps, confessing to a crime he hadn't committed? Was there really a body on Dartmoor, and if there was, would David remember where he'd buried it? In the end, Louis realised, he had to trust his instincts and his instincts told him that David was telling the truth. After all the years of misguidedly trying to protect the family, if David was lying now about what had happened to Philip, it would be unspeakably cruel. The nineteen-year-old boy had locked himself into a lifetime of lies, but the man, faced at last with the need to tell the truth, had to see things differently. Surely, now was not the time to once again hide from reality.

During the cocaine-smuggling case the previous year, Louis had come across a young constable named Ben Satchel. It was Ben who had used his initiative, disobeyed Louis's instructions and, as a result, probably saved a very dangerous situation from developing into a bloodbath. Based in Truro, Louis had arranged to poach him for the day and it was Ben who was driving David and Jack up to Dartmoor. There was no question, in Louis's mind, of David absconding but Ben was a good man in a crisis and the day was likely to be very harrowing. A specialist team from Tavistock were going to meet them, start the dig and hopefully retrieve the body – well, if it was Philip, it would be a skeleton now.

'Gracious, Louis, you look a lot more cheerful than last time we met,' said Sally, as he walked into the chief super's outer office.

'It's because I am feeling cautiously optimistic,' said Louis, 'and how are you today, Sally dear? You look ravishing as ever.'

Sally, who was very much the wrong side of sixty, was never impressed with Louis's regular attempts at flattery, although she adored him. 'Don't be silly, Louis. What is it you want?'

'To see sir, if he's available. I just need a few moments to update him on the Trehearne case.'

'Have you conquered it, then, dear boy?' Sally asked.

'If I have, then it's more by luck than judgement, and in no small measure thanks to you,' Louis said.

'How do you make that out?'

'You straightened my backbone and gave me a stiff lecture when I was being wimpish the other week and suggested asking for photographs – which turned out to be a stroke of genius,' said Louis. 'I love you dearly, Sal, as you know, but I am also more than a little intimidated by you – your sound rollocking did the trick. I am most grateful.'

'It's a tough job but someone has to do it. I'll pop in and see if sir will see you now.'

John Dent was in a good mood, which improved still further having listened to the tale Louis had to tell him. Louis's concern that Dent would disagree with taking David to court before obtaining the DNA evidence proved unfounded. In fact, Dent's view was very positive.

'I am very pleased you managed to keep a lid on Tom Trehearne's outpourings to the media, but if we delay too long in charging David Reed, it might set him off again. We certainly don't want that, just when, mercifully, his mother's suicide has now become yesterday's news.'

Louis managed to hold his tongue, but only just. *These are real people*, he thought, *a family in turmoil but clearly to John Dent, they are just a threat to the reputation of the police force – just something that needs to be stopped.* Once more, the thought of Adam McKenzie flashed into his mind – Adam, he suspected, would have been seething with fury at Dent's reaction. He smiled; yes, Adam would probably not have kept quiet at this moment.

'What are you smiling about, Peppiatt, and with what hideous crimes are you charging David Reed?'

'Sorry, sir, I'm just relieved we can go ahead with taking Reed to court,' said Louis hurriedly. 'The charges against him are manslaughter and perverting the course of justice. Manslaughter might not stick, it was just an accident. However, the deception in hiding the body and concealing the truth over such a lengthy period is very serious indeed, in my view.'

'Yes, yes, but the important thing is we have solved the mystery of Philip Trehearne's vanishing act, and in answer to any criticism of the police handling at the time, I think it fair to say it would have been unlikely that David Reed would have confessed while he was still little more than a boy. And without that confession, Philip's body would never have been found.'

Louis's temper was now barely under control. 'The body hasn't even been found yet, and I'm afraid I don't agree with you, sir. I would have thought a nineteen-year-old, so close to the trauma of seeing his father die in front of him, would have been a very easy nut to crack. By his own admission, he was a shy, timid lad who, I'm sure, would have spilt the beans almost immediately if interviewed. But, of course, he never was.'

'So what are you wanting, Peppiatt, a thank-you for solving the case? In which case, easily done – thank you very much. However, judging by what you've just said, I don't want you involved in any of the press interviews, which will be inevitable after the hearing. Clearly, you still think the police should have done more at the time.'

'Of course they should have done more, sir. Much was made of the exhaustive search, but within twenty-four hours, it should have been obvious that Philip was no longer in the vicinity of the path to Halsetown Inn, either dead or alive. However, looking at the file, it's also obvious that no one did any research into Philip's past, which is where the answer to his disappearance had to lie. An old farmer neighbour of the Trehearnes summed up the situation perfectly. If there was no body to be found, then it was obvious Philip *must have been took*. If he was *took*, then foul play had to be involved because Philip would never have left his family of his own free will. The other day, you rightly reprimanded me for relying too heavily on Haines, our IT expert. Good old-fashioned police work, sir, is what you suggested and, in my view, that is what was lacking in the original investigation. The lack of it meant the Trehearnes have suffered thirty years of uncertainty as a result. We probably have silenced Tom Trehearne but in my view, he still has every right to be very angry. It is a case that should have been solved at the time.'

'Have you quite finished, Peppiatt?' John Dent asked.

'Yes, sir. Quite finished.'

'You're a clever bugger, Peppiatt, and an excellent detective but you are too much of an idealist. We do our best but it often isn't perfect.'

'But surely, sir, that doesn't mean we shouldn't strive for perfection. The law gives very little wriggle room, if applied correctly.'

'Enough, Peppiatt. All this zeal worries me. You have

got this one right, haven't you?'

'Yes, sir,' said Louis, with a confidence he definitely did not feel.

Back in Sally's office, she looked Louis up and down. 'Oh dear,' she said, 'I assume by the sound of raised voices that you're in trouble again, Louis. What have you done this time?'

'I'm in trouble for being right,' mumbled Louis.

'Oh, that old chestnut,' said Sally.

'I forgot to tell sir, because I was too cross, that I am not going to oppose David Reed's application for bail. He's not any sort of danger to the public, he's definitely not going to abscond and he has funds to support his application. I'm going to contact his aunt to see if she will let him stay with her until the trial. Could you relay all that to sir, please.'

'You're taking a great deal of trouble over this man,' said Sally.

'He's guilty as charged and he did a terrible thing but David is also the man who saved Edward when he got lost on the cliff path in a sea mist. Did you hear about that?'

'Yes, of course I heard about it, but I didn't realise it was David who saved him. That must have made arresting him very difficult for you.'

'Not really,' said Louis, 'he confessed without much prompting. I'm sorry for the man and in a different world, he's someone I would have liked.' Louis smiled at Sally. 'And he saved my boy.'

'Off you go then, Louis. You have got this one right, haven't you?'

'That is what sir has just asked, and the truthful answer is – I bloody well hope so.'

CHAPTER FORTY-SIX

Teresa Gilbert had been reduced to watching daytime television. Not every day, but today was particularly tragic as the sun was shining and she knew she should be outside doing something, anything rather than sitting on the sofa gawping at rubbish. She had friends, of course, but now it was the school summer holidays, many of them were off spending time with children and grandchildren. Teresa didn't have any of those. There had been one man in her life since her husband died, but he was a first-class plonker and not even particularly attractive. She had to face the fact that, for the first time in her life, she was lonely. And then her mobile rang.

'Mrs Gilbert,' said a voice she instantly recognised. She was rather taken with Chief Inspector Peppiatt, but she'd had to recognise he would not be interested in someone of her age. A pity, he was a good-looking man, rather buttoned-up, but one felt there were plenty of seething emotions buried deep. It would be a delightful prospect to unleash them.

'Good afternoon, Chief Inspector,' she said, 'and what can I do for you?'

'I've got a great deal to tell you, Teresa. I wish I could come and see you but I just can't find the time at the moment.'

'A handsome man who has lots to tell me and wishes he could come and see me – wow, you've really made my day, Chief Inspector, or can I call you Louis?'

Louis laughed. 'You're the most accomplished flirt I have ever met and therefore a very dangerous woman. And yes, you can call me Louis but I should warn you, I have a very large favour to ask you concerning your missing – now found – nephew.'

Louis unfolded the full story of Nigel Anstey Junior/ David Reed, complete with his involvement in Philip's death and the secret he had kept from Philip's remaining family.

'So, he's in court tomorrow. What exactly have you charged him with, Louis?'

'Manslaughter and perverting the course of justice.'

'Manslaughter seems rather harsh. It was an accident, wasn't it?'

'I am hoping the manslaughter charge will get thrown out, but I think it's better to put it before the court. David's half-brother, Tom, is going to be very angry – he's volatile at the best of times and when he learns he's spent thirty years working every day with a man who has not admitted to being his brother, he'll be furious. But that's nothing compared to how he will react when he discovers that David was involved in the death of his father – God knows how that's going to work out. I think Philip's family will handle the whole thing better if David is charged with manslaughter, even if the court then throws it out. The court obviously carries far more authority than me, or the DPP. The judge taking the decision that no manslaughter charge is justified will be more acceptable to the family, I'm hoping.'

'You're a funny sort of policeman – fancy hoping that the charge you have made against a man you have arrested will get turned down by the court. I understand your thinking – it's interesting and to be applauded, just rather odd.'

'This is not a straightforward case in very many ways, but it's thanks to you and the photographs you sent me that we are where we are, and I'm very grateful.'

'It's somewhat ironic, though, isn't it,' said Teresa, 'that by sending you those photographs, in an attempt to help, I'm now responsible for sending my nephew to prison? He's my only remaining living relative.'

'Well, that's where the big favour comes in. I am going to support David's application for bail and I think he will stand a very good chance of getting it. If he does, he has to be registered at a specific address and will have to report to a local police station every so often. This arrangement is obviously only until he goes for trial but that will be some months ahead. The thing is, Teresa, could he come and stay with you? Obviously, he can't remain on the Trehearnes' farm in the circumstances, and apart from them and you, he has no other living relatives either –

assuming we discount his stepfather. It sounds like he has enough money to pay his way, with food and utilities – maybe even rent.'

There was a very long pause. 'Money's not an issue; I have plenty of that.' There was another pause. 'He's not violent, is he, Louis?'

'Absolutely not, a very gentle soul. Do you honestly think I would suggest such a thing, if I thought it might put you in the slightest danger?'

'He was a very quiet, shy boy, from what I remember,' said Teresa. 'That bloody man, Nigel Anstey, made sure he knocked the self-confidence out of his wife and sons. Why on earth did the silly boy get himself in such a mess?'

'One decision made by a nineteen-year-old in a state of panic. If he'd had supportive parents, he'd probably have had the courage to call the police when Philip died, but all he had was Nigel.'

'Are you suggesting I let him down, Louis?'

'No, of course not, and nor am I trying to put any pressure on you to take him in. This is very much your decision, which I will respect, whatever you decide.'

'How old is he now?' Teresa asked.

'Forty-nine,' said Louis. 'He's never let anyone get close to him since he arrived at the Trehearnes'. He's been kind and helpful within the community, and is much liked and respected locally. However, he has always kept his distance so he has no real friends, nor ever had a partner. I imagine he's been very lonely.'

Louis, of course, did not realise the impact his words had on Teresa. He had played a winning hand, without knowing it.

'Well, it's what Mary would have wanted me to do, and it will be nice to have a man about the house again. If he gets bailed, when can I expect him?'

'Probably tomorrow night, or the following morning. The hearing's at ten o'clock tomorrow morning. I'll let you know what's happened as soon as we're out of court. Thank you so much, Teresa.'

'There is a condition, though, Louis.'

'What's that?' asked Louis, his heart sinking, just when he thought the arrangement was sorted.

'You'll have to come and see us once David has settled in. You will, won't you?'

'Of course I will. Tell me, are you happy to call him David? It's what he's used to and he did change his name officially.'

'Well, I'm not calling him bloody Nigel, that's for sure!'

Louis had only just finished talking to Teresa when his mobile rang. It was the call he had been longing for and also dreading.

It was the reassuring voice of Jack Eddy. 'Boss, we've found him, we've found Philip, just where David said we would!'

'How can you be sure it's Philip?' Louis asked.

'His wedding ring was still on his finger. It's engraved – *Sarah & Philip* – and there's a date, presumably of their wedding day. Ben's asked Colin to check out the date, just to be absolutely sure. But there can be no doubt, boss. We've found him – at last, we've bloody well found him, after all these years!'

Relief flooded through Louis, but at the same time, an

accompanying sense of sadness. He had achieved what he had been asked to do – to find Philip. But at what cost?

'Right, Eddy. I need you to meet me at the station in St Ives as soon as you can, and bring the ring with you. Ask Ben to take David straight back to Camborne. He will need to stay in the cells overnight and I've arranged for a Crown Court hearing tomorrow at ten o'clock. I'd like you to bring him in to Truro by nine-thirty tomorrow morning. Is that all clear? Oh, and ask David to give a DNA sample and get it express couriered over to Graham Bennett.'

'Yes, boss,' said Jack.

'How is David?' Louis asked.

'He's not good. When the team found the skeleton, he completely collapsed and sobbed his eyes out. Ben took him to the car and did his best to calm him down. You can't help feeling sorry for the poor bloke, boss.'

'Yes indeed, though hopefully in the long term he will find some relief in not having to live a lie any longer. Can you tell him, please, that I've arranged for him to stay in Tavistock with his aunt, his mother's sister, Teresa, assuming he is granted bail. I'll give him all the details after the hearing but obviously he can't remain at the Trehearnes' farm.'

'Will do. Boss, will you be needing me tonight? Only Mrs Eddy—'

'Yes, I will, Eddy,' said Louis, cutting Jack short in mid-flow. 'You, I and the wedding ring are going to the Trehearnes' to tell them everything. I'm sure you understand, they now need to be brought fully up to date.'

'Yes, boss,' said Eddy, wondering how Mrs Eddy was

going to react – he had promised to take her to the cinema. He was not going to be popular.

Louis's next call was to Merrin. He'd toyed with the idea of calling Jago but thought it might be difficult to speak to him alone.

'Merrin, we've found Philip's remains up on Dartmoor. It's definitely Philip; we have his wedding ring.'

'On Dartmoor, why there? Poor Philip, so far from home. How did you find him?'

'David showed us where he buried him. Philip's death was an accident in all probability, but David is being charged with manslaughter. I will explain all this evening.'

'Oh, Louis, how awful that it's David who's responsible,' said Merrin. 'God knows Philip needed to be found but I can't help feeling sad that he has. Daft really, because we all knew he had to be dead.'

'I felt exactly the same,' Louis admitted. 'So, I'd like to have that meeting I mentioned at the Trehearnes'. Could you make it at six this evening and could you tell Jago, Gemma and Tom to be there?'

'Yes, of course,' said Merrin. 'I have all the documentation ready for the transfer of David's half of the farm back to Tom, and I have spoken to Tom's solicitor and agreed that David and I will come and see him after the hearing. Assuming you can fix bail, of course.'

'Good, thank you. Remember, the meeting this evening is a particularly delicate because Tom and Gemma still don't know that David is their half-brother. The thing is, Merrin, I still think we should give David the chance to tell Tom and Gemma himself who he is. He may want me to do it, in which case I will tell them tomorrow after the hearing. But this evening, I feel that Tom and Gemma have enough to cope with – their father having been found and David being responsible for the accident – without immediately adding in the whole relationship thing.'

'I understand your thinking but the trouble is the story doesn't ring true,' said Merrin. 'Why would David bury on Dartmoor the body of a stranger he had bumped into on the way to the pub? It makes no sense.'

'I thought I'd say to them that there was a reason David was trying to meet Philip but I would prefer David told them that reason himself.'

'If you think that's the way to deal with it, then I expect you know best,' said Merrin, without much conviction.

'I'm not at all sure I do, but I'm overwhelmed by your faith in me,' said Louis. 'Let's play it by ear and see how hard they press me. Just make sure Jago knows I may not tell them about the relationship this evening.'

'Yes, boss, as Jack would say,' said Merrin.

CHAPTER FORTY-SEVEN

The six of them gathered round the kitchen table at Trehearne Farm. There was no small talk, no suggestion of tea or coffee. Just a tense silence, while everyone looked expectantly at Louis. For a second, it flashed through Louis's mind that this was like a Hercule Poirot moment but Monsieur Poirot was always triumphant when he had solved his case – Louis just felt sad.

He took a deep breath. 'Gemma, Tom, this afternoon we found the remains of your father, Philip. He had been buried up on Dartmoor. He is now in transit to Truro, to our pathologist, Dr Graham Bennett. I am very sorry.'

Gemma gasped and clutched Jago, who put an arm round her and held her close. Tom remained stony-faced but he trembled as he spoke.

'How do you know it's Dad?' he asked.

Louis drew out of his pocket the evidence bag that

contained Philip's wedding ring. 'We found this on the body.' He carefully withdrew the ring from the bag and handed it to Tom.

Tom looked at the ring and read out loud the inscription *Sarah & Philip*.

'Can I see?' Gemma asked. Tom silently passed the ring to his sister. She began to cry quietly, and, looking at Tom, Louis could see he, too, was fighting back tears.

'Mum's ring had the same inscription, her ring was just a little narrower. We buried it with her,' Gemma said. 'So, you really have found him, at last?'

Louis nodded but remained silent. He knew the questions would come in a moment but he wanted to give brother and sister time to absorb the news.

Strangely, after a while, it was Gemma who started asking the questions. Tom just sat – silent, shocked and tearful, so very out of character.

'How did he end up on Dartmoor? Who did this? Who killed him?'

'We have a man in custody who will be appearing in court tomorrow charged with your father's manslaughter and for perverting the course of justice. He has pleaded guilty.'

'It's David, isn't it?' said Gemma. 'He dashed off yesterday as soon as he heard Tom had been arrested and we haven't seen him since.'

'Yes, it is David Reed,' Louis confirmed.

'Are you sure you've got the right man this time, Chief Inspector?' said Gemma. 'After all, it was only yesterday that you thought Tom had murdered his father.'

'No one murdered your father, it was a tragic accident,

we believe, although Dr Bennett will be able to tell us more once the post-mortem has been completed. I am very sorry about yesterday, Tom, but you had no alibi and then the change of will made me suspicious.'

'What change of will?' Gemma said.

Louis looked at Merrin, who gave him a brief nod. 'Gemma,' she said, 'your mother changed her will just before she died and left only half the farm to Tom and the other half to David.'

'Why didn't you tell me about this, Tom?' demanded Gemma. 'Is this why you've been so odd and drinking too much? This is our family home; surely I had a right to know. And why on earth did she change the will when we'd all agreed it? What did you do to upset Mum?'

'Nothing,' said Tom. 'I have no idea why she changed her will.'

'Tom, Gemma, it's all academic anyway,' said Merrin hurriedly. 'I have been requested to draw up papers that will ensure David's half of the farm is returned to you, Tom. I am going to see your solicitor tomorrow and set in motion the rescinding of the new will. This is David's wish, so the will is one thing you don't have to worry about any more. The farm will be yours, with the small legacy for Gemma.'

More silence.

'It can't have been David who was involved in Dad's death,' burst out Gemma suddenly. 'He didn't come to Cornwall until weeks after Dad disappeared. You've got it wrong again, Chief Inspector.'

'He was in Cornwall, on the path from Halsetown Inn on the evening your father vanished,' said Louis firmly.

'What happened was an accident, but he was there. Your father fell and cracked his head. David said he died instantly, which means he would have felt no pain. We'll know more in a day or so when Dr Bennett produces his report.'

'I've just remembered, David grew up on the edge of Dartmoor,' said Tom, 'which, I suppose, explains why poor Dad ended up there. But if it was an accident, why didn't he tell the police, not bury poor Dad in some godforsaken place?' Suddenly, the old Tom was back. 'And why on earth didn't David tell us what he'd done to Dad?' he raged. 'All those years he worked and lived alongside us, watched us grieve – particularly Mum – about the lack of closure, the not-knowing, the awfulness of that. The man's a monster, he has to be. How could he just watch us suffer and say nothing?'

'He has a reason,' said Louis. 'It's not an excuse for his behaviour, he knows that, but it is a reason. If you can both bear to see him again, then I think it might be best if he told you himself. It's a very personal matter, a secret he's told no one until now. If you don't want to see him and/or he can't bring himself to tell you his secret in person, then I will do so after the hearing tomorrow. Just think about it overnight and decide what you want to do.'

'I want to know about it now, this so-called secret,' said Tom. 'I never want to see the bastard again. I hope he goes to prison for a long time and rots in hell. He didn't just work for us, I thought he was a friend – no, I thought of him as part of the family.'

At that moment, Louis did not dare look at either Jago or Merrin. The temptation to say to Tom – *that's the so-*

299

called secret, he is *part of the family* – was overwhelming. He resisted.

'I would like to hear what he has to say, I'd like him to tell us himself,' said Gemma. 'I agree with you, Tom, not telling us what had happened to Dad is unforgivable. But he's unconditionally supported our family over decades; I thought he really loved us. I want to hear from him in person as to how he could have done such a terrible thing to our family, when he appeared to care for us so much.'

'I agree with Gemma,' said Jago. 'Why not sleep on it and decide in the morning what you both want to do. What's your view, Louis?'

'I don't believe it's my secret to tell, but I will do so after the hearing tomorrow, if you both so wish. Otherwise we can arrange a meeting with David.'

Louis left immediately, wanting to get away before any more questions were asked. Merrin offered to drive him back to St Ives. Jack stayed behind to take DNA swabs from both Tom and Gemma, so he offered to drive Louis's car back to St Ives.

It was a beautiful evening in St Ives, as Louis and Merrin walked down to Miranda's Cottage. The sun was now low in the sky, sending a path of golden light across the water. The harbour was already a mass of lights, not only on the wharf but also from a number of small yachts now moored in the harbour. The serious eating and drinking of the evening had not yet started in earnest, so the waterfront was still tranquil, calm and quite, quite lovely.

'What a contrast to all that unhappiness,' said Louis, stopping to gaze across the harbour. It was high tide, and the sound of the waves gently lapping up the slipway was oddly soothing.

'Come in,' said Merrin, starting to climb up the steps to her cottage. Louis followed her, to be met by a rapturous greeting from William and much exploding of bombs from Horatio.

'What a splendid reception,' said Louis. 'Do you get this "return of the conquering hero" routine every time you come home?'

'Pretty much,' said Merrin.

'Lucky you.'

'It staves off the loneliness.' Merrin hesitated. 'Sorry, it was my intention to cheer you up, not add to this evening's miseries.' She looked him up and down. 'You need a large drink, in fact several. I also bet you haven't eaten properly today. I can only offer you chicken curry and wine and before you say you can't drink and drive, I have an idea. How about you go mad and get a taxi back to Truro tonight? Then Jack can bring your car over to Truro in the morning for the hearing, and I can drive Jack back, and hopefully David too. Now, tell me, if you dare, that my idea isn't a first-class one?' She plucked a bottle of white wine from the fridge and a red from the wine rack and waved them at him. 'Red or white or both?' she asked.

'You remind me of your daughter, who is possessed of some very forceful arguments, which are impossible to resist,' said Louis, smiling. 'Alright, I give in, thank you, although my Presbyterian father would not have approved of squandering money on a taxi. I'll just call Jack and explain the plan.'

CHAPTER FORTY-EIGHT

Having made his call to Jack, sitting on the stone steps outside Merrin's cottage, Louis appeared back at the front door, already looking less stressed and tired.

'All well?' Merrin asked.

'Yes, on two counts, no, three really. Jack was in deep trouble with Mrs Eddy, apparently, as he was supposed to be taking her to the cinema tonight. Anyway, he has been forgiven as he's managed to book a table at Porthmeor Beach Café. A smart move, I think. He's picking up David from Camborne tomorrow in my car to be in court by nine-thirty. Also, and this really is good news, neither Tom nor Gemma want to attend the hearing tomorrow. I was worried Tom's presence might prove disruptive, but that clever brother of yours has managed to talk them out of it, according to Eddy.'

'Jago has his uses,' said Merrin. 'I have an idea. The

chicken curry is in the oven and William needs a walk. So I have packed a bottle of white wine and some cheese straws and I thought we could have an aperitif on the beach. It's such a beautiful evening. What do you think?'

'The only possible answer is yes please, it's a wonderful idea.'

They walked up to the island and then doubled back across Porthgwidden Beach. As they turned the corner by Smeaton's Pier, Merrin pointed to some tiny stone steps, leading down on to the harbour beach.

'Come down here,' she said to Louis. 'It's very sheltered and there's a nice piece of wall to sit back against.'

Louis opened the wine and they raised their glasses to one another. 'I just can't think of an appropriate toast in all the circumstances,' he said.

'How about to Philip and Sarah? May they now truly rest in peace.'

'Philip and Sarah,' they said solemnly.

Merrin passed the cheese straws, after a few minutes Louis topped up their glasses and they sat in companiable silence, gazing out across the harbour, both lost in thought.

'This is a perfect little spot for evening drinks,' said Louis, at last. 'I suppose it's mostly used by the locals – particularly when the tide's in like this, you would expect it to be under water, if you didn't know better.'

'Yes,' said Merrin, 'it's called Kitty's Corner.'

'Really?' said Louis. 'We're sitting in Kitty's Corner, how strange. Tom spent the evening here instead of going to the cinema with the Pascoes. He met up with a girl and they sat here drinking wine while David was meeting Philip on the path to Halsetown. The girl was a visitor;

Tom only met her that once, which meant she couldn't provide an alibi.'

'It is very sad to think Tom left here not knowing that his world had changed for ever,' said Merrin. 'It stuck me this evening, when you were explaining everything to the Trehearnes, that there is no happy ending for anyone. Yes, Tom and Gemma will know all there is to know about how their father met his end. That's helpful but they now have to cope with the knowledge of David's betrayal and ultimately to learn that Philip had a serious affair in college, while their mother was waiting for him at home. David, meanwhile, no longer has to live a lie but he will probably have to cope with prison. As I say, no one wins.'

'Exactly,' said Louis. 'That's what I've been wrestling with – have my findings made things worse?'

'You did your best, you achieved what you had been asked to do. There is no point beating yourself up about it. Look, enough of the Trehearnes for now, the idea of this evening was to cheer you up.' Merrin tossed back her glass and held it out for more. 'Tell me about your Presbyterian father who wouldn't have approved of taxis; in fact, tell me all about your family.'

'It's not very exciting, I'm afraid,' said Louis. 'My family was very conventional. My father, Charles, was an accountant and my mother, Catherine, was a primary school teacher. We lived in a cottage on the outskirts of Plymouth, the Devon side. I was an only child, though I wasn't supposed to be. My mother died in childbirth when I was seven. The baby died too, he was another boy.'

'Oh, Louis, how sad, I'm so sorry. Do you remember your mother?'

'Yes, of course,' said Louis. 'I remember everything, her life and her death.' Somehow, from the way he spoke, it was clear he did not want to discuss any details of what happened to his mother.

Merrin immediately picked up his reluctance. 'Seven, poor little boy, that's an awful age to lose your mother,' she said. 'Did your father remarry?'

'No, Dad tried to build some sort of domestic life after Mum died but it didn't work, so I was sent off to boarding school, which, to be fair, I mostly enjoyed. It would be wrong to say that Dad was embittered, but losing Mum knocked the stuffing out of him. He was always a quiet man, Mum was the outgoing one, but, after my mother's death, his life was, well, it seemed to me like he was simply marking time. He spent his whole life working for the same firm of accountants, and after he retired, he sort of faded away. I saw him as often as I could but I don't think I was a very good son. He was so difficult to reach, he seemed unable to express any sort of emotion. He died at only seventy-four, allegedly of a heart attack, but I've always felt that his cause of death was more the result of his lack of interest in staying alive.'

'What happened to you after school; did you go to university?' Merrin asked.

Louis shook his head. 'No, I joined the army at eighteen and was de-mobbed at twenty-four. My army career began, I think, as an excuse for not being at home but I did benefit from the experience. I think it was also good for me because it gave me a sense of belonging. In the army, you're part of a family, a rough and tough one, but a family nonetheless. I joined the police force as soon as I left the army and I was first stationed at Newton Abbot. Dad had died by then and very shortly after joining the police, I met Stephanie. She wanted to settle in Falmouth, she'd been at art college there, so I transferred to Truro.' Louis smiled at Merrin. 'There you have it, that's my life story.'

'You must miss not living as part of a family,' said Merrin gently.

'Yes, of course,' Louis agreed. 'But Steph and I did have a good divorce, if that doesn't sound too mad a thing to say. We're friends, we don't fight over the children, she's happily remarried and the children are fond of Andrew. It's not ideal, of course, but we've all come out of it pretty well, I think.'

'But for the fact you're alone,' Merrin persisted.

'Says the woman who relies on a very strange-looking dog and a crazy parrot to stop her feeling lonely. Come on, I'll pull you up. Do you think the curry will be ready? I must admit I'm starving.'

'So,' said Louis, once the meal was on the table. 'Tell me about the Tripconeys – a great name, by the way.'

'Our dad, Harry Tripconey, was a real character. He was a fisherman, crabs and lobsters mainly, but all year round he could always find a catch. He came from a long line of fishermen, there was nothing he didn't know about this coastline. He was a happy man, loved his family, loved a pint and was a Cornishman through and through. Mum had a very different start in life. She came from The Potteries, you know, Stoke-on-Trent. Her mother worked for Wedgwood as an illuminator and Mum inherited her talent, she was very artistic. Mum was an only child and when she was thirteen, her father was killed in a car crash. Her mum, my grandmother, remarried, very quickly, an unpleasant man who did a lot of shouting and was fairly handy with his fists as well. He really disliked Mum, it sounds as if he was jealous of her relationship with my grandmother. When her dad was still alive, one year he had taken the family to Cornwall, to St Ives, for a holiday. Mum had adored it so when she was sixteen, she ran away to Cornwall. She got a job in service at a big house in St Erth. They treated her well and when she was nineteen she met Dad in St Ives on her day off. It was love at first sight and they married shortly after her twentieth birthday. She never had a proper full-time job. She helped out crimping pasties, vegetable prep in restaurants and, later, serving behind the bar in the Sloop. But her main interest in life was her family. Jago and I were very lucky. But in a different age and, maybe, a different part of the country, she could've had a career. She was a clever woman. Still, she loved her family.'

'She sounds lovely,' said Louis.

'She was, and she was very well read. After the chores were done, you would always find her with her head in a book. She even quoted Shakespeare at my dad's funeral.'

'Well,' said Louis, 'this explains a lot. We have Celtic blood in common. The Peppiatts were Huguenots from Brittany originally and the Cornish are Celts, of course. Maybe that's why we've had one or two rather fiery disagreements.'

'No, being Celts has nothing to do with it. Our disagreements only occur when you won't acknowledge that I'm right, Chief Inspector!' said Merrin, with a grin.

CHAPTER FORTY-NINE

The hearing was brief and the results as expected. David pleaded guilty on both counts but he was granted bail as the prosecution raised no objection. Louis outlined the plans for David to live with his aunt until the trial, which was deemed satisfactory.

Once outside, Louis suggested that Merrin and David should join him and Jack for a coffee at the Wig & Pen before they went to see Tom's solicitor. While Jack was fetching the coffees, Louis took David on one side.

'Have you decided yet whether you are going to tell Tom and Gemma of your relationship to them, or do you want me to do it?' he asked.

'Do we have to tell them at all?' said David.

'Yes, of course we do. You owe them an explanation. At the moment, they know the details of your meeting with Philip and that you buried his body on Dartmoor, but it makes no sense to them, nor would it to anyone. Why would you hide the body of a complete stranger who died accidentally?'

'I'm so ashamed and they'll hate the idea of being related to someone like me,' said David. 'Also, it will mean they'll have to know Philip had an affair with my mother while he was at college. It will taint their view of their parents' relationship.'

'David, your relationship to Philip is going to come out during the trial. You've misled the family all these years. Do you really want them to find out the truth, either in court if they choose to attend, or in some bloody newspaper? That really would be a betrayal.'

'I hadn't realised it would come out in court,' said David.

'Oh, for God's sake, what planet are you on? It will be pivotal in trying to persuade the judge to throw out the manslaughter charge. You had been longing to meet your birth father for years, you meet him, and yes, he thought, initially, you were some sort of nutter. You put out an arm to stop him moving off, so you could explain to him who you really were, and he slipped and fell. But you didn't want him dead, you very much wanted him alive because he was your father. Of course it will come out in court, and, incidentally, you need to sort yourself out a good solicitor. Your aunt is very worldly-wise, I'm sure she will be able to help you there.'

'If they have to know then would you tell them for me, please,' said David.

'It's the wrong decision, David,' said Louis.

'I can't do it. If they must know, then it has to be you who tells them.'

After coffee, they all walked round to Merrin's car and while David climbed into the passenger seat, Louis spoke to Merrin.

'David insists that I tell Tom and Gemma who he really is,' Louis said. 'So, I'll take Jack back to St Ives now and then go on to Trehearne Farm. David already has the details of his aunt's address and I will call her when I get to the station and tell her David will be on his way shortly, once he's picked up his car.'

'Maybe it's just as well he won't be doing the deed himself. Tom is going to be beyond furious,' Merrin suggested.

'Maybe you're right,' said Louis. 'By the way, thank you for dinner last night, you definitely saved me from myself. At home, it would have been the terrible combination of whisky, baked beans on toast and a double helping of self-doubt.'

'I hope you're not imagining I am flattered to know I was an improvement on that lot!' said Merrin, smiling.

When Merrin and David reached the garage, there was a great deal of grumbling. David's car had been in for an MOT, as a result of which he needed two new tyres. However, not surprisingly, the garage had been unable to get hold of him and so had not obtained permission to carry out the work. After much haggling, it was agreed that they would fit the tyres within half an hour, after Merrin explained that David had to travel up to Devon that afternoon.

They returned to Merrin's car.

'Not having my mobile reminds me that I haven't got

any of my things, it's all at the barn – my clothes, my laptop, everything. Could we go there now and collect a few bits? Then maybe at a later date I can arrange to clear it completely.'

'I don't want us to run into the Trehearnes, particularly Tom,' said Merrin. 'I think we really ought to ask Louis first.'

'My barn's right at the end of the lane, near the main road. No one will be down there to see us.' David glanced at his watch. 'They'll be having lunch now, anyway, and I'll be really quick.'

'I suppose it makes more sense than sitting here waiting for the tyres to be changed. But please don't hang about, I don't want any trouble.'

Merrin turned the car round, and they headed off to Trehearne Farm. After a few minutes, Merrin said, 'Louis told me that you feel you can't speak to Tom and Gemma about who you really are. That's awfully sad, David. To me, it seems like it would be the first stage towards facing the future. Obviously, they will be very angry, initially, but in time they are much more likely to understand if *you* explained, rather than be told by Louis. Forgive me, but it comes across as rather cowardly.'

'Of course it's cowardly. I am a coward, I always have been. I just can't face them, and that's an end to it. Please don't mention it again.'

Merrin pulled off the lane in front of David's barn and turned the car round ready to leave. 'Be really quick,' she urged. She sat in the car as the minutes ticked by, feeling increasingly nervous. Then, in her rear-view mirror, she saw a tractor coming down the lane towards them. The tractor came to a grinding halt. The cab door opened and out climbed Tom Trehearne.

'Merrin, what on earth are you doing here?' Before she could answer, she saw from Tom's expression that he was beginning to understand exactly why she was there. 'You've brought David here, haven't you, hoping to slip in when no one would notice?'

As if on cue, David emerged from the front door, carrying a suitcase and a backpack. Tom ran round the front of Merrin's car and, on reaching David, first punched him in the stomach and, as he doubled up, hit him again in the face. 'That's just for starters for killing my father,' he shouted.

David, with his hands full, was unable to defend himself and fell to the ground. Tom kicked him viciously in the side. 'Get up, you bastard,' Tom screamed, kicking David once again.

Merrin jumped out of her car, ran up to Tom and tried to drag him away. He turned and pushed her aside. 'Stay out of this, it's nothing to do with you.' Merrin tried to grab him again but he hurled her backwards so hard that she was slammed against her car, hitting her head on the wing mirror as she went down.

Louis Peppiatt turned into the lane leading up to Trehearne Farm. He'd only driven a few yards, when his way was blocked by a tractor. Annoyed, he got out of his car. The scene before him took a moment for him to understand. Merrin was slumped against her car, there was blood on her face but she was trying to sit up. David was lying outside the front door of his barn, making no attempt to move while Tom kicked, punched and screamed at him.

'Tom, stop that right now,' Louis shouted.

Tom turned as Louis advanced towards him. 'Why should I? He killed my father, he deserves everything he gets and he won't even stand up and fight me like a man.'

Tom turned back to David. 'Come on, stand up and show us what you did to my father. Try throwing a punch at me and let's see how you get on.'

'I can't hit you, Tom,' said David; his speech was slurred as blood poured from his mouth and nose.

'Why not?' Tom demanded.

'Because you're my brother,' said David.

CHAPTER FIFTY

In the end, it was Louis who told Tom and Gemma the full story of Philip and Mary and their son – who would one day be known as David Reed.

An ambulance had been called for David, who had a broken nose, broken ribs, broken front teeth and possible concussion. Louis and the paramedics tried to persuade Merrin to go in the ambulance as well, just for a check-up, but she refused. It was only a superficial head wound, she insisted, and apart from the odd bruise, she maintained she felt absolutely fine.

As he was being loaded into the ambulance, David managed to call out to Louis. 'I won't be pressing charges, Chief Inspector, please let the matter drop.'

'Nor will I,' said Merrin, standing beside Louis. 'It was just a minor domestic.'

'It doesn't look very minor from where I'm standing,'

said Louis, looking at the wreckage that was David.

'Please,' pleaded David, as the ambulance doors closed.

'He's right, Louis. Bringing charges against Tom really won't help – in fact quite the reverse.' Merrin smiled at him. 'In any case, David and I will deny everything. I'll say, of course, that I walked into a door, and David . . .' She hesitated. 'He will say he walked into about a dozen doors, barn doors at that.'

Tom drove the tractor into a field to get it out of the way. Then he joined Merrin in Louis's car for the short drive to the farmhouse. 'I'm sorry I hurt you, Merrin,' he said. 'The red mist came down and I totally lost control – no excuse, though.'

'Absolutely no excuse,' said Louis. 'Unfortunately, neither David nor Merrin want to press charges. If I'd had my way, you'd be in the cells by now. David's injuries are quite sufficient for a charge of GBH, and throwing a woman around beggars belief.'

'Point taken,' said Tom quietly.

'I should bloody well hope so,' said Louis.

When they all arrived back at the farmhouse, there were gasps at the sight of Merrin, with blood running down the side of her face.

Jago hurtled round the table and took her hand. 'Darling sis, what on earth has happened? Come and sit down; should we take you to a doctor, or hospital maybe?'

Merrin smiled down at her brother. 'Don't fuss, it looks much worse than it is. I ought to go and clean myself up a bit.'

Gemma was beside her now. 'Sit down and let me bathe your wound. I'll fetch some cotton wool and disinfectant and then we can see how bad it is. Still, if it's your head, maybe Jago is right and we should take you to hospital. How did you do it? Did you fall over?'

There was a lengthy silence. 'It was my fault,' said Tom. 'I lost my temper with David, Merrin tried to stop me and I pushed her away. She caught her head as she fell down.'

'Where's David, then?' Jago asked, looking at Louis.

'He's in an ambulance on the way to Treliske,' said Louis. 'He's been very badly beaten, he has some serious injuries, not life-threatening, I hope, though his head has taken quite a lot of punishment. He'll need a scan, I imagine. It was lucky Merrin was there and I turned up, or the situation could have been much worse. I'll put the kettle on and I suggest everyone sits down, including you, Tom.'

There was a tense silence in the room, while Gemma began bathing the cut on Merrin's head and Louis busied himself making tea. Jago wheeled up beside him with a bottle of brandy. 'Put a drop in Merrin's mug,' he suggested.

'The bleeding's stopped,' Gemma said. 'I'll just put a dressing on the cut. It's a nasty one. Tom, how could you do this to Merrin? Of course, I understand how angry and how betrayed you feel about David but putting him in hospital isn't going to help, is it? I expect you'll end up with a criminal record and serve you right.'

'Neither David nor Merrin are going to press charges,' said Louis, in his frustration rather over-vigorously stirring the teabags in the pot. 'Though they should do.'

'Why?' yelled Tom, standing up again and starting to stride around the room. Involuntarily, Merrin flinched as he walked past her. 'He killed our father and now he says he's related to us. Can you believe that? He says he's my brother, so yours too, Gemma, I assume. The man's off his head. Just because he's lived with us for most of our lives, it doesn't mean we're related.'

'Sit down, Tom; you're frightening Merrin, and small wonder,' thundered Louis. Tom did as he was told. 'David has made some very serious mistakes in his life, but he is not mistaken about the fact you are related. He is your half-brother.'

Louis passed round the tea and sat down himself. He then told the story of how David came to Cornwall to find his father and ended up by accidentally killing him. He told them about Philip and Mary, Nigel Anstey and David's poor dead brother, Benjamin. And about an aunt, who Louis was careful not to name, and who David would live with until the trial, once he was out of hospital.

When he'd given them all the facts, he finished by saying, 'I truly believe that Philip's death was a tragic accident. However, what David did next was terribly wrong. Of course, he should have called the police instead of hiding the body. And even if he had, in a panic, buried your father on Dartmoor, once he joined you at the farm, he should have told you what he'd done – particularly when he could see for himself what the lack of closure was doing to your family, particularly Sarah. He kept quiet, not because he didn't care; he kept quiet because his life to date had not equipped him to deal with expressing emotion.' Louis looked directly at Tom. 'But however much damage he did to your family, your sister is right. David did a dreadful thing but beating him to a pulp doesn't help anyone.'

A strange calm seemed to settle over the assembled group, for which Louis was extremely grateful. It was odd, almost as if he had told them something that, subconsciously, they already knew and, at the end of his narrative, their comments seemed to confirm this.

'He looks a lot like Dad, now I think about it,' said Gemma. 'Same floppy hair, same walk and the way he tilts his head when he's listening to you. And, of course, the way the animals respond to him, they all love him, just like they loved Dad.'

'It explains why I was always jealous of him,' said Tom, 'without knowing why.'

Questions, of course, were inevitable. 'Why did Dad come back to Mum, leaving poor Mary pregnant?' asked Gemma.

'Your dad never knew Mary was pregnant. I know this because a close relative of Mary's told me, and I trust the information because they were quite close. As to why he came back to your mum, I don't know but I suspect it was because she was his first love and that the affair with Mary was no more than a college fling.'

Louis had already decided that this was the correct answer to the inevitable question. Teresa's view that Philip came home to ensure he inherited the farm was something Louis intended to keep to himself.

Louis then excused himself and telephoned Teresa to tell her what had happened. 'So, he won't be with you for a few days, I imagine,' said Louis, 'and if he can't drive, my sergeant can bring him up to you.'

'This Tom,' said Teresa. 'Is he under control now? I don't want him coming here and smashing up the furniture.'

'The crisis is past, I'm sure of it,' said Louis. 'He also won't be told of your whereabouts or your name.'

'I'll hold you to that, Chief Inspector. Still, at least the delay gives me a few more days to get David's room ready,' said Teresa.

To Louis, this seemed a promising sign that David would be made welcome by his aunt. Any plus point in this sorry tale, he clung to, he thought as he returned to the kitchen. The atmosphere was still calm, though much discussion was in progress.

'Tom and I have decided we should go and see David while he is still in hospital and Tom is going to apologise for hurting him so badly,' said Gemma. 'His injuries do sound dreadful.'

'That sounds a good idea in theory,' said Louis cautiously, 'but I think you should leave it until David is out of hospital and on the mend, and even then I'm not sure it's a sensible plan. You need time to calm down, Tom, absorb what has happened and put everything in perspective.'

'I'm never going to calm down,' said Tom. 'David was responsible for my father's death and he kept the secret of what had happened to Dad for over thirty years, leaving our family in a state of limbo – a state of limbo that caused my mother to kill herself. Gemma and I lost both our parents because of David – I will never acknowledge him as a brother of mine. I will make my apologies for my violence towards him, only because my sister wants me to. After that, I never want to see or hear from him again. I hurt him today, he has been hurting us for decades. He will get better, we never will.'

'I'm not going to argue with that assessment, Tom, but it confirms that you should not go and see him yet, if ever. David did do a terrible thing but it may help you long-term to try and remember all the good things he did to help the family over the years.'

'There is nothing he could possibly have done for us that could begin to compensate for the lie he lived,' said Tom.

'I've just been thinking,' said Gemma suddenly. 'Did Mum leave half the farm to David because she found out who he was?'

'No,' said Louis hurriedly. 'David never told her because he was very fond of your mother and didn't want her to know about Mary, fearing it would hurt her a great deal.'

'Yeah,' said Tom. 'He was so fond of Mum that he was able to watch her suffering for decades when he could have told her the truth and eased her pain. Very touching. In any event, I don't believe him. Gemma, how long ago did David have that accident with the bull?'

'About two weeks before Mum died. Why?' Gemma asked.

'Because, if you remember, David had to stay in the farmhouse for a few days because he had concussion and Mum had to wake him up a couple of times during the night to make sure he was OK. They spent a lot of time together while he was recuperating and I bet that's when he told her who he really was. That's why she suddenly changed her will and gave half the farm to him, and that's why she killed herself.'

'Tom, I sincerely believe David was speaking the truth when he said he had told your mother nothing about his background,' said Louis.

'And of course we all believe him,' said Tom sarcastically. 'This man who always tells the truth. I don't know how you dare suggest that we should believe anything that David says.'

'I do understand how you feel and with tensions running so high at the moment, I'm going to instruct the hospital to allow no visitors. I think it's for the best.'

'He's right, Tom, we're not ready to see David,' said Gemma.

'Coming back to the will,' said Merrin hurriedly, in an effort to change the subject. 'As promised, David and I visited your solicitor today and David has gifted back his half of the farm to you, Tom.'

'Did you manage to keep my solicitor awake?' Tom asked.

'Only just,' said Merrin, and, miraculously, they managed to exchange a tentative half smile.

'I'm going to leave you now,' said Louis. 'I believe you have David's mobile here. Could I take it with me, please? Also, I'm going to run Merrin home. We'll leave her car where it is overnight and I'll arrange for it to be collected in the morning.'

'I'm fine to drive,' said Merrin.

'No, you're not,' said both Louis and Jago.

'Just one thing I'd like to say to you, Tom, while Merrin is still here,' said Jago. 'If you ever hurt my sister again, what you did to David will be nothing compared with what I will do to you.'

Merrin and Louis sat in silence in his car for a moment or two. 'So much for happy families,' said Merrin. 'That was so unlike Jago. He's such a kind, gentle soul, I just can't believe those words came out of his mouth.'

'The trouble is,' said Louis, 'violence begets violence. Come on, I'll take you home. I bet that head is hurting?'

'It is a bit,' Merrin admitted. 'Actually, I'm fairly sore all over but nothing a hot bath won't sort out. It's one of the hazards of getting older – not much suspension left, I don't bounce any more.'

'In his defence, I have to admit that if I was your brother, I would feel much the same as Jago does,' said Louis.

'And as my friend, how do you feel?' asked Merrin.

'Much the same as Jago does,' said Louis, with a smile.

CHAPTER FIFTY-ONE

It was three weeks before Philip's remains were officially released for burial, but in the meantime, Dr Graham Bennett, in his usual grumpy way, had been able to provide Louis with all the information he needed. The DNA results confirmed that Tom, Gemma and David were all related to Philip and, therefore, to each other. Philip's dental records confirmed identification, and Graham was satisfied that there were no other obvious signs of injury, other than a fractured skull. However, he did have one interesting piece of information.

'Philip Trehearne had an egg-shell skull. It explains why, during the search, the dogs picked up no trace of him on the rock where he fell. There would have been no blood,' he said. 'Would you like me to explain that to you?'

'No thank you, Graham,' said Louis, 'I know what an egg-shell skull is.'

'Bloody know-all, aren't you, Peppiatt?'

'In my defence, I've had to deal with quite a number of fractured skulls in my time. What I do know is that, although it meant that Philip's skull was damaged more easily than most because of its fragile nature, it doesn't help David Reed in any way. It is his actions that he will be judged on, not the state of Philip's skull.'

'In most circumstances I would agree with you, but maybe not so much in this case,' said Graham.

'Go on then, amaze me,' said Louis.

'Well, let's take an ordinary bloke like you, with a thick skull, which I'm sure you have, Peppiatt. If Reed had simply put out an arm to stop you going forward and you had tripped and fallen, I would not expect you to be dead, maybe not even concussed. To polish you off, Peppiatt, I think someone would have had to knock you down fairly hard onto that rock in order to fracture your skull. The prisons must be full of people who would be delighted to do that, I'm sure.'

'Which means what?' Louis asked.

'Oh, for heaven's sake, Chief Inspector, keep up. It means that when I go into the witness box, I can say that the victim had an egg-shell skull, which suggests that he did not need to be pushed or thumped in any way in order to sustain the facture that killed him. In other words, Reed's account is plausible. Understood, or would you like me to write it down for you – can you manage to cope with joined-up writing?'

Used to his ways, Louis ignored him. 'That's very helpful, Graham. I'm hoping the judge will throw out the manslaughter charge.'

'You are a very peculiar policeman, Peppiatt. You go to all the trouble of charging the poor bastard with various crimes, march him into court and then sound positively thrilled that at least one of the charges may be dropped. It's not normal behaviour. Have you thought of seeing someone? I have some good contacts in the psych world.'

'It's a complicated case with many shades of grey,' said Louis lamely, 'though I must admit, you're not the first person to make the same observation.'

'I suppose it wouldn't be anything to do with the fact that Reed rescued your lad off the coastal path, would it?' said Graham, with a sly grin.

'How on earth did you hear about that?' Louis asked.

'I may spend most of my days trying to persuade the dead to talk to me – a fairly thankless task, I can tell you – but I admit to being a slave when it comes to gossip, and you are regularly in the headlines so far as our small crime community is concerned. Is your lad alright?'

'My boy's fine, thank you. Obviously, I'm very grateful to David for finding Edward but, truly, that's not what influences me. The fact is, David Reed is a nice chap, a decent, kind person, who was dealt a pretty miserable hand so far as his early life was concerned. He made a terrible mistake and he's been paying for it through decades. I suppose I feel sorry for him.'

'Dear me, you're going soft, Peppiatt. You'd better get out on the streets again and start kicking a few thugs about before dragging them away in handcuffs.'

The day after the hearing, Louis sat down at his kitchen table and made three phone calls, two of which were not strictly necessary but, nonetheless, he felt they were important.

The first was to Annie Pascoe.

Annie answered her phone almost immediately, as if she was waiting for the call, which she probably was, Louis thought.

'Annie, it's Louis Peppiatt here. I don't know how much has reached you on the St Ives jungle drums but Tom was not involved in any way with his father's disappearance.'

'I know he was arrested and then released and that now you've charged David Reed. It's very hard to believe David was involved but I'm so relieved that Tom is off the hook. Did you . . .' She hesitated. 'Did you tell him how you knew he didn't go to the cinema that night?'

'That was one of the main reasons for calling you, Annie. I didn't have to tell Tom anything. I was going to explain to him that I couldn't reveal my source, but I didn't even have to do that. He never asked.'

'Oh, Chief Inspector, I am so grateful, thank you very, very much. So he won't ever know it was me?'

'Not unless you decide to tell him yourself and there's no reason why you should,' said Louis.

'Thank you so much for calling and thank you for everything.'

Annie started to cry as he ended the call. *That poor girl is still in love with Tom*, he thought.

His second call was to Donald Coleman.

'Hi, Don, it's Louis, Louis Peppiatt.'

'Louis! How's it going? Have you solved your mystery and is the villain safely behind bars?'

'Sort of,' said Louis. 'We've found Philip Trehearne's

remains. Sadly, his son, the son he had with Mary, was involved in his father's disappearance but it was an accident, I believe.'

'That's very sad,' said Donald. 'They were such a lovely young couple, Philip and Mary. If you'd asked me at the time, I would have said their relationship was for keeps. Still, what do I know, or anyone else, come to that, when it comes to other people's relationships. Will the son go to prison?'

'I don't know, probably,' said Louis. 'The reason I'm calling is to thank you for your help – telling me about Mary, in the first place, and then her sister. Actually, it was Teresa who really cracked the case by sending me a photograph of Nigel Junior when he was a boy.'

'So you met Teresa and is your virtue is still intact, Chief Inspector?'

'Absolutely!' said Louis.

'You did well. Dare I say, there are a considerable number of men who did not get away so easily, so I'm told.'

'The other thing I wanted to say, Don, is that you are a real inspiration. From my side of the fence, we send people to prison, often with a heavy heart, believing they will never get over the experience, will almost certainly gain nothing from it and, in many cases, come out hardened criminals. Your story, how shall I put it, keeps hope alive that sometimes the system works. So thank you for sharing your story, I am truly grateful.'

'I'll tell my old girl what you said, she's going to love that. Don't be a stranger, Louis, come and see us again soon.'

The third call was to Stephanie.

'Are you lot doing anything much tomorrow, given it's Sunday?' Louis asked.

'We've actually free all day tomorrow and the weather looks pretty grim so I don't think there will be a demand to take the kids surfing. Can you come to lunch?'

'I'd love that, Steph, if that's OK. It's been rather a gruelling week.'

'Actually, I was going to call you in any event. Edward's picked up on the fact that you have arrested David, the chap who found him on the cliff. We've got that right, have we, it is the same man?'

'I'm afraid it is,' Louis admitted.

'Well, between now and lunch tomorrow, could you think out how you are going to explain to our son that you arrested the man who may possibly have saved his life.'

So much for a relaxed lunch in the bosom of his family, Louis thought.

CHAPTER FIFTY-TWO

Before driving over to Falmouth for lunch, Louis called in at Treliske hospital to see how David was doing. Having discovered which ward he was in, Louis approached the nurses' station and asked where to find him.

'Can you show me where I can find David Reed?' Louis asked.

'I'm sorry, but I'm afraid he is not allowed any visitors,' replied the nurse.

Louis produced his warrant card. 'My name is Chief Inspector Louis Peppiatt. It was me who asked that he should receive no visitors. I just need to talk to him for a few moments.'

'I'm sorry, my instructions are very clear. I am not to allow him any visitors.' She sighed and relented. 'I suppose I can check with Matron.'

'You do that,' said Louis, who was more than a little

frazzled, and was still worrying about trying to explain David's arrest to Edward.

A rather terrifying matron appeared after a considerable wait, and looked Louis up and down. He waved his warrant card. 'It was me who asked that the patient should receive no visitors,' he said again.

'In future, Chief Inspector, it would be more helpful if you could issue precise instructions.'

'Such as?' Louis asked, genuinely confused.

'You should have instructed us that the patient should receive no visitors except for your good self. Fifth bed up on the right, behind the curtain. Don't be long, he's needed a lot of patching up. Heaven knows what you did to him.'

'Thank you,' said Louis, through gritted teeth.

Except for the absence of blood, David looked considerably worse than he had done when he was loaded into the ambulance. His face had swelled up enormously, as had his nose, his lips, too. His eyes were tiny slits and one ear could have passed as that belonging to a baby elephant.

'How are you?' Louis asked.

'Well, if I look as bad as I feel, I must resemble some sort of horror mask.'

Louis smiled at him and made a show of studying his face. 'Yup,' he said, 'you look as bad as you feel, maybe worse.'

'You have a great bedside manner,' said David, trying to smile back but it was clearly too painful.

Louis reached into his pocket and pulled out David's mobile. 'Here's your mobile. I rescued it from the farm kitchen and charged it up last night so it's good to go.'

'That's kind. H-How is everyone?'

'Merrin, Tom and I went up to the farm after you left in the ambulance. I told them the full story of your background and about your mother, Mary. The questions flooded in, as you can imagine, but I think I've told them everything they needed to know. Everyone was mostly calm, except Tom, of course, who had a few explosive moments. I've had no contact with them this morning but I have instructed the ward that you must receive no visitors, just in case Tom wants a re-match. I also told your aunt Teresa about what has happened and she looks forward to seeing you as soon as you can travel. Have you been told how long you'll be in here?'

'No, but I've got to have a brain scan this morning. My head got in the way of a bull a couple of months ago, as well as Friday's fun and games, so they just want to check to see if I still have some brain left.'

'I can tell them the answer to that. Absolutely no brain left at all. What on earth possessed you to go to the farm to collect your stuff without checking with me first? I could have provided a couple of constables to make sure there was no trouble, and putting Merrin in danger like that was not clever, was it?'

'No, and Merrin suggested we should contact you first. I just thought I could be in and out of the barn without anyone seeing. Is Merrin alright? I keep thinking how brilliant she was to try and stop Tom.'

'Merrin's going to be very sore today, I expect, but she's OK. Having thought about it, are you sure you don't want to press charges?' Louis asked.

'Absolutely not, I only got what I deserved,' said David.

A nurse put her head through the curtain. 'Matron says you are to leave now.'

Louis stood up to leave. 'Take care of yourself. I'm just off to see Edward to try and explain to him why I arrested the man who saved him. You do seem to cause an awful lot of trouble, one way and another.'

'More trouble than I'm worth, that's for sure. Send Edward my best wishes.'

Louis turned in to the drive of his former home and parked up. He sat in his car for a moment or two, trying to gather his thoughts. The last few weeks had left him exhausted, with all the emotional turmoil, broken lives and divided families. *Give me a good old-fashioned crime any day of the week, compared with the machinations of the Trehearne family*, he thought.

Louis walked up slowly to the front door and knocked. It was flung open almost immediately by the small figure of his son.

'I'm very cross with you, Dad,' Edward said.

'I'm very cross with me too,' said Louis, 'in fact, I bet I crosser with me than you are.'

'You couldn't be crosser than me, Dad. I'm crosser than anyone could be in the whole world. As cross as cross can be.'

'Ah,' said Louis, 'but I'm much bigger than you so I have a bigger capacity for crossness.'

'Oh, for heaven's sake, you two, you're as bad as each other,' said Stephanie, but she was smiling. 'Come in, Louis, lunch is almost ready.'

Lunch was delightful. The children were on good form, Andrew was more relaxed than Louis had ever seen him, and Stephanie, as always, produced a delicious meal. Afterwards, Andrew volunteered to wash up and the children disappeared upstairs so Louis and Stephanie were left alone for a moment.

'Have you talked to Edward about David?' Stephanie asked.

'Yes, while you were dishing up. I didn't make a big thing of it. I just told him that before a trial, policemen are not allowed to tell anyone about the details of a case, how I couldn't even tell you. I told him that David was a good man who had done a bad thing but hopefully he wouldn't be punished too severely. I popped into Treliske, before coming here, in order to see David. He sent Edward his best wishes, which I passed on. Ed seemed very happy with that – I suppose because it showed that David still liked him, despite what his wretched father had done. I have promised Ed that he will be the first person I talk to after the trial. He's fine. This has been a messy and highly emotional one, Steph, and all about broken families and a man who inadvertently killed his own father.' Louis smiled. 'I don't want to give our boy ideas!' he said.

'And why were you cross with yourself?' Stephanie asked.

'Because I was thoughtless. I should have told you that the story was going to appear in the press. I thought they'd only be interested in the discovery of Philip's remains, I didn't expect them to link it to David's hearing. I'm sorry to have put you on the spot.'

'That's OK. So, you came here to lunch today because

you'd had a basinful of broken families and emotional traumas?'

'Something like that. Lunch was lovely, thank you, Steph.' He hesitated. 'We've made it, haven't we, despite everything? We're a happy family, aren't we?'

'Of course we are,' said Stephanie. 'Come here.' She swept him into a big hug. 'Does that feel better?' she murmured against his shoulder.

'Much,' said Louis.

'Right,' said Stephanie. 'Stay for tea and as it's still raining, let's play Racing Demon.'

Louis eyed her suspiciously. 'Just because I haven't played for a while, don't think for one moment that you're going to win.'

'You've absolutely no chance,' said Stephanie.

Of course, it was Daisy who won, much to the fury of both her parents!

The day was not so tranquil for Merrin. It began badly. When she tried to get out of bed, there didn't seem a single piece of her body that didn't ache. After a very hot bath, which eased the pain a little, she tottered round the harbour in the rain, with William in tow – an experience that neither of them enjoyed.

On her return, she was just making a coffee and Horatio's morning toast, when her mobile rang. It was Jago.

'How are you, sis?' he asked.

'Not brilliant, in fact pretty sore,' she replied, 'but an awful lot better than I imagine David is feeling this morning.'

'I thought I would come over and check up on you. Gemma's having a lie-in and I thought after Friday, it would be good for us to spend some time together.'

'That would be lovely, Jago, but would you mind getting a taxi? My car's still outside David's barn and in all the confusion, I still have the key here – stupid idiot.'

'There's nothing stupid about you, sis. It's OK, I've already arranged for Tom to drop me over and I'll get a taxi back.'

'I don't think I'm up to seeing Tom,' said Merrin.

'Of course not,' said Jago. 'He can drop me at the bottom of your steps and my chair at the top. It's the least he can do in the circumstances.'

Jago's plan did not run smoothly. Having dropped Jago at the bottom of Merrin's steps, Tom carried the wheelchair up the steps and straight into Merrin's kitchen, where she was sitting in Adam's chair, with a hot water bottle pressed against her back.

'I wanted to say sorry for hurting you,' said Tom, opening the wheelchair by the kitchen table, which allowed him to avoid making eye contact.

'You said sorry yesterday, Tom. I'm really not up to seeing you today, please leave and be careful of Jago on the way out.'

'You just don't understand. David watched us suffering all those years and did nothing. It's like a form of torture – the man must be deranged under all that apparent nice-guy stuff. I just lost my temper, you can surely see why?'

'I don't want to talk about it, Tom. I just want you to go.'

'But you must understand why I was so angry, you must, Merrin.'

'I've worked as a family solicitor for over thirty years. I've dealt with marital disputes, children being taken into care against their parents' wishes, several kidnaps and an enormous amount of high emotional family turmoil. But never, in all that time, has anyone tried to hurt me, as you did. We're family, I'll get over it, but right now I want you out of my home and out of my sight.'

Jago had reached the top step, sitting directly behind Tom. 'Do as the lady says, Tom, just go.'

Tom left without another word.

Jago abandoned the idea of coffee in favour of a bottle of red wine. Having poured two glasses, he manoeuvred his chair so he was sitting opposite his sister.

'Cheers,' he said.

'Here's to happy families,' said Merrin, 'and that is intended to be ironic.'

'Point taken,' said Jago, 'but we're all going to be OK, I promise.' He smiled. 'Can you imagine what Dad would have done to Tom, if he'd still been alive – he'd have pulverised him for hurting his precious daughter.'

'He wouldn't, Jago. Dad was never violent and he hadn't a mean bone in his body. But he would have given Tom the most almighty lecture, which would have left him a quivering wreck. Do you remember the worst thing he used to say to us, when we'd been naughty?'

'I'm very disappointed in you,' they chorused.

'Much worse than telling us we were bad,' Jago agreed. 'You're right, Dad certainly had a way with words.'

'Are you and Gemma alright?' Merrin asked.

'We're good. Gemma can't wait to get back to Oz and the kids now, a complete about-face from when we first arrived. We'll be here for Philip's funeral, obviously, then once she's sure Tom is OK and I'm sure you're OK, we're on the next plane back home.'

'There's a part of me that wishes I was coming with you, right now,' said Merrin, 'but I need to stay here and face my demons.'

CHAPTER FIFTY-THREE

The funeral of Philip Trehearne was a very small, private affair. Apart from his children, Merrin and Jago were obviously included, as were the Pascoe family, Clara and Tristan, Chief Inspector Louis Peppiatt and Sergeant Jack Eddy. David Reed was not invited.

It was the height of the tourist season so the police cordoned off an area around St Ia's Parish Church, in order to give the family some privacy, particularly away from the press.

The service was short, poignant and dignified. Everyone remained dry-eyed but it was a different matter when they reached the burial site. Philip's grave had been dug so close to Sarah's that the coffins must have almost been touching. Merrin had tracked down a large bunch of glorious peach-coloured roses, named, appropriately, Peace. A vase of the roses had been already placed on Sarah's grave and the remaining flowers were distributed amongst the small congregation to throw onto Philip's coffin, once lowered into his grave.

Tears flowed, and Louis felt oddly moved as he took his turn to throw his rose. He stood by the grave for a moment, head bowed. 'You led me a right dance, old lad, but I'm so glad we found you in the end. Rest in peace now,' he murmured, as he moved away from the grave.

The service finished, the vicar began leading the congregation down the hill. Tom hurried forward and put a hand on Louis's arm.

'Thank you for finding him, Chief Inspector, I'm very grateful.' Tom nodded towards the graves. 'It's so good to see them back together again.'

'Yes,' said Louis, also looking towards the graves. 'Reunited, at last. I'm sorry it took so long.' The two men shook hands. 'Take it easy, Tom, and good luck.'

Unlike after Sarah's funeral, this time there was a wake. They all drove to Trehearne Farm, where in true Trehcarne tradition, there was plenty of food and drink. Tom made a small speech in which he explained why the wake was now possible – because at last the family had closure. He publicly thanked Louis again for unravelling the mystery.

Louis left quietly soon after, having thanked Jack Eddy for all his help. As he walked towards his car, Merrin spotted him and caught him just before he drove off.

'Are you alright?' she asked.

'Yes, but it was time for me to go – it's a family affair now, no place for the likes of me. How are you, have you recovered?'

'Absolutely, except for a small scar.' She swept hair to

one side to show him. 'Louis, the reason I've dashed after you is that I was going to talk to you about something the night you came for supper, but we got bogged down in our respective family histories.'

'We did rather. Come and sit in the car for a minute and tell me what's on your mind.'

Merrin settled into the passenger seat and turned to face him. 'I've decided what I want to do with the rest of my life,' she said proudly.

'Goodness,' said Louis, 'that's very impressive. What does it involve, may I ask?'

'As a hobby, I'm going to try to learn to be a potter. I'm joining a course in September; I'm quite excited about it. Then, for a job, albeit part time and usually unpaid, I thought I would offer pro bono services as a solicitor. Helping Steve Matthews made me think it would be something I'd like to do. The senior partner at my old law firm is going to try and put some work my way, but I also wondered if you would keep a look out to see if there are any cases where I might be helpful. I appreciate we will always be on opposing sides – you prosecuting, me defending – but there could perhaps be the odd case, like Steve's, where you feel I could be useful.'

'I think that's a splendid idea but just be careful you don't take on too much work. William and Horatio wouldn't think much of that. You know, it's such a shame you can't represent David Reed. He really needs someone sensitive who understands why he got himself, and everyone else, in such a mess.'

'That really would put me on the wrong side and my family would never speak to me again.'

'Oh, I appreciate that. I only mentioned it because it's another situation, like Steve's, where, for justice to be done, it's vital that the full story is given a proper airing. Like Adam said – good people do bad things and bad people to good things. I always try to remember that.'

'Me too,' said Merrin sadly.

'Well, I'll certainly keep a look out for some potential pro bono cases. It will provide the added bonus for us needing to keep in touch, from time to time. I'd like that.'

'I'd like that, too,' said Merrin.

EPILOGUE

Five Months Later

Trehearne Farm was sold. Tom's trip to Australia to see Gemma and Jago was booked. He had barely ever been out of Cornwall so Merrin was going to take him to the airport and see him through to departures. Merrin and Tom were friends again to everyone's relief, particularly their own.

Of course, Annie Pascoe had helped Tom with the farm work after David's dramatic departure, and she had also organised the packing up of the house. Her final task was to clear the office. She had almost finished when she opened a small drawer in the centre of Sarah's old desk. There was a single item in it – a large book declaring itself to be the Trehearne farm accounts. Annie opened it to find an envelope tucked inside. It was addressed to Tom.

Tom was in his bedroom, trying to work out which of his clothes he should take to Australia and which should go into storage.

'Tom, I found a letter for you; it was in your mum's accounts book,' said Annie, trying to smile to ease the tension.

Tom stared at it for a moment and went very pale. 'That's Mum's handwriting,' he croaked.

'I know,' said Annie. 'She probably expected someone would look at the accounts book before now. I'll leave you alone to read it.'

'No,' said Tom, 'please stay.' He tore open the envelope and began to read, while Annie sat on the bed and watched him.

Darling Tom,

I am writing to you regarding my plans because if I talk to you about them, I fear we may end up in an argument and I don't want our last conversation to be an angry one. I love you so much.

I have changed my will to leave half the farm to David. This will come as a big shock, I know, and I'm sorry. Let me explain. I know you have always hated farming and if I had been a half decent mother, I should have sold the farm when it became obvious to everyone, except me, that your dad would not be coming home. But I couldn't. Against all the odds, I've always wanted to believe that one day he would walk back through the kitchen door. And so, I have trapped you in the farming business all these years, and as a loyal son, you have let me do it. You're a good man, Tom, I'm proud of you and so would Dad be. But, of course, your heart wasn't in it and without

David, I don't know what would have become of us. Gone bankrupt, for sure – we certainly couldn't have managed without him.

So, I'm giving David half the farm as a thank you for his years of service. He can run it with some labouring help and you will be free to make a different life outside of farming. You're only halfway through your life, darling – you have time. You will see from the accounts that you and David sharing the profits will give you both a decent income, so you don't have to worry about money, while you decide what to do next. As you both grow older, you may decide to sell the farm. It will be your decision then, not mine.

We both know that marrying Beth was a terrible mistake. Find a lovely, kind woman, and without the black cloud of having to farm hanging over you both, I believe you need to look no further than Pascoes. Annie has always loved you and Geoff can manage perfectly well without her. So maybe??

I'm sorry to leave you and Gemma, but it is time. Why now? Because at last I have faced the reality and accepted that my husband will never return. In short, I have given up hope and without hope, I simply cannot go on. I pray you both understand and please never feel guilty. There is absolutely nothing either of you could have done to stop me doing what I'm about to do.

Have a wonderful life.

MUM xx

As he read his mother's letter, Tom felt his constant companions, stress and anger, miraculously begin slipping away. Clearly, his mother had known nothing of Mary Daniels and of the baby, who was Philip's. She saw David as being responsible for keeping Trehearne Farm alive but certainly not as the man who had caused her husband's death. She had been spared the truth – David had not been lying.

He handed the letter to Annie. 'I'd like you to read it,' he said.

She took the letter and read it carefully. When she finished, she hardly dared look at Tom. When she did, she saw he was smiling and watching her intently.

'So maybe?' he asked.

'Maybe,' she replied.

ACKNOWLEDGEMENTS

I am so lucky to have enjoyed the advice and encouragement in the writing of this book from Dr Lucy Mackillop, Diana Palmer, Edita Goodall, Chris Macfarlane and Sally Cuckson. Also, a big thank you to my children – Locket, Mikey, Charlie and Deets for their kindness and support. And, of course, very many thanks are due to the team at Allison & Busby.

Also By Deborah Fowler . . .

A St Ives Christmas Mystery

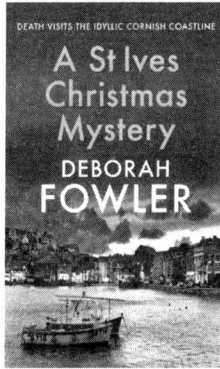

When tragedy brings Merrin McKenzie back to St Ives, she knows adjusting might take time, even with the comfort of Christmas back in her hometown. Stepping back from her career as a solicitor, she agrees to clean holiday rentals for her friends who own cottages nearby. She anticipates dirty laundry and sandy floors, but she didn't sign up for a dead body, neatly tucked up in one of the guest beds.

The police are baffled by the young man's identity and the strangeness of his death. For Merrin, however, coincidences are beginning to stack up. Even though Inspector Louis Peppiatt is sceptical of her theories, something sinister is hiding beneath the festive surface of this charming seaside town. As the case unfolds, a dark side to the Cornish coast emerges.

DEBORAH FOWLER'S first short story was published when she was seventeen. Since then, she has published over six hundred short stories, novels, a crime series and several works of non-fiction. Deborah lives in a small hamlet just outside St Ives and *A St Ives Christmas Mystery* was the first in a new series set against the beautiful backdrop of the West Cornish coastline.